BETWEEN LOVE & LIES

GAMBLING HEARTS SERIES

JACQUI NELSON

Cover design by The Killion Group, Inc

ISBN ebook: 978-0-9936387-3-2
ISBN print: 978-0-9936387-2-5

PRAISE FOR THE GAMBLING HEARTS SERIES...

Between Love & Lies - **Book 1**

"I loved the twists and turns this book takes. If you want a top-shelf historical western romance, you won't go wrong with this." ~ Linda Broday (New York Times & USA Today bestselling author of historical western romance)

"I couldn't read it fast enough and I didn't want it to end either." ~ Bob

"The chemistry in this book sizzles from the very first pages. The characters come to life with vibrant color and intensity." ~ Heather C.

"Held me in its grasp and wouldn't let me go until the oh-so-satisfying conclusion." ~ Diane B.

Between Home & Heartbreak - **Book 2**

"A western romance, thrill ride, filled with twists and turns in every chapter!" ~ A.P.Reader

"A fun, yet nail biting story." ~ Christine W.

"Open the book and get swept away!" ~ Little Piggy's

"Kept my attention until the end! I just loved her heroine Eldorado Jane" ~ Nicole L.

DEDICATION

For my readers who waited so long for this story.

Thank you for your wonderful words of encouragement
while I strove to find my own words to finish this new
venture into the Old West.

PROLOGUE

South of Dodge City, Kansas
May 1, 1876

They were destroying everything: the tiny apple tree she'd sheltered in the wagon during the long, sweltering journey from Virginia; the fence she'd devoted weeks to repairing over the winter with scraps of deadwood; the vegetable garden she'd sown during the first whisper of spring and painstakingly coaxed to life every heartbeat since.

All trampled, devoured, gone.

Sadie glared at the beasts, eyes burning with tears of hopeless rage. Graceless creatures, they wielded heavy horns that stretched out of their skulls like spears. Texas longhorns. The Devil's helpers.

In the middle of them rode Lucifer himself, sent straight up from hell to torment her and tear away everything she'd slaved to build.

She tracked the long-legged, well-built rider as he steered his horse through the milling animals, angling toward her and her father—and their sod house. Dismay tightened her throat, left her bereft of air and hope. Even that stalwart structure was in danger of being leveled by the heaving mass in the care of the man coming ever closer.

The intruder, similar to all the other Texas drovers, was covered in a layer of trail dust so thick it hung on him like a second skin. But it was one of the only things he and the other men had in common. While the rest hollered and cracked whips over the backs of the beasts in their charge—trying to persuade them to return to the trail—this man urged his charcoal-colored mount through the river of hide and horn, making a beeline for her.

His silence, along with his ability to guide his horse with remarkably little effort, infuriated her. As the distance between them shortened, unease crept up her spine.

His gaze was unwavering, never leaving her.

She tightened her grip on the ancient shotgun clutched at her side, then concentrated on her anger and frustration, transferring them from the longhorns to settle solely on him. She did not want him to come any closer.

Yanking the shotgun up to her shoulder, she took aim.

The cowboy straightened in his saddle but otherwise did not acknowledge her hostile action. Nor did he slacken his pace; if anything, he bore down on her even faster.

Damn him to hell. Her finger tightened on the trigger.

Something slammed down on her shotgun, pitching the rusted barrel earthward. The buckshot tore a savage gouge out of the clay in front of her and kicked up a cloud of dust. The blast forced her to stumble back.

Her father's red face inserted itself between her and the cowboy. With a curse, he jerked the weapon from her grasp.

As she stood gawking at him, the cattle, spooked by the shotgun blast, bolted—fast and in every direction. Her father sprinted toward their lone plow horse, scrambled onto its back and galloped away from the melee and her.

She shouldn't have expected anything different. Still, the hurt came. Sharp and deep. Once again, he'd thought only of himself. He'd abandoned her in the center of the herd, alone and defenseless.

I'm going to be trampled. I'm going to die.

Time suspended as she contemplated her life ending. She felt...numb. Her hard work had been obliterated in a blink. She couldn't summon the will to move a single step, let alone face the prospect of starting over.

The cattle's bellowing and their thundering hooves became a single roar. The heat of their breaths hit her first, then their bodies. Walloped square in the chest, they knocked her off her feet. But the surge did not wash over her. Instead, something snared her waist, jerking her up until she crashed into an immovable wall.

She sucked in air and immediately wished she hadn't. Pain pierced her ribs. Dust billowed and shrouded the air. Through slitted eyes, she realized her leather-clad perch was already covered in a blanket of dust—and she was being held against it. She struggled to raise her head and discovered a square, beard-stubbled jaw directly above her.

Lucifer—in the disguise of a Texas cowboy—held her in his lap while waves of cattle buffeted his mount. His grip on her was solid but not bruising as he guided them to safety. When they'd cleared the beasts and the noise level dropped a notch, he peered down at her. Eyes like warm whiskey stared at her from a face etched with concern.

"Are you hurt?" His voice came low and ragged, fanning out in bursts, caressing her face.

Her world tilted, and the air once more left her lungs. She forced herself to remember he was responsible for destroying everything she held dear. Anger flooded her, pushing away all other thought, the same way his herd had swept away her dreams.

Mustering all her strength, she curled her fingers into a fist and struck him in the abdomen. Pain ricocheted up her arm. He didn't budge. He merely blinked, his brows lowering. Infuriated by his lack of response, she unleashed a flurry of hits, striking him with her fists, elbows, and feet.

Beneath them, his horse whinnied shrilly and reared up.

Blind to everything but her need to make him hurt as much as she did, she launched her entire body at him. They tumbled from the horse and struck the ground, him landing first on his back, her on top of him. He released a grunt of surprise, but his hands stayed around her waist. She scrambled to her knees. His hold tightened, not letting her go farther. She struggled to break free. And failed. That didn't stop her from trying, over and over.

"Hold still. You don't want to spook my herd again. I want to help you."

His voice caught her off guard and held her immobile. The tone was gruff and demanding, but edged with a note of pleading. Its undercurrent tugged at her.

She shook her head, refusing to yield to him. "Help me?" She slammed her fist down on his chest. "Do you know how long it took me to plant that garden? Or make that fence?" She hit him again.

He didn't move, not even to flinch. Couldn't he feel her punches?

Exhaustion and frustration clenched her hands so tightly that her bones ached. "You've destroyed everything I built!" She pounded out her fury on him until she couldn't lift her arms.

Only then did he move. He pulled her close, drawing

her into the curve of his body, guiding her head onto his shoulder. His palm cradled the back of her head, while his fingers smoothed the wild tangle of her hair.

No one had held her with such care in a long time. Not since her mother had died. Great sobs shook her. She slumped against him, unable to contain her sorrow.

The callused pad of his thumb traced her cheek. He brushed away each tear as it fell. Did he honestly believe he could make things better with his gentle persistence? She hid her face against his tear-dampened coat, smelling of leather, wool and the earth—and tried to think.

His scent reminded her of her farm. Straightforward. Stalwart. Steady. Her land may have challenged her, but it'd never abandoned her. Her insides tightened with a longing so intense it hurt.

"If I could undo the damage, I would." His words caressed her ear. Soft and husky like silk and sand. "You can't stay here. Come with me to Dodge."

He wanted her to leave her farm? The realization unleashed the storm in her belly, like a herd of pronghorn antelopes spying a mountain lion.

She jerked away, scrambling off him. This time he didn't move to stop her. She didn't go far, though. She didn't have the energy. Sitting stiff-backed beside him, she stared at the rubble that had once formed her home. The salt of her tears stung her skin and her eyes ached, mirroring the pain in her heart.

His leather chaps creaked as he stood and stepped closer. The din associated with the longhorn herd had faded. The cattle had returned to the trail, once again heading north toward Dodge. The drover didn't follow them, nor did he touch her. The heat of his body did, though, intensifying the unsettling fluttering in her stomach.

"It can be rebuilt." Plainspoken words, without a trace of doubt. "It's not—"

A bitter bubble of laughter burst from her. Maybe miracles happened in his world. She clenched her teeth. She wouldn't let him see how much he'd hurt her. See that a scream was building inside her. One so big that, if she let it out, she was certain she would shatter.

He exhaled a long breath. "I know it won't be easy."

You have no idea. She swallowed her reply as she spotted her father steering their aging swayback mare toward her. She lurched to her feet.

Behind her, the cowboy's hand, strong and solid, found her elbow and kept her upright. "At least no one was hurt."

She shrugged off his hold and forced her own legs to support her weight. She refused to look back. Instead, she stared at her father and dreaded what was certain to come. She knew this side of him too well—his manipulative mind, his greed, and his lack of love for her, his own flesh and blood.

But when her father reached them, the cowboy surprised her by speaking first. "It's a right shame, my herd moving through your homestead like that, Mr.—?"

"Sullivan. Timothy Sullivan. And yes, it is."

What her father lacked in stature, he made up for with a classically-boned face and a thatch of white hair that a long time ago had been as red as hers. With looks as compelling as his smooth-talking tongue, he should have pursued a career in the theater. Then maybe he could've made a contribution to their meager funds rather than draining whatever she earned. Unfortunately, he was more interested in drinking and gambling.

He eyed Sadie briefly before he looked at the man standing behind her, his familiar features settling into a look of mournful loss. "Me and my daughter worked hard building the place."

Liar!

He hadn't spent a single minute on their farm. He'd left that all up to her. She cringed at his charlatan nature, knowing he'd ply the cowboy with a consummate actor's skills as he strove to extract a reward for something he played no part in creating.

The cowboy astounded her again. "I'll compensate you fairly for your loss, Mr. Sullivan. It's the least I can do for you and your daughter."

Not wanting to witness any more, she turned away. She couldn't block out the scrape of his footsteps, the jangle of his spurs, as he approached her father. They rang harsh against the tender earth of her home. He murmured something in a deep rumble that she couldn't decipher.

The surprise in her father's gasp was unmistakable. "You are most generous, sir!"

She spun to face him. A stack of greenbacks rested on his soft, white palms. The cowboy assumed giving her father money would help her? Her plummeting prospects stole the starch from her spine. When her gaze found the cowboy, her eyes blurred with more useless tears.

His brows drew together, and he took a step toward her. She took one back, shaking her head, forcing all the emotion from her heart and, she hoped, from her face. She kept moving away from him, to where her home had once stood.

Giving that much money to a compulsive gambler was a sure-fire recipe for disaster. It'd be gone come morning, and so would her future.

CHAPTER 1

Dodge City, Kansas
One year later

"*I*'m glad you saw fit to return to our fair city, Mr. Ballantyne."

Robert Wardell's simpering words grated on Noah. He had no interest in what the rich cattle baron thought or didn't think.

"Only here as a favor. Mr. Adams owns the herd." He jerked his thumb over his shoulder at his friend, Lewis. "If you want to buy the cattle, talk to him. This time 'round, I'm no more than a trail boss."

Noah hoped that'd be enough to discourage Wardell. He didn't like him, didn't want to talk to him. The man was too full of himself, loud and showy as a jaybird. Nothing was overstated about Wardell's countenance, however. His eyes were a watery blue, his chin nonexistent, and the flesh of his neck loose and sagging, like the wattle of a turkey.

Luckily, Noah's words had the desired effect. Wardell dismissed him, turning his eager eyes and broad smile toward Lewis. "Welcome to our town, good sir," he said. "We're honored that you chose our humble rail stop for shipping your herd."

Lewis laughed. Noah had known him since they were boys growing up on neighboring ranches. Lewis had always matched him in height and muscle while somehow appearing lighter. He retained the unflappable spirit of his youth, plus his windswept blond hair. Not once had Lewis lost his temper during the two months it'd taken them to inch up the six hundred miles of the Western Trail.

Noah couldn't say the same for himself.

"How could I resist after your trail agents arrived in Texas, enticing us with tales of Dodge's unrestrained hospitality?" Lewis flashed the perfect grin that never failed to draw everyone to him like a stampede.

More often than not, Noah was left standing in their dust. With Wardell, he welcomed the experience.

Wardell thrust out his chest like a bantam rooster. "Did they exaggerate?"

The town hadn't changed much in the year since Noah had first visited, had only gotten more crowded. The streets swarmed with life: a handful of bankers, blacksmiths, merchants, grocers, and a horde of Texas drovers with their wide-brimmed hats and stacked-heel boots inlaid with a lone star. Fresh-faced youths, hardened trail bosses, dandified cattle barons. Men of all sorts, but mostly that—men.

Since their arrival yesterday, Noah had been searching Dodge's streets, but he hadn't found her. No slender-boned redhead with mesmerizing freckles and blazing emerald eyes.

In the last miles before Dodge, they'd ridden right by her farm. He hadn't been surprised to find the homestead abandoned and sinking back into the earth. Last year, he'd had no idea how destructive the cattle drives could be on the small farms between Texas and Kansas. He'd heard that many went under when their crops were trampled and their cattle fell ill with fever from the longhorn tick. It ate at his conscience that he'd destroyed someone's livelihood and, more than likely, their dreams as well.

Hoping to find Timothy Sullivan's daughter in Dodge was a long shot, yet he couldn't stop himself from searching.

He cleared his throat, reluctant to engage Wardell in further conversation now that he'd shifted the man's focus to Lewis. "How're your local folk holding up?" he asked, continuing to scan the crowd.

"As you can see, our town's prospering."

"Was wondering more about those *outside* of town."

"The sodbusters?" Wardell's voice overflowed with scorn. "Don't concern yourself with them. They're a dying breed in these parts. Better to do business with a free-thinking Texas rancher than an uncouth Kansas farmer."

"Free-spending, don't you mean?" Noah grimaced. *Leave it alone.* He prayed for the good sense to say no more. He wasn't here to argue about right and wrong. He was here to ensure he'd righted a wrong.

Wardell shrugged. "One has to make a living. Mine is buying and selling cattle. I'm a businessman first and foremost, and there's no business to be gotten from a farmer. Clear your mind of them. Everything you need is here, including a good saloon. Try the Northern Star. After those long months on the trail, you and Mr. Adams could probably use some womanly comfort."

Lewis looped an arm around Noah's shoulders. "Mr. Wardell makes an excellent suggestion. Let's get off this dusty street. Whatever you're searching for—surely it'll survive the next hour without your attention."

Noah shrugged off his hold. "I'm not searching for anything."

Lewis snorted good-naturedly, then leaned closer and lowered his voice. "Save your bullshit for someone who hasn't spent most of his days by your side. Until lately. You've been avoiding me and my questions ever since you came home from Dodge last year. Confounds me why you agreed to help drive my herd north."

"You asked. I agreed. Simple. End of story."

"Like hell it is." Lewis blew out a long breath. "Whatever your reasons, I'm grateful. I'm not complaining. Much." His familiar grin returned. "All I want is a break. Who knows, maybe we'll find what you need in one of the saloons."

Noah shook his head. "Not a chance in hell." He needed to find a farm girl, not some strumpet.

HEAVEN HELP HER, the saloon was packed tonight. Sadie had seen the Northern Star busy, but this was ten times that. Every chair was occupied, every wall lined. Patrons were three deep at the bar, calling for whiskey in voices as grating as the bawling longhorns they'd been herding an hour before.

The one difference was that after a mad dash down to the barber and bathhouse, the men were all scrubbed clean. Otherwise, the dusty, trail-smelling drovers would've been barred from the saloon. One had to keep up standards. Madam Garrett insisted.

Forget standards. What about survival? They'd all be lucky if they lived through the evening with this mass stampede for entertainment. The men may have been all tidied up, but their manners were unchanged.

Sadie stood hidden behind the ruby curtains framing the stage, considering turning tail and running. She wouldn't get far, though. Not with Handsome John standing so close.

Among other things, John was the Star's box herder. He kept the ladies in line and fetched them back if they took any ideas of independence. Moments ago, Gertie Garrett had instructed her right-hand man to keep watch over Sadie. He was to protect her from the crowd, and from her own self. He'd have to punish her if she ran. Those were the rules.

John looked her straight in the eye. His stare jolted her with an inescapable truth. He shared her apprehension. Rightfully so. A giant of a man with a battle-scarred face, he towered over everyone and outweighed most men two to one, but he was only one man against a hundred. His gaze dropped to the floor, his lips compressing into a resigned line before disappearing beneath the snarl of his beard. He drew himself up and stepped onto the stage and out of Sadie's sight, entering the lion's den.

"Settle down now, boys," he hollered.

Nothing happened. If anything, the noise increased.

Her guardian tried again. "I said, pipe down!"

Curses and jeers turned the air blue, followed by the shattering of glass. Close by. On the stage where John stood. His calls for order had their attention.

Sadie flattened her spine against the wall. The rough-cut boards dug into her flesh, reminding her that the men couldn't see her. Still safe. Still a coward. She squeezed her eyes shut, gulped for air, and began to sing.

"Amazing grace, how sweet the sound..."

She grimaced, but didn't stop. Why had she chosen such a song? Was it because this morning she'd been pondering her past, both before and after she'd come to live in Dodge? Was it because she'd figured God would never forgive her for all the sins she'd committed of late?

Whatever the reason, her selection didn't matter. The men were too busy kicking up a ruckus to listen to her. *Damn them and their gracelessness. Damn them all to hell.* If it was possible to send them there with a song, then she'd give it her best.

She raised her chin and her voice as well.

On the other side of the wall, all went quiet. She kept singing as if her life depended on it. And it did.

Her every move at the Northern Star was a step deeper into hell. The role she'd concocted to slow her descent was a precarious one. She'd saved herself with a series of lies that now might lead to her death. But the lies were all she'd had. *Too late to do anything differently. Keep lying—and singing.*

Heart hammering against her ribcage, she opened her eyes and mid-sentence stepped onto the stage. A sea of faces stared up at her, unmoving. Liquor bottles and glasses hovered in their hands. Forgotten. A new indulgence had captured their attention.

All too soon, the last line of her song slipped from her lips. She drew the words out, holding on to them, dreading their departure. Without her song, she feared chaos would return.

And then there was silence. Not a word. Not a footfall. Nothing.

"God in heaven," a man standing in the front row said. His words echoed in the stillness, making her flinch. "You sing like a preacher's daughter. But if I'd wanted a sermon, I'd 'a gone to church."

Laughter slipped from her lips, a bubbling, carefree sound that took her by surprise. When was the last time she'd laughed? She couldn't remember. Didn't want to remember. The past was gone and the future uncertain. All she had was today.

"Well—" She drew in another breath for courage. "We can't have you believing this is a house of the Lord." Or that she was pure. She needed to maintain the appearance of a seasoned saloon girl.

She forced herself to lean forward and prop her hands on her knees so she could stare directly into her reluctant disciple's eyes.

His gaze fell to her cleavage and stayed there.

"Now you see what you want to see." Bit by bit, she straightened, sliding her hands up her legs until they settled on her hips. She assumed one of the poses she'd observed the other girls at the Star employ—and put some thought into her next song.

> "There's a yellow rose of Texas
> That I am going to see."

Shrill whistles and a volley of shouts greeted her choice. But it was the guttural gasp behind her that drew her attention. Handsome John's jaw hung so low that it rested on his chest.

Didn't believe I had it in me, huh? She gave him a mock salute. *Wasn't certain I did either.*

With a shake of his head, John settled the contours of his scarred face back into its usual scowl and lumbered off to tend the bar. Sadie faced her audience again and strove to make the next line of her song as sultry and breathless as she could.

"No other fellow knows her,
No other, only me."

The men's appreciation grew louder.

Texans. One of their statesmen had started her descent. The one with eyes like fine whiskey. *Nothing fine about him.* He'd destroyed everything she had. Then he'd left. His memory didn't deserve to linger in her thoughts.

By God's hand—no, by her own hand—she'd get out of Dodge. She'd be beholden to none. She'd be free. Completely free.

But first she'd give these Texans something to remember.

Strident piano music, so unlike Edward's masterful playing, joined her song. He'd insisted she had her own talents, hidden ones waiting to surface. A surge of confidence made her buoyant and lifted her voice above the clamor. She was pulling it off, holding the men's attention and more. They'd bought her act. They believed she was one of Gertie's girls, just another prostitute with only her wits and her will to keep her alive.

Her gaze skimmed the sea of faces: clean-shaven and bearded, young and old, drunk and sober—then jerked to a halt on one she recognized. Disbelief stole the strength from her voice.

Lord in merciful heaven, it couldn't be.

The face from her past. A face better left there. She kept singing, but every fiber of her body begged to retreat from the stage, to crawl away so she could hide her wounds. Unwelcome memories—her father's betrayal, Madam Garrett's ownership, Edward's death—surfaced, so vivid they could've happened yesterday rather than during the last year, making her voice more breathless, her song more emotional.

She closed her eyes, opened them again ever so slowly. She wasn't dreaming.

The face remained. Solid and unmoving. A face so compelling it was sinful. She cursed every line of his features, from the straight slant of his nose to the robust square of his jaw—and his whiskey-colored eyes.

You took my home. You took my future. You cannot be trusted. The sorrow constricting her chest splintered into anger. *May the devil take* you *straight back to hell.*

AWARENESS PRICKLED the nape of Noah's neck as he and Lewis stood in the doorway of the Northern Star Saloon.

"Jesus," Lewis whispered. "An angel is singing about Texas. I must have died and gone to heaven."

Sweet Jesus, indeed. He'd never heard a voice as compelling as the one that washed over him now. The husky rawness awakened every nerve in his body. It drew him like a parched man to a watering hole.

His step quickened as he pushed through the crowd in search of the voice's owner. Cowhands, trail bosses, and wealthy cattle barons pressed shoulder to shoulder, all focused on one thing—the redhead on a raised stage in the far corner.

His redhead.

The air abandoned his lungs in a rush. He blinked and forced himself to take a second look. Nothing had changed. She was still onstage, but oh, had *she* changed since he'd last seen her. Gone was the tangle of red tresses, replaced by a mass of curls artfully arranged atop her head. Her pretty gingham dress had been swapped for a shiny sapphire creation with a high hem, a tight waist, and a plunging neckline.

Equal parts shocked and mesmerized, he watched her chest rise and fall with the words of her song.

> "She cried so when I left her,
> It like to break my heart,"

Lord, his heart was liable to break right here and now. It missed a beat, tightened as if she'd reached out with her small hand and twisted it. What in the blue devil was she doing dressed like that and in a saloon?

> "And if I ever find her
> We never more will part."

He'd found her. Hadn't even taken a day. But what had happened during their year apart? Dread made his stomach churn as a dozen possible answers, each one more sordid than the last, flashed through his mind.

> "She's the sweetest rose of color
> A fellow ever knew,"

The red of her hair shone like a beacon. He'd remembered it perfectly these last twelve months. But her face was different—paler, while the blush on her cheeks was too vivid.

> "Her eyes are bright as diamonds,
> They sparkle like the dew."

From this distance, he couldn't see the color of her eyes, but he didn't have to. They'd be green as a summer meadow and glittering with tears. Tears he'd caused.

An avalanche of regrets roared in his ears, blocking out all sound. The one person he'd loved was gone, wiped out much like he'd destroyed this woman's farm. Now there was only her, haunting his dreams, both sleeping and waking. Her memory had called to him in Texas, same as her voice broke through his grief and called to him now.

> "We'll play the banjo gaily,
> and we'll sing the songs of yore,
> And the Yellow Rose of Texas
> Shall be mine forevermore."

With that last line, Noah made a promise—to God, to himself, and the whole forsaken town of Dodge. He wasn't leaving until he fixed the wrong he'd done.

CHAPTER 2

"And you scoffed at my suggestion," Lewis said in a voice hushed with both appreciation and amazement, "that we'd find anything of worth in a saloon."

Noah wrenched his gaze from the stage to stare at his friend. "Why is she here?"

"You know her?" Lewis' eyebrows rose even further. "Is she what you came searching for?"

Noah spun on his heel and made a beeline for the bar. He ordered a shot of whiskey and drank it in one gulp. The cheap liquor burned a path down his throat, making him grimace. The bartender reached out a hand as big as a dinner plate to remove the bottle.

"Leave it," Noah growled, then poured himself another glass and tossed it back even faster. Out of the corner of his eye, he saw that Lewis had joined him.

"Last year, your trip to Dodge…" Lewis' voice lacked its usual hint of merriment. "I always wanted to ask… You came home awfully cut up about your brother, but there's more, isn't there?" He glanced at the stage. "I'll admit she's mighty pretty, but you could pay dozens of saloon girls to help you forget about—"

Noah seized Lewis by his shirtfront. He wasn't sure if he did so to shut up his friend or keep himself from keeling over. A sudden dizziness was making it difficult to breathe. "I don't deserve to forget. I deserve to rot in hell."

Lewis' face went as white as bleached bone. "Noah, you're scaring me. Tell me why you came back to Dodge."

Noah released him, but only so he could pour himself another whiskey. He knocked back the third drink, despairing when it still failed to numb the guilt stabbing his conscience. First his brother, then her. He'd destroyed both of their lives. Jacob was dead, and she was working in one of the roughest saloons in the West.

What happened to her farm? To her father? To the money I left them? He poured another drink and rotated the glass in his hand, searching for answers in the amber liquid.

"For God's sake," Lewis said. "Say something."

"Yes, she's the reason I came north with you," he managed through gritted teeth. "Only she wasn't a *whore*—" the word stuck in his throat, had to be forced out, "—when I met her last." The full weight of the situation pressed down on him, crushing him. "I'm responsible for making her one."

Lewis' eyes flared with disbelief. He opened his mouth to reply, but a cool, feminine voice behind them interrupted.

"Well, I declare. I reckon I've never laid eyes on two such eye-catching men in all my life." A delighted chuckle followed, then the woman announced, "And that's saying something. Name's Gertie Garrett. Welcome to my saloon."

The middle-aged madam's squat frame sported a massive bosom and red hair, like Timothy Sullivan's daughter, but there was a world of difference in the color. While

Miss Sullivan's mane gleamed with gold and strawberry tones, this woman's hair was harsh and brassy as old copper. Her cloying floral scent made him wrinkle his nose. Everything about her was overstated, overpowering.

Right now Noah welcomed her vulgarity. The force of it, the distraction, anything to halt his careening thoughts and wandering gaze. Despite his best efforts, he was staring at the stage again.

"Ah, you are intrigued by my Sadie," the madam observed.

The word "my" raised Noah's hackles. He gave Gertie Garrett his full attention. The hint of a smile curved her scarlet mouth, as if she were a mother mentioning a beloved daughter. But shrewdness narrowed her kohl-painted eyes. His hands tightened into fists. Madam Garrett owned this saloon. She owned Sadie. She was making that relationship clear.

The madam raised a brow at his continued silence. "Many have been interested. The girl caused a bidding war when I first got her. But tonight I can arrange for her to spend time with you."

Noah fought the urge to punch Madam Garrett—and every person in the room who might have forced Sadie to do anything against her will. His inclination must have shown in his stillness, because Lewis stepped between him and the madam.

Anticipation shone in the woman's eyes. "Sadie deals a fine hand of poker. I'm certain one of you gentlemen would enjoy trying your luck with her."

Lewis shook his head. "Neither one of us is much for playing cards. We should be going."

Noah shouldered Lewis aside. "I'm not leaving." With folded arms, he faced the madam. "The sooner you set up

your game, the better. I want to sit down with Sadie immediately."

SADIE DOGGEDLY AVOIDED MAKING eye contact with the
brooding man seated across the card table. Her thoughts
were harder to control. The Texan had been back in her life
less than an hour, and every second of that hour she'd spent
recalling his self-assured manner when he'd saved her from
being trampled and told her that her farm could be rebuilt.

Then he'd left.

Anger and disappointment made her hand tremble, like
a drunk letting go of an empty bottle, as she dealt the last
card.

She glanced up and caught him frowning, his whiskey-
colored eyes locked on her fingers. She dropped her hand,
palm down, onto the table, anchoring herself while she
concentrated on suppressing her reactions. Unable to look
away, she followed his gaze upward, over her gaudy dress,
pausing for a heartbeat on the exposed flesh of her chest
where—if possible—his eyes narrowed even more before
they rose to her face.

Noah Ballantyne. When he'd arrived at her table, intro-
ductions had been made. He'd spoken in the same rumbling
deep voice that continued to befuddle her. She knew his
name now. She knew who to curse.

Deciding it was safer to concentrate on the others at the
table, she assessed the two men seated with them: a fair-
haired man named Mr. Adams and a cowhand still damp
from a scrubbing at the bathhouse. The cowhand fidgeted
with the collar of a too tight shirt and the brim of a too large
hat, seesawing between praising and condemning his new

clothing. Mr. Adams' smile and cordial replies never wavered. He was a handsome man, but nowhere near as striking as her cowboy.

Damn it. Noah Ballantyne wasn't her anything. Desperate for a distraction, she scanned the table again.

Cora's stare, coming straight down the woman's upturned nose, snared her attention. Perched on the arm of Mr. Adams' chair, the ebony-haired beauty's ample curves and charm made her feel dull and dimwitted. She cared little about her looks, but in Dodge a dearth of knowledge could prove deadly.

Eyebrows arched in challenge, Cora traced a slow but precise finger down Mr. Adams' chest. Only after her hand disappeared below the table did she give Mr. Adams her full attention, along with a murmured invitation from him to accompany her upstairs.

Sadie imagined herself and Mr. Ballantyne climbing the steps to the second-story rooms, his arm around her waist, binding her close. What would happen if they were alone in her room? She pictured him lying down with her, strong and sure, holding her on her bed instead of the trampled earth of her farm.

Around her, the cacophony of braying voices faded to a dull roar. The heat in her cheeks spilled over, spiraling down to curl low in her body. The tension arched her back, making her sway toward him.

Mr. Ballantyne reached out as if to steady her. His tanned, work-roughed fingers hesitated short of her arm.

The wholesome scents of soap and leather tickled her nose, enticing her to remove the gap between them and touch the faded blue shirt hugging his arms, the rough-cut leather vest encasing his chest, the sheepskin coat on the back of his chair. The same coat he'd worn when they first met.

He hadn't bothered to buy new clothes.

A sudden chill chased the heat from her body. He wasn't here to impress anyone and, judging from his lack of attention for his cards lying on the table, he wasn't here to play poker either. So why was he here?

"Why are you so pale?" Mr. Ballantyne's unexpected question made her jaw drop.

His eyes searched hers.

Behind her, Gertie cleared her throat, snapping her back to reality. Gertie always had a way of doing that. The heartless woman needed to pay for what she'd done to Edward. And when she did, Sadie could stop dealing cards to men who, when they stared at a woman like Mr. Ballantyne was looking at her, desired one thing. The one thing she not only wouldn't, but couldn't give.

She edged back in her seat.

"Hey!" The cowhand sitting next to her slapped his cards on the table, making the chips rattle. "You ain't leavin', are you?" He jumped out of his chair. His damp hair stuck out at all angles like a rooster with its feathers ruffled. "You haven't answered my question."

She struggled to guess what he might have asked.

The cowhand's face darkened with a flush of annoyance. "You think yer too good to talk to likes of me." He yanked her out of her chair and up against his side. "Well, I've five dollars that says yer mine for ten minutes, same as any whore in this here room."

Her gasp of surprise and then pain, as his grip tightened on her arm, was drowned out by the screech of a chair being shoved back. Mr. Ballantyne had launched to his feet. The card table between them pitched violently. The chips scattered and struck the floor with the clatter of a rockslide.

Gertie bellowed Handsome John's name. An instant later he stood by his employer's side. He didn't stay there long. The Northern Star's peacekeeper pressed forward, looming over her unwelcome suitor, who had yet to release her arm. John was anything but handsome, having come out the other side of a knife fight the hands-down loser, but Sadie welcomed the sight of him.

Another shadow fell over her. Glaring at the cowhand's grasp on her arm, Mr. Ballantyne towered over her, like a storm cloud ready to descend. His eyes had lost all warmth. The change chilled her to the bone.

She didn't want him or John to get hurt. Only Gertie deserved that level of retribution.

Fixing her attention on the cowhand, she said, "You have misinterpreted the situation, Mr...."

"Miller. See! You can't even remember my name."

"Mr. Miller, let me assure you that it is I who is not good enough for you." She'd spoken as politely as she could, trying to keep her voice calm even with his fingers digging into her arm. *Hold steady. Don't panic.*

Mr. Ballantyne took a step closer to her, robbing her of logical thought and whatever words she might have uttered next.

John moved in on Miller. "Yer new in town and wet around the ears in more than one way. You don't want this lady. Pick another. One without—" his gaze cut to her before locking on Miller again, "—Cupid's Disease. In case yer still confused, I'll put it plainly. You dally with her, you get syphilis."

Mr. Ballantyne flinched as if he'd been slapped, while at

the same time Miller dropped her arm faster than a coyote learning a porcupine has quills.

"The French pox?" Miller's words broke the bubble of silence that had briefly cocooned her.

She fought the urge to lay a protective hand over her aching arm. Feeling the weight of everyone's attention on her, her skin prickled then flushed with heat. What must Mr. Ballantyne be thinking?

An increasingly familiar sickness tormented the pit of her stomach. Then her gut heaved. Dread made her abandon all pretenses. She wrapped her arms around her abdomen. But what alarmed her most was the sudden impulse to deny that she had the disease.

In the past, she'd embraced every opportunity to maintain the illusion of her illness—to the point where she really had become sick. Just not in the way everyone assumed. The medicine the doctor prescribed was making her ill, giving her symptoms that mimicked the pox. The doctor wasn't aware of that, and she couldn't tell him. Not if she wanted to maintain the lie that she had syphilis.

Her lies were all that stood between her and a life of prostitution. It was too late to chart a new course.

Miller's face wrinkled in disgust as he scrubbed his palm over the front of his shirt. "What good's a whore you can't bed?"

John shoved Miller back into his seat. "Would you rather look at me all night while I dealt your cards?" John placed a hand on either side of the chair and leaned over the man. Unforgiving white scars crisscrossed John's face.

"Point taken," Miller grunted and picked up his cards.

As John left, Sadie's stomach dropped back into place. She sat down with a similar swiftness, not trusting her legs to hold her up. She dared a glance in Mr. Ballantyne's direction. He didn't say a word but sat as well, his attention on the card table—a location that had held no interest until he'd been told she was ill.

A profound sadness squeezed her heart.

Miller laughed, his ruffled feathers soothed. "Having you deal my cards beats looking at Squirrel Tooth Alice across the street at the Crystal Palace, too." He leered at her with a grin that made the aforementioned lady's imperfections appear flawless.

Jarring piano music abused her ears and her heart. A cruel reminder that Edward should've been here playing the instrument like he'd done whenever he needed to revive himself during lengthy gambling matches.

Sadie met Miller's stare and refused to look away. She must face each challenge until she came to the one that mattered most. She'd honor her promise to retrieve what Gertie had stolen from Edward. And in doing so, she'd be free. Free to leave Dodge. Free to go far away where she could then worry about her health and her future.

She gathered the cards that lay scattered across the table. Life had dealt her a losing hand, but she was making the best of it. Only two people knew her secret. One was in the grave; the other had vanished. With them had gone the truth—she was a whore in name only. The assumption that she had syphilis, a card she played daily, ensured she stayed that way.

"We all make do with what we have, sir," she replied as sweetly as she could, leaning toward Miller as if she considered him the most fascinating man in the room, and proceeded to deal him his own losing hand.

NOAH STARED AT HIS CARDS, seeing none of them.

Merciful Mother of God, that was why Sadie looked so drawn, so pale, so fragile. She was sick, and not with just any illness. He didn't know much about the French pox, but he knew she could go blind or insane. She could die. Hadn't some even ended their lives by their own hand, too overwhelmed by the stigma of their condition to continue living?

Noah's lungs seized, his guilt pressing down on him from all sides. He was to blame. First Sadie had lost her farm, then her innocence when she came to work in this saloon. And now she battled a disease that could end the one thing she had left—her life.

Shame filled him, but he forced himself to look at her. He was certain he'd find hatred etched onto her face. Instead, she sat serenely across from him, as if she didn't have a care in the world. She should've been railing at her fate, at him. She must despise him. How could she not?

He remembered the spitfire he'd met a year ago. She'd launched herself at him with fists and ferocity, and rightfully so. Tonight she'd barely graced him with a glance. Perversely, he wished she would yell at him again, accuse him of being responsible for her situation. Anything to ease the remorse that drilled into his soul with the grim determination of a longhorn tick.

He continued playing without interest, lasting two more hands before he folded, rose and excused himself from the game. His feet refused to move, though. Sadie's red curls enticed him. The curve of her neck begged to be touched. So did the freckles scattered across her cheeks. He reached out, then drew back. She'd suffered enough. The last thing she needed was the unwanted attention of another man.

He retreated to the bar. Choosing a spot with an unobstructed view of Sadie's table, he slouched with crossed arms over its worn surface and pondered the woman he'd ruined.

A thump shook the counter. Gritting his teeth, he straightened his shoulders and faced the mammoth barkeep who'd served him last time before kicking Miller into line.

The giant inclined his shaggy head toward a bottle of red eye he'd deposited in front of Noah. "From the looks of you, you'll be wantin' me to leave the bottle again."

The whiskey was welcome; anything else was not. He wanted to be alone to think. Praying the man would leave, he poured himself a glass. The amber liquid was halfway to his lips when the barman's words stopped him.

"That be a cryin' shame," he said, thrusting his chin in Sadie's direction. "How she came to town lookin' for work, ended up here, and then got sick. Not five months in Madam Garrett's employ, and she comes down with the pox. Now she's off-limits as an upstairs girl, but downstairs she's a gem." He sighed and turned his attention to polishing a row of glasses behind the bar. "Edward taught her well. You won't find a quicker hand with the cards."

Noah fought the urge to haul him over the bar and lay into him. A moment ago, he'd barely restrained himself from smashing his fist into Miller's face. Now he wished he hadn't. The barkeep had been helpful in preventing any bloodshed, but the reminder of Sadie's downfall made him writhe with equal parts rage and remorse. He wanted to punch someone. He needed to strike out at the world, desperate to right a wrong that couldn't be fixed.

The saloon was too loud, its walls too close. The open range called to him. The compulsion to run flayed his nerves, screaming for him to leave. He couldn't stay here; he didn't have the strength to face his mistakes. And he was a fool to hope he could mend them. He should head for Texas right now and never look back.

But he remained rooted to his chair, staring at Sadie again.

She held him stronger than any guilt or fear. His pulse slowed, allowing a sliver of his old determination to dig in.

He would not abandon her again. He'd figure out a way to help her...to free her from this life. The wariness he'd seen in her eyes, heard in her voice, sensed in her every move—despite her best efforts to conceal it—troubled him.

He had to gain her trust. A trust he didn't deserve.

CHAPTER 3

*T*he next day the sun was high overhead as Sadie guided Gertie's fancy rig and palomino mare toward the cemetery southeast of Dodge. A sudden desire to use the horse and buggy to go even farther flared. She tamped it down.

The first time she'd attempted to flee Dodge, Handsome John had easily found her. His two-tailed leather strap had stung like a horde of irate hornets. It taught a lesson while allowing a girl to return to work. She was dead certain she never wanted to feel its bite again. Nor did she want to live her life on the run, always looking over her shoulder.

But what really held her in Dodge was her vow to Edward. No matter his original motives, he'd been her salvation after John caught her and brought her back to Gertie. She couldn't ignore that debt. And now, as long as the patrons shied away from her because of her distasteful history, she had no need to run. What she needed was more chances to finish searching the Star for all that Gertie had stolen.

She was safe. An uncertain safe, though. Too many things could go wrong, like her dwindling health.

"Concentrate on something positive," she muttered to herself.

The mare's hooves made a comforting thump every time they found the earth, while the harness rattled, adding a merry jingle. Although she enjoyed driving such a fine horse and buggy, she longed for the days when she could saddle a mount and ride. Unfortunately, dizzy spells made staying seated an uncertain venture.

The soft spring air soothed the slight fever prickling her skin. She closed her eyes, savoring its caress. From a corner of her heart, memories of her old life tugged at her. A snug house standing on the very earth it was hewn from, the wind skimming the open prairie like a giant hand bending the buffalo grass so the blades flattened and sprang back with a rustling sigh. Her farm and its peaceful seclusion called to her.

Shaking her head, she strove to cast out her yearning. That part of her life was gone, as incapable of resurrection as those buried in the graveyard before her. She jerked the buggy to a halt, set the brake, and jumped to the ground. Her haste caused the warmth simmering beneath her skin to erupt in a wave of burning heat.

Her pulse pounded and her vision blurred. She latched onto the buggy wheel to keep from falling. So much for the hope that this excursion, and a bit of fresh air, might help rally her strength.

She needed help, but she couldn't depend on anyone but herself.

Even Edward, with whom she'd developed a fast friendship, hadn't held her best interests at heart when he bought her from Gertie. He'd needed Sadie to fill a missing role in his life. And she'd missed her one true opportunity to escape.

Foolish woman. You traded freedom for the need to feel wanted.

The memory of Mr. Ballantyne standing close beside her invaded her thoughts. His attention made her feel wanted. When they'd first met, he'd said he wanted to help her. But his version had been to give money and disappear. She swayed and clutched the wheel with both hands.

Had he already headed home to Texas? Had he left her again?

With her pulse now roaring in her ears, she fought not to collapse. Although she might welcome the opportunity to slumber here among the dead, rather than return to the saloon and match wits with the living.

After a while her headache faded and her vision cleared.

The cemetery sprawled around her, a field of haphazardly planted graves. Their headstones represented a mishmash of lives and loved ones: sizable boards with round cut tops and effusive epitaphs; simple crosses of whitewashed wood etched with a name and date; a few markers created from whatever was at hand—scraps of wood tied together with rope, cloth and even belts. White asters and daisies blanketed the ground, their blossoms overlapping until she couldn't tell where one flower began and another ended.

She released the buggy wheel. She strode past the graves with her attention on the only one that mattered. She'd come to visit her mother. Nothing else was worthy of her time. But the useless compulsion to lash out at a dead man slammed her to a halt beside her father's final resting place.

Damn you. Damn me as well. Why had she tried so hard to prove her worth to him? She'd worked their farm from sunup to sunset. She'd cleaned and cooked and had his meals on the table like clockwork. She'd strove to do every-thing as well as her mother. *Why weren't either of us good enough to earn your love?*

Her only answer was a sudden clatter behind her—hooves on rock and sod, claiming purchase up the rise. A dappled gray galloped toward her with a tireless stride. The long-legged cowboy riding the horse looked equally at ease.

Damn him as well.

Her curses went unheeded. Noah Ballantyne pulled his mount to a halt next to her buggy. He dismounted with effortless grace, not a hint of weakness about him. Their differences riddled her determination with the persistence of a tick.

It always amazed her how a creature as tiny as a tick could be so strong, so relentless. She'd do well to find a way to be as unstoppable.

She studied the man who'd moved to stand within an arm's reach of her.

Deep lines framed his mouth and dark smudges under-scored his eyes, but his mood remained a mystery as he assessed her as well. His attention traveled from the teardrop-shaped boat hat perched on her head down to the delicate front-laced boots below the ruffled hem of her dress. The skirt displayed an immodest portion of her stockinged calves, while the hat was so tiny it offered scant protection from the glaring sun. All perfect for suggesting a profession she was trying hard to maintain.

She forced herself not to squirm under his perusal. Finally, his attention shifted to the graveyard and stopped on her father's headstone. He tugged his weather-beaten Stetson from his head.

"Wasn't aware your father had passed." A long silence elapsed before he spoke again. "I'm sorry, Miss Sullivan."

His hushed tone made her guess he was sorry for a heck of a lot more. But he didn't share his thoughts with her. He just kept frowning at her father's grave.

She swallowed the urge to yell at him like she'd done on her farm. Dredging up her sweetest tone, she said, "Do not trouble yourself, Mr. Ballantyne. My father wasn't worthy of anyone's condolences."

His gaze jumped back to her and narrowed even further. "Then why are you here?"

"To say a final goodbye to my mother." She immediately wished she could take back the words. Talking to him about her father was one thing, but her mother?

Feeling the need to put some distance between them, she hastened through the graves to a plain headstone with the words: *Margaret Sullivan. Loving mother, devoted wife.*

Gone seven years now, her mother had died from a lung fever after they'd traveled from Virginia to Kansas. A journey her mother had made only after her husband forced her to put his need to escape his creditors ahead of her health. A wave of sorrow swept over Sadie—for being separated from her mother, for accepting she'd never be with her again. Not even in death.

Her soul was tainted. She'd be buried in the *other* cemetery—the one for the immoral, the outcasts who died violently with their boots on. If her life ended, her bones would reside in Boot Hill.

Death stalked her. Time was running out. This was the last time she could afford to visit her mother. Dropping to her knees by the grave, she removed the weeds and smoothed the dirt into a tidy swell. She hadn't heard Noah follow her, but she knew he was beside her. The scent of soap and leather, infused with spring air and sweet grass, curled around her. The soulless oppression of Dodge felt a thousand miles away.

Glancing up at him, she whispered, "She was worth a hundred of his kind." Her shoulders slumped. Why had she told him that? Only friends shared such truths. And he was no friend of hers. Was she losing her mind as well as her health?

Brows low over unblinking eyes, he held her gaze. "The money I gave your father—what happened to it?"

Her chin went up, and with it came a terse laugh. She clenched her teeth. *Don't let him control you. Stop jumping at his every word and glance. Or he'll have you swooning at his feet and revealing all your secrets.*

Rounding up her jumbled emotions, she composed her face into what she hoped was an aloof expression. "Is that why you returned to Dodge? For your money? Well, it's long gone. My father was a gambling man. Your money vanished in a week, which is longer than I assumed it'd last."

He moved closer. "That's not what I came for."

She stared at him through narrowed eyes as she considered his reply. "You came with your precious Texan longhorns, pursuing the almighty dollar."

"It's not my herd this time. I'm here for another reason entirely."

Her breath shot out in a huff. "Men. You talk in circles and bend your words to suit your purpose—and your conscience." Overcome with frustration, she stood abruptly and then wished she hadn't.

Stars burst behind her eyes, blinding her, making her sway. A large, work-roughened hand supported her arm. When she gasped, the warmth of Noah's touch retreated. She didn't move again. Not until her vision cleared. When it did, she realized he was standing close, his worried face peering down into hers.

Slowly, carefully, he took a step back. "Are you...all right?"

Alone, the prospect of passing out hadn't seemed so bad. Allowing this man to witness such weakness was unbearable.

"Mr. Ballantyne, it makes no difference to me why you are here." What was one more lie when she'd already told so many? She added a truth to steady herself as she looked him hard in the eye. "What bothers me most is that you are disrupting my life again. *Go home.*"

He matched her glare with one of his own. "No."

She threw up her hands. She was better off sticking to lies. "Suit yourself. I really don't care." And if he wouldn't leave, she would. Carefully, so as not to drain her remaining strength, she moved to step around him.

He moved too, blocking her way. "What happened? Why are you at the Northern Star?" The intensity in his expression stole her breath like a lover stole a kiss. Instead of disgust or disappointment, reactions she'd grown used to seeing on the faces of those who were informed that she was ill, she found interest.

Noah Ballantyne was a far greater danger than she'd first feared.

"Why are you working in a saloon?" he demanded.

Resentment churned inside her chest, threatening to boil over in an endless stream of caustic comments. *Leave me alone!* she cried silently before answering him with as little emotion as she could. "Because you put me there."

The color drained from his face.

"Your herd trampled my garden, destroyed my fence, scattered my cattle. I managed to round up four of the seven.

A useless endeavor when not long afterward they staggered and drooled with the fever from your longhorns' ticks. I had no way to pay the bills, so the bank took back the farm."

He shook his head. "I should've left you more money."

"Why?" She surged forward, making him stumble away from her. "So the money would've lasted two weeks of drinking rather than one? The end would've been the same. We had nothing." She bit back her laugh. "Or rather, *I* had nothing. Or so everyone in Dodge told me when I came begging for a job. But my father had something." She paused, waiting for him to make the connection.

He stared at her blankly, blind to what so many couldn't see. Or didn't want to see.

"Do you have any idea how many girls end up in a saloon because their families needed money?" she asked.

Every muscle in his body went rigid. "A father couldn't—"

"My father could. He sold me to Madam Garrett." She fixed her gaze on the graveyard. The markers blurred with her tears. She blinked them back. No good ever came from crying. "I'm told the madam's money lasted him for a month of drinking...then his liver finally gave out and so did he."

"Jesus, Sadie," Noah growled and grabbed her arm, whether to steady her or himself she knew not.

She stared at his hand, befuddled once again by the gentleness of his hold. How very different from last night's cowhand at the Star.

When he finally released her arm, her heart constricted with regret.

"Do not concern yourself with the details of my past, Mr. Ballantyne. That part of my life is over. It cannot be restored." She marched down the slope toward her buggy.

Noah strode alongside her in silence. When they came

to the buggy, he reached out to assist her, then stopped. She marshaled her flagging strength and climbed in. Flicking the reins across the palomino's back, she set the buggy in motion, only to have Noah grab the bridle.

Her horse snorted and tossed its head. Noah stroked her mane, calming the skittish mare with his touch. A sudden desire to feel that strong but kind hand holding her again overwhelmed Sadie.

"You may be right about the past, but what about the future?" His question jarred her out of her daydream.

"I—have—no—future." Her voice rose with each word until she was yelling.

"That's not true," he shouted back, then clamped his lips tight. After a long pause, he patted the mare's neck again. "You must have dreams."

She jerked back. Was her yearning written on her face for all to observe?

"If you were free to leave Dodge, where would you go?" he inquired in a voice as gentle as his hand on her horse.

The question, as much as his tone, startled her. It was as if he'd opened a door and let in the fresh air she craved when she'd driven out to the graveyard. Her anger snuffed out as easily as a candle flame. But the more she pondered his question, the faster her mind spun. She stared at him, unable to speak.

Where would she go?

Since Edward's death, she hadn't contemplated much beyond taking back what Gertie had stolen and then going somewhere—anywhere—far away. The woman had destroyed too many lives to go completely unpunished. To hope for more seemed greedy.

But she wanted to control her own destiny, to determine

who she associated with and who she did not. The rest of her feelings were too complex to put into words. And even if she could, she wouldn't share them with the man standing next to her. She was loath to confide in anyone, especially him. Everything had gone downhill since the moment he'd ridden into her life.

His hand slid along the mare's neck toward her own clutching the reins. A hand toughened by work and the weather. A hand good with animals. A rancher's hand.

"My farm," she blurted as her gaze jumped to his face. "I'd go back to my farm."

Her impossible request brought a pained look to his brow. She felt a similar pinch in hers. Unlike most of Dodge, this man didn't have a heart of stone. But no matter how much he regretted what his cattle destroyed last year, he'd never hurt as deeply as she did.

The instant he released her horse, she urged the mare toward town.

She gritted her teeth when he showed up on his gray beside her. He might not be hardhearted, but he was definitely bullheaded. Did he intend to shadow her all day?

The heat of her fever flared again. So did her desire for privacy. She craned her neck in search of the Star. He couldn't follow her into her room upstairs. Not without paying. And in her condition, she had nothing he'd want to buy. Oddly, her bedroom was her one sanctuary. She craved the tiny room's solitude more than ever.

The corridor of Dodge's Front Street, crowded with livestock and wagons, thwarted her. Even those on foot experienced delays while weaving through the chaos. Her progress slowed to a crawl. Noah reined in his mount to match her pace.

Determined to ignore him, she stared at the street ahead.

Crossing the fairway was the good Mrs. Dunne, who had refused her employment at the boarding house. Long in the face and round in the middle, Mrs. Dunne had informed Sadie she would be too much of a distraction in her establishment. Even though Mrs. Dunne could use help with the cooking and cleaning for her many guests, she said she wouldn't hire a young, unmarried woman such as Sadie.

The portly, well-dressed banker, George Fairfax, strolled along the boardwalk with the measured stride of a contented man. When Sadie had approached him searching for work, she'd surprised him with her mastery of reading and writing, and a natural inclination to summing. He'd still insisted a woman's place was at home, with her husband, not in his bank. He wouldn't hire her either.

Everyone she'd approached had refused to help, first when she'd inquired politely and again when she'd returned to beg. In the end, her efforts hadn't mattered. It'd been an illusion to believe she controlled her own destiny.

Her father had put an end to her quest to find honest work when he sold her for eighty silver dollars. She recalled the dazzling orbs sliding through his fingers, shining so brightly they hurt her eyes. That was the last time she'd seen him, head bent, counting the coins to make sure he hadn't been cheated.

She might not be able to trust anyone, but she couldn't give up either. The heirlooms Gertie had pilfered—Sadie's ticket out of Dodge—couldn't stay hidden forever.

She stole a glance left, then right. Noah no longer rode beside her while down the street, the Northern Star's faded green balcony beckoned. She exhaled a sigh of relief laced with an annoying amount of disappointment.

Be careful. You can't afford to become dependent on Noah Ballantyne or anyone else. With her attention set on the Star, she counted the strides it'd take the mare to reach the swinging double doors.

The buggy lurched to a halt. She half expected to discover Noah's firm grip on her rein, wanting to control her life again. Instead, she found a much paler and softer hand. Its owner was a slope-shouldered man dressed in a tailored jacket and a paisley waistcoat. A lofty top hat gave him height, but the stiff band collar of his shirt did little for his receding chin.

Robert Wardell.

A chill snaked up her spine. Last autumn, Wardell had bid for her company and lost. The defeat hadn't sat well with him. One of the richest men in town, he was accustomed to getting what he wanted. He'd wanted Sadie. But Edward, riding a wave of luck with the cards, had more ready cash, so she'd been auctioned off to a gambler instead of a cattle baron.

Wardell had left town in a sour mood. Rumor had it he'd gone to Abilene or Wichita. Now he was back. And Edward was gone, dead and buried under six feet of Kansas clay, but not before he'd left his legacy, his mark. The assumption that she had the French pox was her only salvation from Wardell and all the other men who visited the Star.

"Well, well, well," Wardell drawled, his pale-blue eyes raking her. "If it isn't the lovely Miss Sadie. Feeling better today? On the road to recovery, I hope?"

The French pox wasn't a death sentence. Doctor Rhodes said many things about the disease were still a mystery. Some people recovered and lived normal lives, as if they'd never been touched by the symptoms and stigma of the disease. Others weren't so lucky. Their journey on Earth came to a painful and horrific conclusion.

Too many in town were waiting to learn which direction her life would take.

When Gertie demanded a timeline, Doctor Rhodes said they might only have to wait a month, maybe less. If the doctor deemed her recovered, the madam would inform the entire town. Wardell would be the first one at her bedroom door.

She couldn't allow that to happen. She also couldn't continue taking the medicine if she valued her life. The day she defeated Gertie, she'd stop. Hopefully, that day would come soon.

She willed Wardell to release the mare and return to the veranda of the Great Western Hotel. A sideways glance revealed his entourage entrenched on the hotel's elegant terrace, smoking cigars and observing their exchange with interest.

Her grip on her reins tightened. "How considerate of you to inquire about my health, Mr. Wardell. You truly are a gentleman among the crude and callous."

He chuckled, unperturbed by the scorn in her voice. "That's one of the things I've always enjoyed about you, Miss Sadie—your fiery temper. It matches your hair. Your precious Edward may have outmaneuvered me last year, but I'll have you soon. I look forward to bending you to my will with a firm hand in that red mane."

Her courage left her in a startled gasp, abandoning her to face Wardell's vulgarity alone.

A guttural growl erupted on the other side of her mare, cracking Sadie's last bit of composure as swiftly as a wolf could break a brittle bone.

With a shrill whinny, her horse reared as high as the harness would allow. Caught off balance, Wardell released the bridle. The mare lunged at the reins, eager to bolt. All that stopped her was the flash of Noah's broad-shouldered frame, now dismounted and crossing in front of her. The mare shuffled back until her hindquarters bumped the buggy.

She had no place to go. Much like Sadie.

Murderous intent twisted Noah's face. He grabbed Wardell by the collar and jerked him off his feet. "You'll pay for that comment, you son of a—"

"Gentlemen. Gentlemen!" Sadie shouted as Noah's free hand drew back in a fist. She forced her tone lower, striving for a calm that eluded her. "This *conversation* is useless, a moot point, a frivolity." Noah's hand halted, hovering in the air. "I urge you to remember my condition, which makes all talk about such matters ridiculous."

Noah released Wardell with a shove.

Attention locked on Noah, Wardell lifted shaking hands to straighten his jacket and ribbon necktie before saying, "Until next month then, Miss Sadie. When you are either fully recovered, and we can take up where we left off, or you are—" His gaze, filled with a chagrined yet aggravated expression, cut to her. He cleared his throat.

She held onto her smile and her determination not to let his statement go unfinished. "Or I'll be what? An inhabitant of the asylum or the boneyard?" She snapped her reins, and the mare leaped forward, forcing both men to jump out of the way. "I should be so lucky," she called over her shoulder. "Then I'd be of no more interest to you or anyone else in this godforsaken town."

Let them believe she welcomed her own death. The only

death she cared about was Edward's. Gertie may have taken his life, but Sadie had pledged that the madam wouldn't keep the two items Edward cherished most. The heirlooms he'd refused to gamble or sell.

Unfortunately, upholding that promise might be Sadie's quickest route to the grave.

CHAPTER 4

$\mathcal{L}$oading two thousand head of cattle into a series of narrow stock cars was a sight to behold. The din and dust were spectacular. The swirling haze swallowed the vermilion sphere on the western horizon, while the ground beneath Noah's feet vibrated like a living thing. Dodge's railroad depot was a plain affair, a few corrals with a series of chutes and ramps on the edge of town. Nothing fancy. Only what was needed to get the job done.

The trains didn't stay long. The instant this one arrived, the depot men had hauled open its sliding doors and bent their backs to the task of unloading supplies for the town. Refilling the compartments—this time with cattle—was taking even less time. Soon the firebox would be stoked, the engine would belch black smoke, and the iron horse would pull its cargo east to the Union Stock Yards in Chicago.

Noah's work would be done. He could go home.

What he deserved was to stand here choking on the dust until the mild spring weather transformed into a sweltering summer that better represented the hell that was Dodge.

He shot another glance over his shoulder. Lewis still

conversed with Robert Wardell, the purchaser of the herd. Noah recalled every vile word the cattle buyer had said to Sadie earlier that day, and his fists clenched, once again itching to lay the bastard out cold. Instead, he remained rooted by the loading pens, stewing in silence.

Lewis and Wardell shook hands and then parted.

A satisfied grin split Lewis' face as he approached Noah. "Well, two months of chewing dust behind those beasts is history. That's the last we'll see of them." He raised his voice to be heard above the racket. "And fifteen dollars a head makes the parting even sweeter. I can finally buy the land beside your ranch and my folks' and begin building my own spread."

"You've worked plenty hard for every cent. Don't squander too many of them here. A smart man doesn't stay long in Dodge." *Unlike me, who hasn't got a lick of sense.* He turned his back on the stockyard and headed for the center of town.

Lewis fell in beside him. "Don't worry. Never been more eager to start something and, to tell the truth, I'm a mite lonesome for home." He laughed. "Dodge isn't for me. Too brash. Too wild. Exactly as you said it'd be."

They followed the railroad tracks, careful to stay on the south side. The town called the band of metal the "deadline" because carrying a gun was only legal on the south side. Noah wasn't giving up his revolver. Plus, the Northern Star and Sadie were on the south side.

"When we heading out?" Lewis asked.

Noah cast him a sidelong glance. Lewis stared at him, head cocked, eyes narrowed with curiosity. Noah recognized that look. His friend had more on his mind than the journey home.

"Thought I might stay...for a few more days," he answered, trying to choose his words carefully.

"I can wait a day or two."

"Could be more."

Lewis waved a hand, dismissing his amendment. "That's all right, too. You helped me out, agreeing to drive my herd. I—"

"You got a ranch waiting for you. Don't want to hold you up."

"Humph. You got one too." Lewis' tone rumbled with concern. "Or have you forgotten?"

In the last year, he hadn't given his home much consideration. Unusual for him. For as long as he could remember, the land had meant everything.

He'd been eleven when his father and mother died— him in a range dispute and her not long after while giving birth to Noah's brother. He thanked the Almighty for the ranch foreman and his wife. The pair had raised Jacob and held the ranch together until Noah could take up the reins.

Working the land and dreaming of ways to improve it had always filled him with an unwavering satisfaction. Now he felt...empty.

"Nothing at home needs my attention. Hurrying back won't make any difference."

"Noah, I'm worried about you."

"Don't be."

Lewis drew in a deep breath, then blurted, "It wasn't your fault—what happened to Jacob."

A familiar tightness constricted his chest. "Whose fault is it then? My brother's dead. Someone should answer for that."

"It was an accident."

"An accident that could've been prevented."

"No, it couldn't have."

Noah quickened his pace, his pulse accelerating as well. "You weren't there. You don't know."

Lewis matched his stride, sticking close. "You're right. I wasn't there. I don't know. But I want to know, and you won't talk to me or anyone."

"Let it be," Noah growled. They were drawing a fair bit of attention as they stormed down Front Street. It was the least of his concerns. He wanted the conversation to end.

"Jacob was killed," Lewis continued with an unusual persistence. "I believe it was an accident, but you don't. So, what are you contemplating—an eye for an eye?"

"I don't want to talk about—"

"Your brother was a grown man. He wasn't a kid anymore. Beating yourself up for his death won't do any good."

Noah ground to a halt. Every muscle in his body coiled as he spun to face Lewis.

One of Lewis' brows arched in challenge. "Beating me up for speaking the truth won't do any good either."

Inhaling hard, Noah struggled to rein in his anger. "I was the one with Jacob when he died." The pain of that day returned tenfold, leaving him as weak and vulnerable as a newborn calf. "I was riding an arm's length away from him," he bit out in a strangled voice, "when the storm struck and our herd stampeded." He closed his eyes against the memory. "One moment he was there, the next he wasn't. Knocked down and trampled while I didn't even suffer a scratch."

"That doesn't mean you're responsible, and shutting everyone out won't help. You should've told me sooner."

Noah cleared his throat. The rasp that came out shocked

even his ears, like an animal's rattling death cry. "He was my brother. I should've been able to save him."

Lewis grasped his shoulder and squeezed. Hard. "His death wasn't your fault."

He accepted the pain. Welcomed it. He refused to open his eyes, though.

Lewis shook him enough to rock him on his heels. "Look at me."

When he finally did, Lewis' grip eased, but he didn't release him.

"For as long as I've known you, you've taken on too much. You've been like this since we were kids, and inheriting your ranch at such a young age didn't help. Some things are beyond a man's control. You can't save everyone."

Tears stung the backs of his eyes. He jerked free of Lewis' hold and walked away so his friend wouldn't see. "You're right. I can't even save a single person."

Lewis dogged his side. "But staying in Dodge? What good'll that do?"

"I might be able to make a difference here."

"You said yourself that a smart person doesn't stay long in Dodge." Lewis scrubbed his hand over the back of his neck. "Others say not a week goes by without someone dying. The drink and debauchery turn men into easy targets for the swindlers, who grow richer and more corrupt every time a new herd and its drovers arrive."

"I ain't disagreeing."

"Then why not leave?"

Noah shrugged.

"Are any of them worth the risk? They're either ruffians or loafers. None are worth the cost. What if the price is your own death?" Lewis grimaced. "Or is that what you're really after?"

A bitter snort of laughter escaped Noah. "Stop worrying. I'm not done living. Jus' want to do something with a purpose."

"Like what?"

"Rightin' a wrong."

Lewis kept silent longer than usual. Then he said quietly, almost reverently, "Oh, now I get it. The siren."

Noah frowned. "What're you blathering on about?"

A smile curved Lewis' lips. "The pint-sized redhead who has you buffaloed, that's *who* I'm talking about. You're pining over that gal who made pulp of your brain with her song." He let out his breath in a whoosh. "At least that shows you're still kicking. You're not touched in the head. You're merely feeling your oats."

"I want to help her," Noah snapped. "Not bed her."

Lewis grinned. "You could do both. I hope she makes a full recovery."

Noah's prayers for the same were overcast by the harsh reality of the past. "Her being sick and working in a saloon happened because of me. She hates me. I don't blame her. So as soon as I do right by her, I'll get out of her way and head for Texas." Pain, sudden and deep, lanced his heart. He crossed his arms to prevent himself from rubbing his chest in an attempt to ease his suffering. He lengthened his stride. His future held only one path.

"You're as stubborn as ever." Lewis released a long-suffering sigh. "I might as well get out of *your* way. I'll leave tomorrow, but first I want a proper sendoff." He laughed and slapped Noah on the back. "Don't reckon you need coaxing to visit a saloon today, since we're heading straight for one." He gestured to the Northern Star up ahead.

Noah suspected he wouldn't like what came next. Nevertheless, he maintained his course. He'd take a wagonload of punishments as long as Sadie stayed safe.

THE STAR WAS in full swing, overflowing with raucous voices and a barrage of discordant piano music that had taken over in the absence of Edward's talented playing. Outside, an inky sky shrouded the town, while inside, kerosene lanterns glowed from every corner, illuminating the revelers and beckoning lost souls from the street. Gertie had invested a lot of time in making her saloon one of the most popular watering holes in Dodge.

Any improvements or allure were lost on Sadie. Even Edward's absence didn't consume her thoughts like before.

Tonight, her mind and body were tuned to one thing—the man once again sitting with her. After his friend departed with Cora, Noah had come straight to her table and hadn't left. Her breath caught in her throat, aggravating the increasing dryness there.

Why must he keep looking at her instead of his cards?

Ignore him. You have bigger worries.

To her right sat Robert Wardell. He'd joined her table as if their ugly encounter in the street this afternoon hadn't occurred. Or was he here because of it? Did he seek to strengthen his claim on her? A troublesome notion. Probably absurd as well. But then, what did she know about the peculiarities of men?

The cards didn't lie, though. Wardell's poker playing was a reflection of his personality, all bluster and show. He bet heavily, expected the cards to run in his favor, and became surly when they did not. In contrast, Noah played without a trace of emotion. He made the most of the cards he was dealt, but gave the impression that he had no real interest in the outcome.

The thin man who'd introduced himself as simply Davenport before sitting down on her left was harder to nail down. Dressed in the swanky garb common to professional gamblers, he reminded her of Edward. On her first evening at the Star, Edward had paid Gertie an outrageous amount for Sadie, sufficient for five months of exclusive companionship. He'd been her first lesson in the good that money could do.

Davenport even had similar mannerisms, but something about him made her wary. She looked closer. *There it was.* His expensive clothing was frayed around the collar and cuffs. Edward always said an unkempt gambler was a man down on his luck.

When luck deserted this man completely, what would he do?

She frowned as Davenport's slender fingers tossed more chips on the pile, and he raised the bet. Had he ever seen a day's labor? Her gaze jumped to Noah's hands, capable and tanned, deftly holding his cards. When he ran his thumb over their tops, she tensed for another reason.

This unwanted desire could ruin everything. Distracted people forgot the plans they'd crafted so carefully. They also lost track of the dangers sitting right next to them.

The memory of Miller's bruising grip on her arm had her scanning the other men at her table.

A pair of cowboys, fresh from the trail, rounded out their group. They wore snow-white band-collar shirts and pinstriped trousers, most likely purchased this morning from Wright and Beverly's Mercantile. They played impulsively and flamboyantly with dollars she suspected were as new as their pockets. Come morning, they'd only have the pockets.

A wave of fatigue flooded her. These nights were becoming more difficult to endure. Her condition had taken a turn for the worse. Tonight, her body ached while the dry cough hovering in her throat was relentless. Stiffening her backbone and her resolve against her weakness, she focused on the cards lining the table and those she dealt off the deck.

She might be ill, but she must only show a hint of poor health, enough to support her ruse. Gertie was strict about appearances, and her motto: *give the customers what they want or, failing that, the illusion they're getting it.*

She'd use the madam's own advice to beat her.

A victorious hoot pulled her from her musings.

One of the cowboys leaned across the table and pointed his finger at Davenport. "This time I've got ya! Yer winnin' streak's over."

Davenport's luck tonight was indeed remarkable. She hadn't caught him cheating, but she didn't need to see something to know it was true. If he was playing the table, now was the time to be sensible—fold a hand or two, let the cowboys have a few wins.

Noah folded, as did Wardell. All eyes turned to Davenport.

He tossed more chips onto the pile. "I don't know, gentlemen. I believe Lady Luck remains on my side." He winked at her and then addressed the cowboys. "Shall we see if she's on yours?"

One of them slapped down his cards: three queens and a pair of jacks. "A full house! You'll need more than luck to beat that."

Davenport revealed his hand: four aces and the king of clubs...the highest fifth card.

Sadie stiffened. The fool. The arrogant fool.

"That's... That's impossible." The cowboy swallowed convulsively. His bulging eyes finally narrowed. "Yer a low-down cheat."

"And you are a poor loser." Davenport laughed and reached for the pot. The cowboy seized his arm. Davenport struggled to shake off his hold. A pair of kings fell out of his sleeve.

Everyone froze. Except for Davenport. His gaze darted around the table, scurrying from face to face before halting on hers and flaring with hope. She was his way out.

Alarm snapped her nerves tight. She sprang to her feet at the same time as Davenport. He jerked free of the cowboy and grabbed her, yanking her in front of him. One arm encircled her throat, while the other leveled a derringer at the rest of the room.

"Stay back, or I'll shoot."

Everyone complied except Noah. He advanced as Davenport shuffled backward, dragging her with him.

"I said, stay back." Davenport turned his palm pistol toward her. The elaborate floral scroll engraved on the barrel flashed close by her eyes before disappearing. Only to be found again when the mouth of the barrel came to rest against her temple.

Terror, swift and unstoppable, wrenched a gasp from her lips.

Noah halted.

"That's better. I don't want to hurt the lady." Despite his words, he jammed the gun harder against her skull. "But if anyone tries to stop me, I will."

Her lungs seized, depriving her of air and hope.

"You're going to be fine. Just fine," Noah said in a low, unhurried drawl. The honey-brown depths of his eyes warmed her, chasing away her fear. Then his gaze shifted to Davenport, and his expression became so cold and unforgiving that her blood turned to ice.

"You, on the other hand, are a dead man." Noah's vow cut the air like a whip.

With her as a shield, Davenport retreated toward the rear door that opened to the alley. Noah moved with them, never once taking his eyes off Davenport.

"You have no say in the matter." Davenport's back hit the door, and they stopped. The arm around her throat tightened, but the hand holding the derringer lowered.

The removal of the gun barrel from her temple left her shaking with relief. Now was the time for her to break free. Free of everyone in this room, free of Dodge. She drew in a breath for courage and strength.

"As you can see, I still—" Davenport fumbled with the door handle, trying to open it while maintaining his grip on the gun as well.

What if he succeeded in forcing her outside? Into the murky alley? And the endless black beyond? She couldn't let that happen. Keeping her arm close to her body, she raised her hand.

Behind her, the door squeaked. A gust of frigid air raised gooseflesh on her already chilled skin.

"I still hold the winning hand," Davenport finished in a triumphant tone. The chest behind her shook with laughter. "I'm leaving and taking this pretty card with me."

Her fingers curled into a fist. She swung her arm down and back. Her elbow struck the paltry flesh of Davenport's midsection. His gasp echoed in her ear. She wrenched sideways, aiming to slip her chin under the noose loosening around her neck—until it jerked tight again.

A shot rang out. The acridity of gunpowder stung her nostrils. Suddenly, she stood alone. She was free!

The desire to remain free overpowered her. With it came the impulse to leap to the second part of her plan—to take the steps she'd arranged for her flight from Dodge without being caught. She spun toward the door.

The flash of an engraved derringer caught her eye, then the man holding it despite otherwise sprawling limp on the floor between her and escape. Blood seeped from a tiny hole in the center of Davenport's forehead. His wide eyes stared sightlessly up at her.

He'd passed from this mortal realm into the next. For him, Dodge wasn't even a memory. Would death be the only way she'd leave as well?

The room tilted, and she joined him on the floor.

CHAPTER 5

"*W*hy's she shivering like this?" Noah laid his hand gently against Sadie's forehead, and his concern grew. "Her skin's cold as winter. What's wrong?"

After Sadie had collapsed, he'd carried her, under Gertie's watchful eye, to the Star's second floor and placed her on a narrow bed flanked by an ancient bureau and a sliver of a window. The cramped room held faded red walls, yellow curtains, and rough-hewn floorboards unadorned by any rug. There wasn't even a single chair.

Gertie had said this was Sadie's room, but it wasn't the kind of room he would've pictured her residing in. It resembled the lodgings of a maid more than a painted lady. The madam stood at the foot of the bed while he knelt by one side and the town doctor hovered by the other.

Doctor Rhodes blew a tangle of coffee-colored hair with a single streak of white away from his eyes as he bent to inspect Sadie's pallor and breathing. "Chills and fevers are common symptoms of syphilis, but this could also be from shock brought on by tonight's events."

A rumpled dark-blue suit jacket hung from the man's stooped shoulders, making Noah guess he hadn't seen his bed in a while.

Rhodes rummaged through his beat-up case before he shut it with a snap and a sigh that spiked Noah's frustration. "Not much we can do besides make her comfortable and give her some quiet."

Noah glared at him. "There must be something more."

The doctor's hunch became more pronounced, like a porcupine curling up in defense. Why wasn't he offering options? Didn't doctors swear oaths to cure people?

Rhodes turned toward the door.

"You're not leaving, are you?" Noah roared in disbelief.

Spine ramrod straight, Rhodes spun to face him. Anger flashed in the depths of the man's dark eyes. "There really is nothing I can do. Meanwhile, a dozen more patients are waiting on me." Inch by inch, the hunch reclaimed his shoulders as he muttered, "Maybe I can help them. Maybe I can't. Some days I wonder if I'm doing any good for anyone in Dodge, what with the shootings and the like." His gaze cut to Gertie. "Has she been taking the medicine I prescribed?" When Gertie nodded, his expression turned remote. "Then she's in the Lord's hands."

Noah fought the urge to shake the doctor until he said differently. Instead, he pulled the thin blanket over Sadie's trembling body. Worn and threadbare, it was the only covering on the bed. She continued to shiver beneath its meager weight. He felt his scowl deepen.

He removed his sheepskin coat and draped it over her. The garment engulfed her slight frame. When her tremors lessened and her breathing eased, he hunkered down by her bed again and stroked her hair away from her face. The vibrant red strands highlighted skin as white as death.

His heart clenched at that possible outcome. "This medicine you mentioned—"

A knock on the door cut him off.

Grumbling at the intrusion, Gertie crossed to open the door. A man in his twenties with dark hair and a compact body stepped over the threshold. Gertie's downturned mouth lifted into a welcoming smile.

"Marshal Masterson," she purred. "Wonderful to see you. It's always a pleasure when you visit the Northern Star."

Masterson tugged the brim of his hat. His eyes crinkled at their corners as he returned Gertie's smile. "Pleasure's all mine, Madam. Unfortunately, this ain't a social call." The lawman's expression turned unreadable as he surveyed the other occupants of the room. His gaze lingered on Sadie's prone form before coming to rest on Noah. "Heard tell a man got killed tonight."

Noah had never been on the wrong side of the law before. He regretted that he'd ended a life, but if he had to do it all over again, he'd still pull the trigger. He'd save Sadie.

"By all accounts, the deceased was a cheat 'n abuser of one of our lady folk. However..." Masterson's eyes narrowed, but his hands had yet to go anywhere near the pair of Colt revolvers resting in their silver-studded holsters. "Doling out punishment in Dodge is my business. So you'll have to come with me. We need to discuss you...getting between me 'n my business."

Noah glanced at Sadie. She was resting easy under his coat. "I'll be back," he promised her, even though he knew she couldn't hear him. Then he rose to his feet and addressed Gertie and the doctor. "I want to learn more about Sadie's medicine." A handful of strides brought him to the door and the lawman filling it.

Masterson stepped aside and gestured for him to go first. "Jus' follow yer nose until you reach my office across the street."

He could guess what awaited him *across the street*—a sturdy brick building with bars on the windows.

When he paused on the jailhouse porch, Masterson snorted a laugh. "Don't you reckon you've come too far to turn back?"

Noah glanced over his shoulder at the Star.

"Eyes to the future, boyo. My door's open." Masterson exhaled a long breath. "Didn't have time to lock it after I heard yer gunshot."

Inside the jail, a cell with its door wide open greeted Noah. So much for his future.

"Have a seat." Masterson pointed to a chair on his right, then strolled over to the chair's partner on the other side of a desk. He waited until they were both seated before he spoke. "Well, boyo—"

"Name's Ballantyne."

Elbows resting on the desk's worn oak, fingers laced under his chin, Masterson looked bored, as if he were at a Sunday social that had gone on too long. Noah wasn't fooled. Masterson's gaze was sharp as steel, assessing him. "Well, Mr. Ballantyne, it appears yer pretty handy with a gun."

Anchoring his thumbs on his belt, Noah suppressed the urge to fidget and aimed for a casual tone. "They say you are as well. You made a name for yourself with that gunfight in Sweetwater."

Masterson flicked his fingers. "That was Texas. This is Dodge. Difference is I'm the law here along with my brother 'n Wyatt Earp. Wyatt 'n us go a ways back. I met him in seventy-two hunting buffalo. So, if I shoot someone, no one's gonna toss me in a cell, 'cause I'm the one wearing a badge 'n I've got friends looking out for me. Understand?"

He didn't. At least not how any of this pertained to him. He shrugged and let his attention wander around the lawman's headquarters.

Behind Masterson, a cabinet full of polished guns was impressive. So were the thick bars and heavy padlock guarding the collection. But what snared his interest was the half-open door on the other side of the room. It afforded him a view of an unmade bed surrounded by trunks and valises. The addition of dirty plates and coffee mugs scattered about the room amplified a chaos at odds with the Spartan neatness of the main room.

"The baggage ain't mine." Masterson's chair creaked as he leaned back. "When someone dies without people to stand up for 'em, we bury 'em in Boot Hill 'n store their belongings here. Wait for their next of kin to show up."

The marshal didn't mention the other clutter. It appeared he'd spent many hours eating and sleeping in the jailhouse, which wasn't surprising, since a town as rough as Dodge probably kept a lawman busy at any hour of the day or night.

Masterson reclined even further in his chair and propped his feet up on the corner of the desk, at ease, as if he'd made a decision. "You got plans to stay awhile in Dodge?"

"Maybe."

A smile tugged Masterson's lips. "Yer sort always over-complicates things," he said, pointing his index finger at Noah. "That much's certain. How 'bout we lay all our cards on the table? Dodge needs—" he turned his finger on himself, "—I need another hand in this marshaling business."

Noah stifled a snort. Masterson probably needed a dozen hands. Hell, maybe double that.

"Mr. Ballantyne, are you interested in being my deputy 'n helping me live to see November?"

Despite cautioning himself not to react, Noah sat up a little taller. Become a lawman? He respected Masterson, so assisting the man wouldn't be a hardship. When he'd left Texas two months ago, he hadn't expected to remain in Dodge for more than a handful of days. But the minute he'd walked into the Northern Star, his plans had blown away like tumbleweeds across the open prairie.

"Still waiting on my answer. You willing to buy-in to my game? Or is it time to fold 'n skedaddle?"

"I can't leave Dodge," Noah admitted.

"'Cause of the redhead over at the Star."

It was a statement, not a question. Nevertheless, Noah found himself nodding.

Masterson blew out a low whistle. "You got an uphill battle with that one. I should know, 'cause I had a similar challenge. My Lizzie used to work in a saloon in Ellsworth."

"Where is she now?"

"Across the street in our room at the Dodge House Hotel, waiting for me while I sit here jawing with you."

"Sounds like you got dealt a losing hand tonight."

"So did yer redhead last year, from what I heard."

Noah nodded, remembering that when he'd last been in Dodge, a lawman named Deger had been in charge.

"And still she has a way about her not common to her profession. Can't count the number of times I seen her blushing like a schoolmarm as she captivates a roomful of ruffians with her singing, or watches in dismay when those fools bet every dollar they own at her card table. A smart man would haul her down to the preacher's 'n end the game she plays."

An image of himself standing with Sadie before an altar invaded Noah's mind. Marriage afforded a woman a measure of safety...if she married an honorable man, one who wouldn't force her to do anything against her will.

Masterson dug in his desk drawer and tossed a silver star onto the desk. It landed with a ping. The light from the oil lantern caught the metal, glimmering as the badge spun in a circle before coming to rest between them. "Being a deputy might give you an edge in settling whatever business you have with Miss Sullivan."

"Might get me killed." Regardless of his words, Noah had already picked up the badge.

Masterson gave a hoot of laughter. "That it might. What-ever happens, I don't reckon yer the type to stand by 'n watch a wrong being perpetrated. That much's clear from tonight's events. Could mean you'll end up participating in more of the same for the duration of yer stay in Dodge. So might as well make it legal 'n get paid for it. Plus, you can bunk here."

Noah couldn't contain his grimace.

"The baggage has to stay." Masterson cracked a grin. "But tidying up everything else can be yer first duty as my deputy."

"Why me?" Noah scanned the marshal's face. "You don't know anything about me."

"I know that without you a woman might've died tonight. I gotta gut feeling. And out here, where trouble comes at you faster'n greased lightning, it pays to listen to yer gut."

The badge weighed heavy in Noah's hand.

Masterson's fingers drummed on the desk. In spite of his impatience, he hadn't lost his smile. "Well? Do I have myself a new right-hand man?"

He pinned the star on his vest. "Until I get what I came for, Marshal Masterson."

Masterson inclined his head in acceptance, which Noah took as his cue to leave. He was halfway to the door when the marshal spoke. "By the way, my name's Bat...or William Barclay or Bartholomew. But most folks call me Bat. Out of curiosity, Deputy, you got a plan where yer redhead's concerned?"

Noah sighed. His new boss enjoyed sticking his nose where it wasn't welcome. It appeared Bat had hired him for more than the role of deputy. He was to be a source of entertainment as well.

"No, but I'm working on one," he called over his shoulder.

Bat's laughter followed him out onto the porch. Directly across stood the Dodge House Hotel, Bat and his lady friend Lizzie's place of residence. To the left was the Northern Star.

Counting off the windows along the saloon's second story, he retraced his route when he'd carried a trembling form. His gaze came to rest on the room at the far corner, the one with the yellow curtains concealing worn wallpaper, a narrow bed, and a small but devilishly stubborn woman.

He ransacked his mind for a plan. All he created was a chaos that rivaled Masterson's storage room. What the hell was he going to do?

SADIE WOKE SLOWLY, struggling through heavy layers of sleep. Memories hounded her, shrouded in fog, and then flashed bright as lightning. An arm tightened around her neck. Metal gouged her temple. A gunshot banged. Davenport sprawled at her feet with a bullet in his head.

The gambler's face morphed into Edward's. His eyes opened and his lips moved. *Find them.*

She surged upright, her gaze ricocheting in every direction.

All she found were faded scarlet walls, the shade of a dying rose. A window aglow with late morning light snagged her attention. Beyond the thin curtain and cracked glass came the rattle of wagons and the clomp of hooves. A steady, rhythmic song of life. A life outside her cage. A life still beyond her reach.

She was in her bedroom above the Star. Nothing had changed...except for the homey scent of soap and leather tickling her nose. More memories skimmed her mind. A rock-hard strength and warmth holding her, followed by an unwavering sense of security.

Curling her fingers into her blanket, she pulled it closer. The scents that had danced through her mind grew stronger: beeswax saddle soap and not only leather but wool. Something thick and unfamiliar lay beneath her hand.

Noah's sheepskin coat was draped over her. How did it get into her room?

Understanding dawned. Noah had been here. He'd killed Davenport. After she'd collapsed, he must've carried her upstairs, placed her on her bed, and left his coat to keep her warm. Yesterday it had clung to his broad shoulders; now it hugged her body, making her skin tingle.

Smoothing a hand down the length of the garment, she imagined Noah's strength beneath it.

She jerked her hand back. This was madness. Noah, and

the hope he infused in her, increased the risk of discovery or worse. Davenport's death was a stark reminder of her precarious position.

What did Noah want? The answer eluded her. Only one thing remained certain. She couldn't trust him. She couldn't trust anyone.

Her father had used her, first to tend the farm and then to pay his drinking and gambling debts. Gertie had sold her to the highest bidder and now held onto her for her voice, her card dealing skills and the hope that one day she would recover...then the madam would sell her again.

Noah had decided he could fix the damage he'd done with money, then he'd ridden away. Now he was back. He couldn't bed her, so why did he continue hanging around the Star? He was too inquisitive. What if he unraveled her lies and exposed her secrets? What if Gertie found out?

One of Edward's favorite sayings came to mind. *You can't bluff if your opponent knows the cards you hold.*

Failing would mean betraying Edward and all he'd done for her. All he'd promised to do as well. He'd agreed to pay Gertie whatever price she asked to let him take Sadie with him when he and his partner, Orin, left Dodge. Then Edward had died a painful death.

She hadn't been able to help him or herself.

It was common knowledge that she'd been the one to find him, in his hotel room at the Great Western—in a pool of his own blood, a suicide note in one hand, a pistol in the other. What everyone in Dodge must never learn was that when her shock sent her crashing to her knees beside him, Edward's eyes had opened.

He hadn't been dead. Not quite.

"Find them," he'd whispered.

Hope had shot through her. For an instant she'd thought

she could save him. He'd been the one person in town who'd helped her, the only one she counted as a friend. It was unthinkable that she might not be able to help him in return.

She'd jumped to her feet. "I'll fetch the doctor."

"Too late." His eyes had beseeched her to stay. "I caught her robbing my—" His breathing had grown labored, and when he spoke again, his words had tumbled out in harsh gasps. "Don't let her keep them. Steal them back. Use them to leave Dodge. Promise me you'll find—my father's watch —my mother's box." His breath hissed between his teeth. "My letter."

She'd glanced at the piece of paper clenched in his hand, then back at his face.

Anger twisted his features. "Not—mine. Not—" His entire body spasmed. "Not suicide." He stared past her, his eyes bulging with pain and fear.

She'd wrapped her hands around his, so he'd know he wasn't alone. "I'm here. I'll help you. I promise."

His eyes had flared even wider and then closed.

"No! Stay with me. Talk to me. Tell me who hurt you."

His hand went limp in hers as he breathed one last word, "Gertie."

She'd made her vow to a silent room. "I swear I'll make her pay...in whatever way I can. She won't keep what she stole."

It'd taken all her willpower to release his hand, to leave the suicide note in its place and not rip it to shreds. Gertie couldn't suspect that Edward had spoken to her. She couldn't discover the card Sadie meant to play, for Edward and herself.

The moment she fulfilled her pledge to retrieve Edward's most cherished possessions, she'd stowaway on a train for Chicago, make a sale there, and use the funds to run even farther. No one would catch her. She'd disappear. Far away and forever.

She couldn't let Noah Ballantyne interfere with her promise or her plans for the future. Not again.

CHAPTER 6

"*I*t's a shame you won't reconsider and keep me company on the trail home." Lewis slapped Noah on the back. "Fully understand your reasons for staying now though."

Noah propped his shoulder against the jailhouse post and stared at the Northern Star. Standing around trying to figure out how to help Sadie was becoming a habit. A damned frustrating one. He needed that plan Bat mentioned. Now.

Even though they were alone on the porch, Lewis leaned closer, his voice taking on a confidential tone. "If you hadn't shot that worthless son of a sidewinder last night, I sure as hell would've. There wouldn't have been a rock he could've hidden under. I'd have found him and brought your girl back to you."

Noah swallowed his retort that Sadie wasn't "his girl." Buried deep beneath Lewis happy-go-lucky temperament was a territorial streak as wide as it was long. The only time Noah had witnessed his anger was when someone threatened to take what belonged to him or those he cared about.

As quickly as Lewis' ill humor surfaced, it vanished under an easy smile. He stepped down to the street where his horse stood at the hitching post. With sure movements gleaned from a lifetime on the range, he checked the ties on his bedroll and saddlebags. "Having said that..." He paused to tighten the cinch. "You'd best take good care of Miss Sullivan or, friend or not, I'll come back, sweep her off her feet and make her mine."

"I told you before. I only want to—"

"Help her. An honorable wish." Lewis rested his elbows on his saddle. The worry etching his brow made the muscles along Noah's shoulders bunch. "Fact is, if you don't claim her, someone else will. If not you or me, then probably... Wardell."

The name struck Noah like a punch to the gut, making him suck in his breath. "Don't suspect she'd take kindly to anyone *claiming* her," he muttered, shooting another glance at the Star. "All she wants is her farm back."

"So give it to her."

"And then what?" He shook his head. "Let her work herself to death trying to farm a strip of land that'll be flattened every spring by the first cattle drive?"

Lewis laughed. "A lot of things can change on the way to granting a lady her wish."

Anger coiled in his gut. "Friend or not, I'm gonna slug you if you suggest anything inappropriate. She may work in a saloon, but she doesn't belong there."

"Ever considered courting her?"

The image of him standing beside Sadie before an altar rose in his mind again. He shook his head. "I can't marry her."

Lewis raised one brow. "Because you don't find her attractive?"

"Because," Noah growled, "she won't willingly spend a single minute with me."

"Use her farm as an incentive."

His entire body went rigid in rejection. "You're suggesting I bribe her?"

"Entice her."

"Impossible," Noah scoffed, but his muscles had lost their stiffness. He wasn't leaning against the blasted porch post either. When had that happened?

"How many acres are the farms 'round here?" Lewis asked.

"Not sure...maybe a hundred."

"That's not even a tenth of your ranch. Your earnings for helping drive my herd north could buy that with money to spare." When Noah shrugged, Lewis' head tilted at a contemplative angle. "Well, at a hundred acres, her farm won't be difficult to acquire, but it'll make the *rest* of my idea harder."

"Which is?" Noah asked, not sure he wanted to hear the answer.

"You give her one acre every time she agrees to see you. She gets her farm back, and you get a hundred reasons why she should talk to you, to spend time with you. The *rest* I leave up to you. If you can't woo her under those terms, you don't deserve her. That's when you write me, and I'll return and—"

"You'll do no such thing." Noah was now poised on the top step.

Lewis raised his hands. "Hey, like I said, if not me, then—"

"She's been through too much. I won't take advantage of her."

"Of course you won't force her to do anything. Give her

the option. She can always say no and await your next request. But that'll mean she has to wait a little longer for her farm."

Noah felt his jaw drop. It might work. "Sweet Jesus, you're diabolical," he said in growing wonder.

"Hey, don't knock a sound plan. Or in this case, the only plan you've got." Lewis grasped Noah's hand and gave it a firm shake. Then he mounted his horse and reined the animal south. "Good luck," he called over his shoulder. "You're gonna need it!"

Noah watched Lewis ride away. When he couldn't see him anymore, he turned in the direction of the bank. No more standing around waiting. It was time to return what he'd taken from Sadie, time to give her what she desired most—her farm.

Pressing against the glass of her bedroom window, Sadie gave up on rubbing the chill from her arms so she could concentrate on the two men standing across the street. She'd been watching the Star's veranda, looking for Gertie, when the conversation between Noah and his friend snared her attention.

Mr. Adams adjusted a bedroll on the back of his saddle and then several saddlebags. He packed enough for a long trip. Was Noah leaving as well?

A shiver rocked her and sent her gaze darting back to him. He stood with one shoulder resting against the jail's porch post. The sturdy gray that he'd ridden out to the cemetery was nowhere in sight.

She realized she was holding her breath and let it out.

Distance and the wagons rattling down the rutted street

made it impossible to hear their conversation, but the range of emotions—frustration, alarm, anger, disbelief—flitting across Noah's face and frame fascinated her.

Noah's gaze followed his departing friend. Then he spun on his heel and strode off in the opposite direction.

What had they discussed? And where was he now heading, so purposefully?

The familiar creak and reverberation of the Star's swinging doors jarred her from her thoughts. Pressing against the window again, she peered over the balcony to her right.

The top of Gertie's head appeared, followed by her narrow shoulders and broad backside. She stepped off the boardwalk, opened a copper-colored parasol that matched her hair and dress, and set off in the direction of the Great Western Hotel. The wind was at her back, propelling her forward like a ruffled sail of taffeta and lace in pursuit of lunchtime entertainment.

She couldn't guess how long Gertie would be gone. She only knew her future hung on rare moments like these. Moments when she could continue her search with less chance of being caught.

Edward's most cherished possessions remained missing. He'd told her he'd faced financial ruin many times. Not once had he contemplated gambling his mother's silver Fabergé jewelry box or his father's gold Cartier pocket watch. The watch never left his waistcoat pocket, and the box always graced a shelf over the card table in his hotel room. Reminders, he'd said, that some things were too precious to risk losing.

According to the townsfolk, Orin had most likely run off with both heirlooms.

If Orin had them, Edward would've been content.

Edward said they'd both enjoyed many partners of both sexes until they'd found each other, fallen in love, and became monogamous. He'd concluded they should live with a woman to confuse the gossipmongers, especially when they returned to his home in Boston.

Edward's syphilis made it imperative that they go east to find better care for him. Before they could, another tragedy had struck.

Sadie was convinced that Edward had interrupted Gertie's thievery. The madam had killed him rather than face the consequences. Convincing anyone else would be impossible. Although she longed with all her soul to bring Gertie to justice, no one would believe her. The law wasn't on her side. No one was.

Edward was gone. The debt she owed him wasn't. Because of him, she'd survived her first role as a prostitute untouched and a whole lot better prepared to deal with Gertie.

She couldn't afford to be distracted by Noah. She must find Edward's treasures. Then she'd head for Chicago and disappear.

She hastened across her room and out onto the second-story landing overlooking the main floor. She forced herself to saunter, so as not to draw any attention. Below her, only a pair of old timers slouched over the bar. Hardly daring to breathe, she halted by Gertie's bedroom door and, keeping her back to it, glanced right then left. The landing remained empty.

She swept her fingers over the door behind her until she found the latch. It didn't budge. Steeling herself, she plucked two hairpins from her hair and bent the U-shaped metal straight.

Her time with Edward had been enlightening in many ways. He hated being bored. Teaching her had become a form of entertainment. Her education had gone beyond dealing cards when Edward instructed Orin to take the reins. With night-black hair and eyes, Orin was breathtakingly beautiful in a boyish way, yet he had an edge to him. Once she'd dared to ask him about his life before he met Edward. She'd never asked again.

She inserted the pins in the keyhole and applied every trick she'd been taught. Finally, the lock clicked. The door opened. She slipped inside and closed it behind her.

Slumped against the wood, she fought to slow her racing heart. Despite having new skills, she wasn't at ease with her new life. Each day she did things that would've been preposterous a year ago. Picking a lock so she could rifle through a person's belongings were additions to an already lengthy list.

Nerves stretched tight, she forced herself to push away from the door.

Twenty minutes later, her nerves were close to snapping. She'd found nothing. Not in Gertie's dresser drawers, not under her mattress, not even under her floorboards. Each tick of the grandfather clock in the corner chipped away at her courage. She feared the door would swing open at any moment.

Hugging her arms around her waist, she stared at the one place she hadn't searched. Gertie's safe. The iron-gray box stood, solid and impenetrable, against the wall opposite the bed. Frustration churned inside her until she was tempted to kick the blasted thing. Opening a strongbox lay far beyond her knowledge. She couldn't give up, though. There had to be another way to get inside.

Merely a temporary defeat, she consoled herself as she went to the door and pressed her ear to it. Not a sound came from the other side. She eased open the door enough to peek through.

The landing remained empty. Thank the Lord for small blessings.

She stepped out into the hall, pulled the door closed and inserted her hairpins in the keyhole. Once again, the lock resisted before finally complying.

Relief swept over her as she shoved the pins into her skirt pocket. Exhaustion rapidly followed. She needed time to establish her next move. Intent on making a beeline for her room, she ran straight into a wall of leather and muscle.

Strong hands held her arms, steadying her. A familiar face towered above her.

"Whoa, there." Noah Ballantyne's voice was low and soothing, as if he was calming a skittish mare. "Didn't mean to startle you."

Sadie gaped at him for a heartbeat, and then pasted on what she hoped was a guilt-free expression. As far as Noah was aware, she'd every right to be in the room she'd exited. He'd only been in town four days. Odds were he didn't know the location of Gertie's private domain.

She didn't like the look on his face, though. Not suspicious, but something equally disconcerting. Something that hadn't been there when they'd last met. He'd always appeared robust and capable. The exact opposite of how she felt. Now the man before her wore an air of determination, like he'd made up his mind and wouldn't take no for an answer.

The notion made her stomach knot for a different reason.

When his hands dropped from her arms, she lowered

her gaze, hoping to conceal her irrational disappointment. His faded shirt and rough-cut leather vest confirmed he still hadn't bothered with the fancy clothing the majority of the newly arrived Texans purchased from the local mercantile. Her attention locked on a silver star over his heart.

He cleared his throat. "Marshal Masterson made me his deputy."

"Is that why you were standing in front of—" She pressed her lips tight, mortified that she'd almost revealed she'd been observing him. A bigger concern leapt to the forefront. "You've been collaborating with the marshal for a long time?"

"Only met him last night after I carried you to your bedroom." The words sounded wicked, especially with him standing so close.

Her face grew hot. So did the rest of her. A delicious heat that coiled low in her body. She hadn't been warm since she'd lain under his coat this morning. She should return the garment. She wanted nothing to do with him.

And still she couldn't bring herself to say the words and give up his coat. Not when she'd previously been so cold. Since leaving her bed, she'd been harassed by the disturbing chill from last night. She'd been looking forward to returning to her room and snuggling under his coat's comforting warmth.

All intentions of going back to her sanctuary fled. What if he followed her? The prospect of being alone with him in her bedroom filled her with alarm, but also made her body tingle in a very worrying way.

Careful not to touch him, she slipped by and headed for the stairs and the saloon below. Noah matched her every step, staring at her as if he wanted to say something of grave importance.

The sun flooded through the ground-floor windows, filling the saloon with light and warmth, making her burn even hotter. No additional patrons had entered the Star, and for once, she missed the crowd. The quiet made her exceedingly aware of the man beside her.

When he removed his hat and held it in front of him, she drifted to a halt beside the piano with her fingertips trailing across the smooth mahogany surface. Her memories of Edward playing it were swept aside by a new musing. The wood's hue reminded her of Noah's hair. The sunlight picked up the auburn highlights running through the thick waves. Her fingers itched to explore them instead.

She folded her arms and pressed her elbows against her sides, pinning down her traitorous hands.

"I hope you feel better today." His softly spoken words flowed over her like a caress.

"I'm as well as can be expected. Thank you for inquiring, Mr. Ballantyne." Aware that she owed him for a lot more, she forced herself to continue speaking. "And thank you for coming to my aid last night."

"Glad I could help." His mouth lifted at the corners, the first time she'd witnessed him smile. The most sincere and long-awaited smile she'd ever won. It pulled at something deep inside her. Something wonderful...and dangerous.

"Will you sit a spell with me, Sadie?" The rumble of his voice grew even deeper, reminding her of the way he'd spoken to her a year ago, when his cattle had destroyed everything she held dear.

You know you can't trust him. So stop being foolish.

Erecting a wall around her heart, she spun away from the piano and Noah, angling for the bar and the two old-timers. "I should inquire if I'm needed—"

He jumped to block her path. "I want to discuss your farm."

The heat she'd felt since bumping into him on the landing drained away. "Don't be cruel. Nothing more can be said."

"I disagree. And I'll be coming back every hour until you hear me out."

She sank onto the nearest chair and clenched her hands in her lap to stop them from trembling.

Noah pulled up a seat and sat facing her. "I need to talk to you about the day we met." She shook her head, but he didn't stop. "After I left, I went over what happened, every single day, and wished it could've been different. That's why I came back."

She felt her eyes grow round. "I don't believe you."

"I don't blame you. But it's true. When we met, I was at the lowest point in my life. One I haven't recovered from." His grip on his hat tightened. "My herd had been days without water. Then came a rainless thunderstorm. The cattle stampeded and trampled several of my men."

A cold apprehension made her gasp. "Did they survive?"

"All except my brother, Jacob."

Her heart ached for his loss. She hadn't experienced the joy of having a brother or sister, but she could imagine the torture of seeing one die in front of you.

The lines of his face twisted with sorrow and guilt. "I should've kept Jacob safe. I failed him. Then I met you and —" he swallowed roughly, "—failed you, too. I'm sorry I made you lose your farm. If I had known the damage that cattle drive would cause, I'd have never come north."

That he was tortured by this much remorse astounded her. She'd never viewed him as anything but strong and self-assured. Wanting to remove the sadness from his eyes made her forget her own troubles.

"I'm sorry your brother died." The urge to comfort him made her lean toward him. "From what you've told me, I don't see how you failed him. You shouldn't hold yourself responsible for his fate."

His brow lowered along with his gaze until he was staring at her hand clutching his arm. When had she—?

She jerked back, then covered her embarrassment by clearing her suddenly dry throat. "As for me and my farm... it doesn't matter anymore."

"It does to me." His voice sounded raw, wounded.

"Go home, Mr. Ballantyne," she whispered, dismayed to hear her voice crack.

"Not until you're safe."

"Mr. Ballantyne—"

He gestured to the walls around them. "I'm not leaving you in this godforsaken place."

She raised her chin. She couldn't risk relinquishing what little control she had to anyone, including him. "You have no say in where I go or where I stay."

The furrows on his brow deepened, but his tone remained even. "I'm going to help you."

"Your help in this particular matter isn't welcome." She considered him through narrowed eyes. "Last time you gave my father money and left me with nothing. You departed without a backward glance."

He nodded. "I wish I'd stayed."

"Yes, you should've stayed in Texas."

"Stubborn little hellcat," he muttered.

She drew back with indignation. "Pig-headed oaf."

The lines etching his brow relaxed and the corners of his mouth twitched. "Call me Noah."

Unfortunately, the back of her chair prevented her from leaning even farther away from him. "You also have no say in what I call you, *Mr. Ballantyne*."

"What if you had your land back?"

The abrupt return to their original topic took her off guard. She shook her head, hoping to dispel the sudden sting of tears in her eyes. "I'll never see my farm again."

"I bought it."

"What?" Her voice was no more than a squeak.

He drew a bag from each of his vest pockets and emptied their contents on the table, scattering a stream of one dollar poker chips. "How many acres was your farm?" He pulled his chair closer, and his knee brushed hers.

The all too brief contact brought the warmth back to her cheeks. Twisting on her seat, she stared out the window and huffed out a breath, seeking to cover her discomposure. "If you'd bought my farm, you wouldn't have to ask its size."

From his pocket came a crisp white piece of paper, which he unfolded and placed next to the chips. The deed to her farm, bearing his name.

Her blood roared in her ears. "Well, since you apparently do own it, you already know how many acres you bought."

"Indulge me," he insisted, pulling his chair even closer until she sat between his splayed knees, within the solid, unyielding curve of his body.

In an effort not to touch him, she tucked her feet under her chair, then scolded herself against any further retreat. A soiled dove wouldn't care how close a man sat, especially not one as eye-catching as the man before her.

She struggled to remember his question. How large had her farm been? She blinked, bewildered by his persistence and uncertain of such a conversation's purpose. The shadows where the sun didn't penetrate were no less dark, but with him sitting so close they somehow seemed less worrisome.

"My farm had one hundred acres."

Noah scooped up the poker chips and stacked them. She counted ten stacks of ten chips.

"I'll give you one acre for every request you grant me," he said.

Her jaw dropped in disbelief, while the rest of her snapped to attention. The desire to have her farm back was deep-rooted but illogical. She couldn't live there without a new house. And even if she accomplished that, she had no idea how she'd keep it from being demolished by the endless herds of cattle. The dream of recovering all she'd lost faded, leaving her to focus on Noah's proposal.

"You mentioned requests? What kind? What if I find them...*distasteful?*" Warmth flooded her face.

"Then you should tell me."

She snorted. "And?"

"We find something you're comfortable saying yes to."

"Humph." She drummed her fingers on the table, trying to distract herself from the urge to touch the chips. "Might I remind you of my condition? I can offer you nothing."

"There's plenty. I want your company and for you to drop this act, to be yourself when we're together."

Her hand froze, and she forced her lips to form a smile. "What makes you think there's anything more to me than what you see before you?"

His amber eyes inspected every inch of her. She refused to turn away.

"Half the time I wonder if you want to hit me like you did a year ago. Instead, you do something unexpected like smiling. Don't get me wrong, it's a lovely smile, but a false one. I'd rather have the real thing."

"You are grossly mistaken, Mr. Ballantyne," she replied, keeping her counterfeit smile firmly in place.

"Call me Noah."

She arched an eyebrow at him.

He picked up two poker chips and held them out to her. "Call me Noah, and you'll have your first acre back. Join me for a picnic this afternoon, and you'll have your second."

CHAPTER 7

$\mathcal{N}$oah guided the rented buckboard north, away from Dodge and all its noise. Soon the peace of the open prairie cocooned him, emphasizing the silence of the woman seated by his side.

He'd suggested this picnic in the hope that some distance from town might persuade her to envision the future differently. The land here was pristine in contrast to the trampled crops and churned up earth south of Dodge. The longhorns never reached these northern plains. Their march ended when they entered the town and its rail station.

His dislike for Dodge had grown. Take away the cattle drives and the town would wither, might even fold up and disappear. Out here, he was reminded of Texas. A stalwart cottonwood grew in a gully, surrounded by miles of bright-green spring grass.

These plains bore both new and old growth. They gave him strength. They made him breathe a little easier.

Until one of the wagon wheels hit a rut, and Sadie slid across the seat and her leg, from hip to heel, touched his. A wave of desire, hot as a wildfire, roared through his veins. All of his thoughts settled on Sadie as she shimmied back to her side of the seat. Bracing his feet on the wagon floor, he fought not to follow her.

His body might be misbehaving, but he would not. He meant to take things slow. He couldn't afford to spook her again. Lewis' parting words invaded his head and spiked his pulse. *Court her. Entice her.*

A frown tightened his brow. He wasn't sure he was up to the task. Not with the stakes so high and with all his failings sitting so heavily between him and Sadie. What if he made her life worse?

If you can't woo her under those terms, you don't deserve her.

The idea of Lewis returning to court Sadie in his place made him clench the reins, while the memory of Wardell promising to claim her made him jerk the buckboard to a halt. And what if her condition worsened, as Wardell had suggested? What if she didn't survive till next month? His worry and anger vanished, snuffed out by a cold dread.

"Do you wish to return to Dodge, Mr. Ballantyne?"

He sighed, but his tension eased. "Call me—"

"Noah." The hint of a smile curved her lips. "Calling you Noah earlier and now, plus agreeing to this trip...that's three acres. At this rate, I'll have my farm back in a month. You really are a terrible businessman, not to mention a poor gambler, going by your track record at the Star."

"I don't come to the Star to gamble. I come for the same reason that keeps me in Dodge."

He watched her lips part in surprise and longed to press his mouth to hers. He focused on the field of purple wild-flowers where the wagon had stopped. The sweet, fresh scent made him inhale deeply. "Shall we have our picnic here?"

When she nodded, he climbed down from the wagon, came around to her side, and held out his hands. She regarded him warily, like a fawn thirsting to drink from a stream but doubting the wisdom of leaving the woods.

"Don't be afraid, Sadie."

"I'm not," she snapped and reached down to accept his help.

Her hands settled on his shoulders with a rightness that made his heart sing. He clasped her waist and lifted her down. Her slender frame and light weight drained his happiness. Turning away to hide his concern, he unloaded a blanket and the picnic basket and set them out on the grass. It was time she ate a decent meal. But once they were seated, she merely pushed her food around on her plate.

His worry grew. "You don't like the food?"

"I'm sure it's very good."

"Maybe. Maybe not. Why don't you take a bite and find out for sure," he coaxed.

She released a weary sigh. "I don't have much of an appetite these days. But sometimes I'm hungrier in the mornings."

Was this another symptom of her illness? He didn't have the right to ask, but a sudden need to know more overwhelmed him. "How do you feel?"

She glanced up at him, then down again. "Fine."

He shook his head. "I asked you to be honest with me. Fine's not an answer, not a truthful one at least."

"What do you want me to say?"

"The truth. How it feels to have...syphilis?"

The line of her shoulders went rigid.

He'd pushed too hard. He'd get no more answers. That didn't stop him from asking the question he feared most. "Are you in pain?"

She drew in a deep breath. "My body aches, and quite often my head does as well." The words left her in a rush, as if she needed to get them out fast or not at all. "On bad days I have chills that make me believe I'll never be warm again. Like the sun is a burned-down candle with no heat. If the damage done to my body is permanent, I'll have to accept that fact. Life's a gamble." She looked him straight in the eye. "And that will cost you one more acre."

She may have been ill, half his weight, and more than a head shorter, but he was wise enough to admit when he'd been outmaneuvered by a stronger opponent. Her grit and vulnerability only made him more determined.

He would not let Dodge destroy such a combination of extraordinary contrasts. Nor would he let her shut him out without a fight. The return trip to Dodge flew by too quickly. Much too soon, Sadie disappeared through the Star's doors without a backward glance.

His gaze rose to the saloon's balcony. Sadie's window inspired a new way for him to see her again. His gut churned with hope and apprehension. His idea meant waiting till morning. And at a place like a saloon, danger could strike at any hour.

SADIE DREAMED of a field of vibrant purple poppy mallows and prairie phlox...of a picnic...of Noah. He whispered her name. His fingertips brushed her hair, then her cheek, gentle as the wings of a butterfly.

She sighed and pressed her face into the warmth of his large palm, wanting more.

The rumble of her name came again, like thunder on a distant horizon. Low and beckoning. Hot against her ear.

Her eyelids popped open. A broad-shouldered silhou-ette crouched by her bed, ominous as a storm cloud against the bright light behind her buttercup-colored curtains. She lurched up on her elbows.

A single finger touched her lips, halting her scream.

"Shh, sweetheart. We don't want company," the voice from her dreams murmured. Familiar and foreign. A grav-elly velvet. Too many things all at once.

She pushed Noah's hand aside. "Why are you in my bedroom?" She winced when her voice cracked on the last word. She'd wondered what would happen if they were ever alone in her room. Now, here he was.

Her heart thudded in her chest. Could he sense her jumpiness? Maybe even see it? She drew her blanket up under her chin.

"You said you were hungrier in the mornings." His gaze dropped to her hands, to the coat draped over her bed sheet. His coat.

Her fingers tightened in its heavy folds, dreading its departure but knowing she must let go.

"You keep warm." He moved toward her bureau. "I'll get your breakfast."

Relief made her finally able to fill her lungs. With the blessed air came the aroma of bacon, eggs, and buttered toast. For once her stomach growled in anticipation.

"Move over." Balancing a plate heaped with food in his hands, Noah nudged her sideways with his hip and sat in the space he made. He reclined against the brass headboard and stretched out his legs on the mattress.

Gawking at his long frame wedged beside her on her narrow bed, she blurted the first words that leaped into her mind. "This isn't a good idea."

"Nothing's going to happen...that you aren't comfortable

with. I promised, and I keep my promises. Eat something, and you'll have one more acre." With a finger under her chin, he raised her gaze to meet his. "That'll make five," he added and graced her with one of his all too rare smiles.

Ah yes, his tempting and perplexing bargain concerning her farm. She'd spent too many moments since he'd outlined his proposal seesawing between conviction and doubt. She couldn't afford the distraction. Despite telling Noah that she wanted her farm to goad him, the desire to regain her home had always lurked in her heart.

The truth hit hard. Any future with her farm would be no different from with his coat. As soon as she had the land, she'd have to let it go. She couldn't keep her vow to Edward and live near Gertie. One didn't stay anywhere near a rattlesnake once you disturbed its nest.

She couldn't even sell the land and use the money to start a life far away from Dodge, and Noah. A sale would take too long to organize. Her flight must be executed with haste. The return of her beloved farm had become a bluff card, a distraction to keep Noah from getting too close and derailing what mattered most—fulfilling her promise and earning her freedom.

So why did she continue clutching his coat and sitting in bed beside Noah? Because she didn't want to be parted from the coat or its owner. That conclusion didn't bode well for her plan's success.

She jumped off the bed and thrust his coat at him. "You should take this back."

His smile faded till not even a shadow of it remained. The sight chilled her more than the loss of his coat or the warmth of him sitting beside her.

A bang on the door made her jump. The sound came

again, low near the floor as if from a booted foot. The rattle of china followed.

"Sadie," a muffled but unmistakably feminine voice called. "Get up, you lazy thing, and open this door. My hands are full."

Sadie gestured wildly at the window. When Noah didn't move except to arch a brow in question, she shoved his chest. Unmovable as a mountain, he stared at her palms touching him. A jolt of unwelcome attraction made her jerk back.

She pointed at the window again and mouthed the word, *Go.*

With a sigh, Noah rose and set her breakfast on the bureau. Then he went to the window, disappearing through it and onto the balcony in one fluid movement. She stared forlornly at the billowing lace curtains—the only sign that a second ago she'd not been alone.

Another knock vibrated the door.

"I'm coming," Sadie yelled.

The voice outside grumbled, "Hurry up. This food's heavy."

The food! Darting around the foot of her bed, she grabbed Noah's plate. Where could she hide it? In a room this size, she had limited options: her bed or her bureau. She opted for the latter and stowed the food in the bottom drawer. Then she rushed to open the door.

Cora greeted her with a glare before giving her an astute once over. "Gertie thought you needed to eat. I thought I heard voices." She shoved the tray into Sadie's hands and pushed through the doorway.

Sadie stifled the urge to tell the woman to leave.

The ebony-haired beauty had been with Gertie longer than anyone at the Star. The other girls whispered that as

Gertie came west, she'd visited a string of orphanages to gather unwanted children. Cora had been among the first. There was a reason she'd outlasted them all. She had brains as well as beauty. If she figured something was amiss, she'd tell Gertie.

Trying to conceal her secrets, Sadie stared at the chipped plate containing two black squares and a gray blob. She shifted the tray. The blob jiggled. A congealed egg, perhaps? She contemplated the squares next and wrinkled her nose at the smell of burnt toast.

The contrasts between Cora's and Noah's offerings made her want to both laugh and cry.

Cora's skirts swished as she completed a circuit of the room before returning to Sadie. She didn't apologize for the intrusion or the inspection. She pointed at the tray in Sadie's hands. "The food was Gertie's idea. The medicine was mine. Didn't want you running out."

A brown glass bottle sat next to the plate. The liquid inside would be a pale, chalky blue. Her medicine. Her poison. She fought the urge to hurl the bottle at Cora's head.

The floorboards squeaked. She glanced up to find Cora heading for the window. Like a hound that'd picked up the scent of a juicy morsel, Cora wouldn't stop until she'd searched everywhere. What if Noah was still on the balcony? The possibility made her heart take off at a gallop.

She had to stop Cora. She had to say something the woman didn't want to hear. Something that might put her plans to escape Dodge in jeopardy. She drew in a quick breath and told the truth. "I want to stop taking the medicine."

Cora's fingers halted on the curtain. She sauntered back, scooped up the bottle and waggled it under Sadie's nose. "There's only one reason for you to stop taking this—if you weren't sick. You telling me you're faking your illness?"

Sadie's stomach plummeted. Was Cora saying she suspected Sadie didn't have syphilis? Had she guessed that Edward never bedded her?

Cora's toe tapped a beat to the seconds ticking away before Sadie's demise. How long before Cora ran and told Gertie?

"Don't fight me. You'll lose. You're sick. It shows in every faltering step you take, not to mention the pasty color of your skin. So take your medicine." Cora collected a spoon from the tray, filled it with blue liquid, and held it up for Sadie. "Take your medicine, an' there's no need for me to tell Gertie about this conversation."

A chill crawled up her spine. Could Cora have discovered, like Sadie had, that the medicine was toxic? She couldn't ask without making her situation worse. Cora's words rang in her head: *Don't fight me. You'll lose.* If she challenged the woman today, she'd lose. But tomorrow might be different.

Sadie opened her mouth and accepted her bitter salvation.

Cora put the stopper in the bottle and set it on the tray. "Remember what I said when you first started taking the medicine? About getting the girls to help monitor your health, to check your chamber pot? Is it time to tell Gertie you can no longer stomach your medicine? That she needs to get involved?"

Cora's continuous harping on the complexity of Sadie's situation held her mute. The woman was as big a threat as Gertie. All Sadie wanted right now was to be left alone to think.

Luckily, when she didn't reply, Cora crossed to the door and closed it behind her with a satisfied click.

A heavy silence filled the room. She deposited the tray on the bureau and opened the bottom drawer. Setting Noah's plate next to Cora's, she stared at the better of the two meals. A strange dejection stole over her as she contemplated Noah's premature departure. With a curse, she grabbed the medicine bottle. When a hand seized hers, she jumped.

Noah stood beside her again. Attention riveted on the bottle in her hand, the contours of his face had hardened. "What's in it?" he demanded, prying her fingers open. "Blue mass syrup..." He rotated the bottle and kept reading the label. "Hollyhock, rose honey, licorice, and mercury." His attention cut to her. "Why are you taking this?"

"Doctor Rhodes prescribed it."

"I don't trust him. I don't want you swallowing any more of this swill."

"Do you believe it matters what you want? It doesn't even matter what *I* want." Her voice rose dangerously high. She pressed her fisted hand to her lips.

"How long have they been forcing you to take this?"

She shook her head and stared at the door, refusing to look at him.

"Answer me, Sadie. How long?"

"Since I was diagnosed."

He swore under his breath. "I'm getting you out of here if I have to carry you out."

"The first chance I got, I'd leave you and come back."

The silence that followed gnawed at her resolve not to give in to him in any way. But it was her dread of what she might glimpse if she looked at him that kept her focus on the door.

"You'd rather stay here than leave with me?" he asked in a much too quiet voice.

"I'd rather say goodbye to Dodge on my own terms. That way I won't be a whore—to you or anyone else."

"It's too late for that."

His words hit her like a slap in the face, rocking her on her heels. She squeezed her eyes shut to hide her pain from him.

"Damn it, Sadie. I'm sorry. I shouldn't have said that. I don't think of you as a—"

She forced herself to cut him off. "I work in a saloon with a brothel above it. Don't lie to yourself. I'm a whore. But right now my illness saves me from those duties. The doctor, Gertie, Cora—they all tell me to take the medicine. If I do what they say, they leave me alone, and so do the men. If you had control over one thing in your life, would you give it up?"

"Sadie, you can't go on like this. Whatever happened when you first came to work at the Star, it doesn't have to be like that. Let me show you."

Disbelief made her gaze careen back to his. He couldn't mean—

"Will you listen to reason?" he asked.

"You haven't said anything reasonable."

"You're right. I was never good with words, but I'll listen. Tell me to stop, and I will."

For every stride he moved closer, she took one back until the wall against her spine halted her. He planted one palm on the faded wallpaper next to her head. She waited for him to raise his other hand and hem her in. He didn't. He'd given her a chance to escape.

She didn't take it. She was too busy trying to stop herself from leaning into his strength. "I was fine before you came along, last week and a year ago on my farm." Her growing anticipation made her words tumble out uncensored. "Every time you show up, you kick the foundation from under everything I've struggled to build."

He leaned down until his lips hovered over hers. "Let me make it up to you. Let me in, Sadie."

She closed her eyes again. "I can't."

His mouth brushed hers, light as gossamer. She held her breath, waiting for him to deepen the kiss, hoping. The feathery touch disappeared. She knew without looking that he'd left as well. Out the window, the same way he'd arrived. The damned curtain flapped again.

Only with his overwhelming presence gone could she think clearly.

Noah still believed she'd been a whore, that she had syphilis. The disease held everyone, including Cora and Gertie, at bay. But not him. He wanted to come closer. That wasn't her biggest problem. She was. She wanted the same.

 oah swung his legs over the Northern Star's balcony. Using the gaps between the rough-cut siding, he climbed down. He halted in the alley entrance leading onto Front Street, mind and body still focused on the frustrating yet compelling woman he'd left upstairs. His tongue brushed his lips, savoring the taste of her, however faint.

He battled the urge to climb back into her room and kiss her soundly. He wasn't sure how she'd react.

She retreated from him, but when she'd reached the wall, she'd chosen to stay there. She hadn't told him to stop. Was she starting to trust him? Now was the time for him to retreat as well, but only on certain matters.

Digging into his pocket, he withdrew the bottle. It lay in his hand, a small and ordinary cylinder of brown glass. Was it medicine after all? Whatever it was, it held Sadie's future.

A group of riders thundered by, cowboys whooping like hellions as they raced down the busy street amid shouts from those they endangered. Two women, with more face paint than clothing, called encouragements from the Star's veranda. Behind them, a thin brakeman in soot-covered overalls shuffled through the saloon's doors and joined the throng, heading toward his duties at the rail depot.

A familiar figure in a dark-blue jacket caught Noah's attention. Head and shoulders bent, Doctor Rhodes advanced with a rapid-fire stride. He lurched to a halt and stared into the distance at some unknown destination. Then he trudged at a lethargic pace back through the crowd until he reached the black maw of a doorway on the opposite side of the street and disappeared within.

Doctor Rhodes had prescribed Sadie's medicine. He should have the answers.

Noah made a beeline for the door. A swaggering group of cattle barons, sporting oversized top hats and flashy frock coats, Wardell's friends no doubt, brought him up short. The men's scowls faltered when they spotted the star on Noah's chest. Their puffed-up bravado vanished when their gazes rose to Noah's face. They wisely refrained from engaging him in conversation and lit out for safer ground. Others followed their lead.

The crowd parted as Noah crossed the street.

At his destination, he paused in the doorway to let his eyes adjust to the murky interior. The stench of stale smoke and strong moonshine, edged with the kerosene used to fire the boiler, offended his nose. A dozen scruffy men, smelling as bad as their surroundings, slumped in chairs, too intent on drowning their demons to acknowledge him hovering on the threshold of this most derelict of rum-holes.

The doctor sat hunched over the bar, his face shrouded by a heavy fall of coffee-colored hair in dire need of a trim. A haircut wouldn't erase the white streak, however, or whatever caused its appearance.

Noah claimed the stool next to Doctor Rhodes. The

bartender, after an initial questioning glance, busied himself elsewhere. Rhodes stared at his drink, oblivious to Noah's presence.

"How's business, Doctor?"

Brushing aside his hair, Rhodes squinted up at him. "Have we met?"

Noah leaned closer. "The other evening at the Northern Star."

The doctor blinked and then nodded. "You were in Miss Sullivan's room the last time I was summoned to check on her. You were concerned about her welfare, asked about her treatment." His focus drifted to the star on Noah's vest before returning to his drink. "Looks like you got a promotion."

Noah placed Sadie's medicine beside the doctor's glass. "It's making her sick." His struggle for a civil tone failed.

The doctor's jaw tightened. "She was ill to begin with."

"She's not getting any better," he countered, his voice growing louder.

"Or any worse."

"How can you say that? She collapsed the other night. And what about the fever, the chills, the—"

Surprise widened the doctor's dark eyes as he swiveled in his chair to face him. A ghost of a smile curved the man's parted lips. "Well, I'll be. You're smitten. This puts things in a whole new light."

Noah huffed in frustration. "I'm here to help her."

The doctor's smile widened. "Don't pay me no mind. I'm glad Miss Sullivan's got someone looking out for her now." The haggard look returned to his face. "She hasn't had it easy. And when I say she's not getting any worse, I'm talking about the tertiary phase of the affliction. She's shown none of those symptoms. At her current stage, the disease isn't contagious, but I haven't shared that detail with anyone but her." His gaze returned to his drink. "Until now."

"Not contagious?" The room spun like he'd been kicked in the forehead by an ox. He shook his head, struggling to focus. "How can that be?"

The doctor shrugged. "She hasn't any visible lesions. That's mainly how the disease is transferred. And regardless of her fevers and chills, I'm hopeful for Miss Sullivan's recovery. We were able to start administering the medicine before any of those first symptoms appeared. Early knowledge of her condition was a godsend. It increases her chances of survival."

Unable to move or speak, Noah continued to gape at the doctor.

The man's expression turned remote. "You still don't believe me."

"I wasn't expecting you to say..." At a loss for how to continue, Noah waved his hand in the air.

"That's human nature. We often hear and see only what we want."

Noah tamped down his shock. Only one thing mattered: making sure Sadie got well. Anything else could be pondered later. "The medicine—"

"Listen. I like Miss Sullivan. I wish she wasn't ill. I wish I could offer her better treatment. But out here, this—" he picked up the bottle, "—is used for everything from toothache to tuberculosis. It's the best option we have." He set it down with a thump in front of Noah. "It's the *only* option we have."

"Sounds like you've given up." Noah's fingers curled into fists.

The doctor stared at a point on the ceiling. "I'm not God. I can't save everyone."

His words hit Noah like a punch to the gut. He'd said almost the same thing the day Lewis had sold his herd, and they'd walked back into town. *I can't even save a single person.* Maybe he and the doctor weren't that different.

He wasn't aware he'd made a sound, but suddenly Rhodes peered at him with concerned eyes. "Sometimes all we can do is hope for the best and leave the rest to the Almighty."

Noah strove to imagine all the patients the doctor must have been asked to assist: the men, the women, the children. Those he'd saved, those he'd attempted to help and couldn't. "Had a bad day, Doc?"

"Can't remember when I had a good one," Rhodes replied in a weary voice.

"Let me lighten your load." He held out his hand. "Sadie's under my care now, as well as yours."

Rhodes didn't hesitate, but took his hand and shook it.

Noah's reaction was instant as well. He started second-guessing his impulsive gesture. Joining forces with the doctor was a gamble he hoped he didn't come to regret, especially when Sadie's well-being depended on the outcome.

Mind over matter, Sadie reminded herself as she strove to squash the growing unease her surroundings evoked. It was dark in Gertie's room, even darker under her bed. The splinters in the floorboards poked her chest and legs. She forced herself to ignore her discomfort and stay put.

Damned if she'd give up now. She had a direct sightline to her salvation. If she waited long enough, she'd learn the combination to Gertie's safe and discover if Edward's watch and jewelry box lay inside.

Daylight had prevailed when she'd picked the lock on Gertie's door and crawled under her hiding place. A tight squeeze, to be certain. And as time passed, and the light faded with the setting sun, the mattress seemed to press down on her even more.

Mind over matter, she repeated, focusing on the wall opposite. Against it stood Gertie's strongbox, an iron-gray slab that she fancied was devouring any remaining illumination. The safe's unalterable solidness taunted her.

Every Wednesday night, Gertie wore her scarlet gown and ruby necklace. Gertie's rubies weren't in the room. Sadie had checked. So they had to be in the safe. All Gertie's jewelry was paste, but she enjoyed telling her customers her baubles were real. Fake touted as genuine was best kept locked away.

The door handle rattled as a key slid into the lock. With a bright beam of light came a cacophony of voices and jarring piano music. The door closed, and the room once more plunged into a hushed obscurity. A pair of pale calf-skin boots crossed to the dresser. Their soles flashed like crescent moons under the hem of a midnight cloud.

A match scratched a surface, and the glow of a kerosene lamp banished the gloom to the corners. The light did little to slow Sadie's racing heart.

Holding her breath, she watched a teal-green gown puddle around Gertie's feet. Dust motes danced in the muted lamplight as Gertie's foot swung in a ghostly arc, kicking her dress away. Then the hem of a scarlet skirt dropped into view, skimming the tops of her ivory ankles before swinging left and right. A satisfied sigh followed.

Sadie guessed Gertie had assessed her reflection in the mirror and found everything to her liking.

She tracked Gertie's feet as they moved across the room. When the madam crouched beside the strongbox, Sadie pinned her attention on the plump fingers spinning the brass dial. She might not be able to blink, but she gave the smile tugging her lips free rein.

On the last rotation, Gertie shifted sideways. Her broad backside blocked the entire strongbox. Sadie stifled her groan.

The madam reached inside the safe and lifted something to her neck, most likely her ruby necklace. The safe door snapped shut, followed by the whirl of the dial.

Gertie stood and spun toward the bed. Sadie's heart clambered up her throat. Each step Gertie took toward Sadie caused the boards to vibrate under her palms and her heart to shimmy farther up her throat. The calfskin boots stopped so close to her nose she made out the scuff marks on the toes. Gritting her teeth, she prepared to be discovered.

Above her, the whisper of cloth sliding across the coverlet hissed in her ears. Then a silver gossamer shawl fell to the floor, making her flinch and almost bolt from under the bed. Gertie's hand appeared and snatched up the shawl.

At long last, the woman pivoted on her heels and marched out of the room.

Only after the key turned the lock did Sadie's heart drop back into place. On wobbly limbs, she crawled out from under the bed and plunked herself down in front of the safe. A quick swipe of her damp palms over her skirt, then she went to work on the dial. The last number would have to be determined by trial and error.

The minutes ticked away on the grandfather clock, more

than she'd hoped for and less than she'd feared, until the strongbox opened. Inside rested Gertie's rainbow collection of paste jewelry, flanked by stacks of greenbacks. No silver or gold. No Fabergé jewelry box or Cartier pocket watch. Sadie's shoulders slumped with disappointment.

Why weren't they inside?

Because if Edward's missing valuables were found in Gertie's safe, it would raise ugly questions.

Giving up wasn't a valid option. She had to keep searching. The saloon held other hiding places. Like the multitude of crates in the storeroom.

Mustering her resolve, she closed the strongbox and glanced at the door. At this time of day, with the landing outside and the saloon below at their busiest, departing that way would be foolhardy. She crossed to the other door, the one that led onto the balcony. Under cover of night, the balcony now provided her best escape route.

Even crouched on her heels, her hairpins made quick work of unlocking and relocking the door behind her. Then she hurried, with bent knees and back, the short distance to her bedroom window.

Her feet had no sooner touched the floorboards of her room than someone drawled, "However did you get on the balcony? You weren't there a moment ago."

Sadie whirled toward the voice. In the shadows, a murky figure reclined on her bed. A match flared, followed by a dull light that revealed a woman holding Sadie's rusted lantern on her lap—an ebony-haired woman with a surplus of curves and a deficit of manners.

Cora laughed and rose to set the lantern on the bureau. "Surprised to see me? You shouldn't be. Didn't take long for me to question your absence downstairs. Where have you been?"

Sadie racked her brain for an adequate response.

Cora grabbed her wrist and shook her till her teeth rattled. "Tell me."

She couldn't. All she could do was track Cora's hand, rising open-palmed to strike.

Satisfaction lowered Cora's voice to a throaty purr. "I'm gonna enjoy making you talk."

"Tell her, Sadie. I won't let you conceal our visits and suffer alone."

Sadie spun toward the window she'd crawled through. Noah sat on the ledge. He looked calm, but when he stood and moved toward them, she glimpsed the muscles bunching in his jaw.

Cora's eyes narrowed as she glanced from him to Sadie and back again. "What's going on?"

"This." He reached past Cora to thrust his fingers deep into Sadie's hair and tug her close. His lips brushed hers. Warm and welcome. Like the last time he'd been in her bedroom...before he'd left.

She wanted to press closer.

He wouldn't let her. He held her immobile while his fingers moved incessantly in her hair. "Very soon, the next time we're alone, I swear I'm gonna kiss you properly."

Through the roar of her blood pounding in her temples, Cora's outraged gasp snared her attention, along with the words, "I'm getting Gertie."

"No," she whispered, dismay leaching the word of any power.

Noah reached the door before Cora could. He leaned one shoulder against the wood while she yanked uselessly on the latch. "Fetching Gertie isn't in our best interests," he remarked. "I'm sure we can solve our differences without her."

Arms akimbo, Cora spun to face him. "You're trying to slide in an' out without droppin' a dollar for your whoring."

A scowl hardened Noah's expression. He shoved away from the door to tower over the woman.

Cora didn't retreat. "You figure, 'cause you've got that tin star on your chest, you can swagger in here an' have whatever you want for free? Well, you're wrong. You'll pay Gertie, same as everyone."

"Why don't I pay you instead?" Noah said.

Sadie felt her eyes flare as wide as Cora's.

The other woman recovered first and ran her gaze over Noah. "You're a most persuasive man, Mr. Ballantyne," she purred like a cat believing her favorite food was within reach. With a sideways glance at Sadie and a smile twitching her lips, the woman looped her arms around Noah's neck. "Why pay for sullied goods when you can have me?"

Noah untangled himself from her grasp and went back to leaning against the door. "I'm only interested in spending time with Sadie."

His refusal to be swayed by Cora's charms made Sadie's heart leap with joy. Yet his words shouldn't please her. He sounded like a man bent on interfering with her plans. She didn't want that. She couldn't want that.

Noah challenged Cora's silence with a raised eyebrow. "Say the word and I'll accompany you downstairs to continue this conversation with Madam Garrett."

"You're playing a dangerous game, dallying with that bitch." Cora jabbed her finger at Sadie.

"I'll take my chances," he replied without hesitation.

The glare Cora turned on Sadie made her scalp prickle like her hair had been singed.

"So..." Her tormentor snorted a laugh. "You've finally got a man paying to lift your skirt."

A chill swept over Sadie. Cora's barb struck too close to the truth. Was she implying that she knew Edward had never shared Sadie's bed? The only way she could know was if Edward or Orin had told her, and Sadie couldn't think of any reason they would.

"If this one gets in your drawers," Cora continued, "you'll be in real trouble. You're both gonna end up payin' a hefty price." She thrust her hand, palm up, toward Noah. "I'll take my first payment now."

Noah watched Cora pocket the gold eagles he'd given her. When the coins were safely stowed in the ample cleavage on display above her corseted waist, she trailed her fingers up her ivory skin to her hair. A scarlet silk rose set off her glossy dark mane, not a strand of which was out of place. She'd obviously invested considerable time in arranging her appearance.

He opened the door for her, wishing she'd left ages ago, wishing he'd never seen her tonight.

As soon as she'd cleared the threshold, he closed the door behind her and faced Sadie.

Dust streaked her face and hair. It couldn't hide the freckles scattered across her cheekbones or the complete disarray of her red hair. He approached her with measured steps, stifling the urge to fulfill his vow and tousle her hair even more as he kissed her for real.

Would she greet him with the same startled inquisitive-ness? As if he was the first to kiss her?

He needed to derail that train of thought as well. Only a fool longed for the impossible when more pressing matters loomed—like learning where Sadie had been and why.

"I'm as curious as Cora to learn what's got you climbing through windows tonight."

"If I wouldn't tell her, do you believe I'll tell you?"

One rebellious red lock, longer and dustier than the rest, claimed his attention. He couldn't stop himself from stroking the silky strands between his fingers as he held them up for her inspection. "Where could you've picked up so much dust?"

"From my window curtain," she replied a little too quickly, while shrugging one shoulder in a casual gesture that failed to conceal her nervousness.

What made her more uneasy? His questions or his nearness? What would it take to learn her secrets and keep her safe?

He leaned closer until they stood eye to eye. "I came in the same way. Notice any dust on me?"

Her chin lowered along with her lashes. "Thank you for helping me with Cora."

He had her thanks, not her trust. He released her hair and gripped the back of his neck instead. His fingers dug into his flesh as he struggled to stop himself from reaching for her again. "You're the most confounding soul I've ever met. Most stubborn, too."

"You mean more stubborn than you?" She stole a glance at him and, for an all too brief moment, he lost himself in a pair of emerald eyes sparkling with mirth before her gaze dropped again. "Haven't we had this conversation before?" Then, incredibly, she laughed.

The sweet sound tempted him beyond endurance.

Once again, his fingers stole into her hair, so he could tilt her face up to his. "When you lived on your farm, did you ever long for a husband by your side?"

Her wide eyes suggested that his question had astonished her as much as him. What the hell was he doing? The answer came to him in a heartbeat. He was trying to propose to the woman he'd traveled thousands of miles to see again. A woman he now couldn't leave.

He may have held her face in his hands, but she held his heart in hers.

A fierce desire to learn everything about her gripped him. He slid his thumb across her nose and along her cheek, removing the dust so he could reveal the extent of her imperfect but utterly compelling beauty. He pressed a kiss to the last freckle hiding below the corner of her eye. Eyes once again concealed by the fall of her lashes.

"A husband can be gentle with his wife." He concentrated on keeping his voice low and soothing. "Trust me on that account, Sadie."

Every sinew and muscle under his hands and lips went rigid. He stiffened as well, waiting for her to tell him to go to hell.

"A husband, I suspect, isn't so different from a madam." Her breath warmed his cheek in soft, breathless puffs while her words sent an icy shiver down his spine. "He owns his wife. He'd be loath to damage his property. But he would if she didn't...tell him exactly what he wanted."

The chill settled into his bones. Who knew hell could be so cold?

"You're no one's property." Despite his words, his grip on her tightened. He was no better than every other man in Dodge, certainly no better than Madam Garrett. He released Sadie and took a step back. "I can wait for what I want...and for you to want the same." Or at least he hoped he could.

"You can't want me," she said in a strained voice. "You don't want to contract syphilis."

"You're not contagious. The doctor told me."

"He told you—" She gaped at him as if she confronted the devil. "Does Gertie know?"

"Of course not. Your secret's safe with us."

"Us?"

"Me and the doctor."

"He's lying. Whatever he said about Edward—" She sealed her lips and wrapped her arms around her waist.

"You don't have to carry this burden alone. If Edward hurt you, forced you to—" Dreading what he might learn, he drew strength from one certainty. "It won't change how I feel about you. Trust me."

She shook her head so vigorously that her hair escaped its last pin and covered her shoulders. "I can't trust anyone. And I can no longer stay in Dodge." She spun toward her bedroom door.

With his palms raised, he moved to block her. "I'm all for leaving, but where will you go? You haven't thought this through."

"I planned for this eventuality, but not for you. How fitting that you, the one who forced me from my farm, would force me from Dodge and my debt."

"You mean your father's debt. It's not yours."

She raised a shaking hand to her pale brow.

Every muscle in his body tightened with concern. "You might not be contagious, but you're still sick. You don't want to run off and be alone if your condition progresses to the next stage."

Her hand fell to her side. "My condition? Didn't the doctor tell you—?"

This time he scooped her up into his arms before she even came close to hitting the floor. "Your secret's safe with me," he repeated as he cradled her against his racing heart. "So are you. I promise."

"Promises...they can so easily turn into lies when we cannot keep them. Sooner or later, you'll have to—" She hid her face against his chest. The tension in her slender frame felt like iron. "Go back to Texas." Her voice may have been muffled, but it held conviction.

She finally believed in something. His departure. Even worse, she sounded like she wanted him gone. But what if that was now the answer to getting her out of Dodge?

"I'll leave town the minute you do." He couldn't agree that he'd head home. Not without her. He couldn't lie about that...but was a lie of omission any better?

She went motionless in his arms as if she sensed the turmoil in him, as if she suspected he wasn't being completely honest.

His footsteps dragged as he crossed to her bed. His arms were also sluggish to obey as he told himself to place her on the mattress and release her. He spun to face the door. He wouldn't burden her with his weakness, the fierce longing that must burn in his eyes.

"Don't go." Her softly spoken words made hope leap in his chest. "You promised."

"And I'll keep my promise. I'll keep you safe."

"You promised to kiss me when we were alone."

Sweet Jesus. How was he supposed to be gentle when she fired his desire using only a handful of words? "Sadie, you just collapsed. You need to rest. I'd be taking advantage of you if I—"

"I know it's a lie, but I want you to kiss me as if we were married, as if we were in love."

Love was damned complicated.

She released a resigned sigh. "I guessed right. The truth is your promises hold no more weight than a feather in the wind."

He'd be damned if he'd walk out of this room with those words reverberating in both their heads.

Kneeling beside her bed, he gathered her in his arms and kissed her. With his lust pounding through his veins, he wasn't surprised when her body remained rigid, and her lips sealed. He'd broken his promise to show her tenderness.

Cursing himself for a heavy-handed lout, he drew back only to have her lips part with a gasp.

The disappointment in the sound made his heart ache. He apologized with a kiss so soft it might have been the feather in the wind she'd mentioned. Her arms wound around his neck as easily as her hair had curled around his finger earlier, and her lips opened like the petals of a spring flower.

He drank her in, one sip at a time, deepening the kiss gradually, pausing often to receive her response. Every time she replied with a kiss to match the one he'd given. She was a damned quick study. He went from a beggar lost in the badlands to a man receiving a king's feast. He couldn't get enough of her.

He pulled back, shaking as much as the woman in his arms. His body demanded one thing, but his thoughts were chaotic. Sadie's kisses were like fire, but they were also innocent.

No denying the truth. He'd never be her first bed partner, but he was her first kiss.

Did he have the patience to entice her kiss by kiss, instead of dollar by dollar, to stay in his arms, to forget all of the men in her past and wish for a future with only him?

CHAPTER 9

oah stared over his coffee mug at the lawman sitting on the other side of the jailhouse desk. For the last hour, Bat had been sneaking surreptitious glances at him. It wouldn't be long before the marshal's curious nature got the best of him. Then he'd start asking questions.

Questions for which Noah had no solid answers.

He'd endured a long and sleepless night since he'd paid Cora to leave him and Sadie alone, since he'd forced himself to leave Sadie alone to recuperate from her collapse. He wasn't sure he could endure Bat's questioning without confessing he might not have the strength to win both Sadie's trust and her love.

He shouldn't have kissed her, because he now craved a helluva lot more. But Sadie had asked. She wanted to be in love. Gertie hadn't destroyed that longing.

He had a chance. But he was now a man whose patience had worn thin, his frustration ready to be unleashed on the first unlucky soul who rubbed him the wrong way. Not a good state for a deputy, charged with being fair and orderly...or for someone with a notoriously inquisitive boss.

He needed to regain control, to breathe. He couldn't do that under Dodge's oppressiveness.

Bat regarded him openly now, not bothering to hide his interest. The look brought Noah out of his chair.

"Thanks for the coffee and the day off work." He set his mug on the desk and headed for the door. "Need to take care of a few things, so I'll see you tomorrow." Although warning himself not to look back, he glanced over his shoulder to gauge the marshal's reaction.

Bat's face crinkled with laugh lines. "Goin' anywhere special, Deputy?"

Noah retrieved his hat from a peg by the door. "Thought I'd get out of town for a while." He had a task in mind that would keep him occupied and hopefully take his mind off Sadie.

"Is that so?" When Noah made no reply, Bat rose and joined him by the door. "Well, I'll ride with you for a bit. Could do with some fresh air."

Noah bit back a curse. "Don't want to trouble you. Plus, I have to make a stop before I head out."

Bat raised an eyebrow. "At the Star?"

"At Zimmerman's."

Bat's eyebrow rose even further. "Zimmerman's Hardware Store?"

Noah nodded reluctantly.

"You picking up tools or lumber?"

"Both."

"Well, I'd better come with you."

Noah gave him his best look of disapproval. "That's not necessary."

The marshal grinned. "Believe me, it is. I know ol' Zimmerman. He'll swindle you if I'm not there." Folding his arms, the marshal showed no sign of going back to his chair. "Zimmerman owes me. With me along, we can borrow his tools for no charge. How can you refuse such an opportunity?"

"It appears I can't." Slamming his hat on his head, he stepped outside and down onto Front Street.

Bat followed him. "So, why do you need lumber?"

Noah stopped to let a wagon roll by. When he ended up staring at the Star hoping for a glimpse of Sadie, he realized it wasn't the wagon that had brought him to a halt. He spun in the opposite direction and continued toward the hardware store.

Bat didn't comment on his odd behavior but instead said in a casual tone, "Heard you bought some property."

Surprise loosened his tongue. "Where'd you hear that?"

"At the bank."

He grunted in exasperation. "Is there anything in this town you haven't figured out?"

"Wasn't certain you'd planned on staying in Kansas."

"I'm not."

"So, why buy lumber?"

"To build a house," Noah mumbled, quickening his pace.

"Where?"

"On the land I bought, which, if you've been to the bank, you're fully aware is the old Sullivan farm."

Bat released a low whistle. "Let me get this right. You bought land. Yer building a house. But you still ain't planning on staying in Kansas?"

"That's right."

"Who's the house for then?"

Noah bounded up the steps of the hardware store and went inside. The soothing scent of freshly cut wood infused the small space, while the rasp of a handsaw drifted through the back door. The store was empty except for its owner, who stood behind a polished hickory counter. Zimmerman was a stumpy man with slicked-down hair. His welcoming smile displayed a surprisingly fine set of teeth.

"Morning, Marshal Masterson. Morning, Deputy Ballantyne," Zimmerman said, dipping his head toward each of them in turn. "To what do I owe this honor?"

"The deputy wants to purchase some lumber." Bat propped an elbow on the counter and regarded Noah. "You know, building a house for a lady could be considered courting behavior."

Noah gritted his teeth and said nothing. Zimmerman's smile faded as his gaze darted between him and Bat. Noah bit back his groan. This was exactly the type of situation he'd hoped to avoid by getting out of town.

He turned to Bat. "*You know,* if this town didn't desperately need you, I'd—"

"Mr. Zimmerman," Bat interrupted. "How much lumber do you have?"

Zimmerman pulled a pencil from behind his ear and a notepad from his apron pocket. "How much do you need?"

"That's a good question. How many people will be living in this house, Deputy?"

Noah glared at him.

"You should add a fence." The marshal looped his thumbs in his belt and rocked on his heels. "I can see it now —a white picket fence around a flower garden 'n a farmhouse with a porch holding two rocking chairs."

Noah drummed his fingers on the counter and counted to ten.

With every second that passed, Zimmerman's eyebrows rose higher with anticipation. "Is that right? You need lumber for a house and a fence?"

He wanted to give Sadie a home to replace the one his herd had destroyed. A sturdy one that would keep her warm and safe, and entice her away from the Star. A fence might help.

"Yes," he replied, resigned that Bat would be privy to more details about his plan. "Give me sufficient to build a strong enclosure, one that'll keep out the cattle drovers and their herds."

"Sounds practical," Bat commented.

Noah ignored him and addressed Zimmerman. "Can you arrange all this?"

The shop owner scribbled a few notes. "Of course. Only hitch is the delivery. I'm short-handed right now. Got no one to load the wood. So I can't get your order to you until the end of the week."

"If you've got a wagon, I'll load and deliver the lumber myself," Noah said, impatient to embark on the physical labor and rein in his yearning for Sadie. "I can bring the wagon back tonight," he added.

Zimmerman looked aggrieved. "I'm sorry, but I need the wagon this afternoon."

"What if I assist the deputy 'n return the wagon before noon?" Bat asked.

"That would work perfectly!"

Noah was sure it was far from perfect, but he kept his opinion to himself.

"If you'll come this way, gentlemen." Zimmerman

gestured toward the back door. "I'll show you where the wagon is kept."

Noah and Bat made swift work of loading the supplies. Then Noah collected Pepper and tethered his faithful gray to the tailgate, so he didn't have to walk back into town.

"Beautiful mornin' for an outing, ain't it, Deputy?" Bat drawled as they cleared the last row of buildings marking the southern perimeter of town.

Noah grunted and flicked the reins over the backs of Zimmerman's horses. The pair of matching sorrels ignored him, plodding along at their own pace.

Bat stretched out his legs until his heels rested on the footboard. Then he leaned back, looking like he didn't have a care in the world. "Told you it'd be wise for me to come along."

Noah snorted. "Funny how Zimmerman didn't try to 'swindle' me."

"That's 'cause I was standing right next to you."

Noah debated spooking the horses into a gallop and accidentally shoving Bat out of his seat. But when a rabbit darted across their path, the team didn't even raise their heads. The nag on the left hadn't twitched an ear since they'd set out.

"You ever gonna share the truth of why yer in such a hurry to start a-cuttin' 'n a-sawin' on yer mysterious project?"

"I'm in a hurry to get away from *Dodge* for a while."

"I'm sure you are. Dodge, and the folks in it, can be mighty vexing at times."

"So can you."

The marshal laughed. "Well, I hope you know what yer doing."

"I know how to build a house," Noah replied, exasperated.

"I've no doubt you can handle the house." Bat's expression became serious, and more than a little troubled. "Miss Sullivan's a whole different matter."

THE CREAK of the Star's swinging doors combined with the tread of booted feet and the jingle of spurs brought Sadie's head around like a compass needle seeking north. Her spine sagged, along with her spirits, when a freshly shaven cowboy dressed in starched clothes strutted across the threshold. He surveyed the saloon with the curious eyes of a newcomer. An eager grin parted his lips, and he headed for the bar, where Cora and several other girls stood smiling coyly at him.

Another cattle drive had arrived in Dodge, bringing enthusiastic guests and their money to the Star.

Sadie turned back to her cards. She was not looking for *him*—that amber-eyed, mahogany-haired Texan with his earnest promises and decadent kisses. His interest and affection had vanished along with him.

She should be thankful. He was a distraction she could ill afford. His disappearance was a blessing.

Straightening her spine, she fought the heaviness that kept descending on her shoulders. One night and two whole days had gone by without a glimpse of him. Every shadow in the Star grew increasingly ominous without his presence or the prospect of his return.

Unable to stop herself, she sought him again. She sucked in a ragged breath when she found Wardell sitting across the saloon, watching her. Though his jawline lacked strength, his gaze did not. He smiled and tilted his head in acknowledgment. His attention always caused her stomach to clench with unease. Tonight was no different.

She concealed her reaction by once again staring at the deck of cards in her hands.

Despite their many differences, Wardell and Noah had one thing in common. They could derail her plans and hopes. She'd be damned if she gained her freedom from Gertie, only to lose it to Noah or Wardell or any man.

"Concentrate," she muttered. *Concentrate.* Find Edward's watch and jewelry box. Use them to get far away from Gertie. Go to...

After Chicago, where should she go?

Back to Virginia and a string of towns she didn't care to remember? Or to the endless unknown on the edge of the country in a metropolis like New York where she'd be hemmed in by thousands? The idea of living in either location was disheartening. She'd grown used to the West's wide-open spaces, to the idea of independence, if not yet its reality.

Where then?

There had to be some place. Go to...to...Texas.

Texas? Why had that destination come into her mind? She'd never been to Texas. She knew nothing about the place. Her only experience with Texas was the drovers who came north with the cattle drives. Surrounded by laughing men and chattering women, she struggled to stop the avalanche of longing that ripped through her.

Dear Lord. She couldn't have developed an affection for a place she'd never been. Was she losing her wits as well as her strength?

Then the truth hit her, tensing her every muscle. The one good thing about Texas was Noah.

She hadn't lost her mind, but her heart. And to a man who might've already become bored with her. A man who'd only paid attention to her in the first place because of guilt. A man who, if he discovered he hadn't ruined her, would race for his home in Texas with the north wind howling at his back and the devil snapping at his heels.

Because she was the wicked one now, the one who lied and schemed. She'd sunk so low that the truth was a distant memory, as unattainable as the warmth of the sun, or a friend, or a man who might grow to love her.

Something cold and smooth touched her hand. Slender fingers curled over hers, forcing her to grasp a shot glass full of chalky blue liquid.

"You look like Hades warmed over, darlin'," Cora drawled. "Better not let Gertie see. Drink your medicine an'—"

Clutching the glass in one hand and Cora's arm in the other, she pulled the woman into the quietest corner she could find.

"Why, Sadie, whatever's the matter?" A burst of laughter escaped Cora's ruby-stained lips, high-pitched and uncertain.

The sound stole her will to kowtow to Cora in order to keep the woman's meddling contained. She'd never asked Cora for help. Maybe if she did— Her raw emotions spurred her on. So did her stomach now rolling like an unsecured pot in a tinker's wagon.

"I can't take this anymore." She glanced from the glass in her hand to Cora, realizing she was talking about fighting with Cora as much as the effects of the medicine. "Each day, it makes me weaker. The medicine is poisonous."

"I know. That's why I keep insisting you take it." Cora's eyes blazed with satisfaction.

Sadie's heart missed a beat. Before her stood a true devil. She released the woman as if she were made of fire and pressed her arm protectively over her chest. "You want me dead."

"Eventually. First you must suffer."

"What did I do to—?"

"Edward chose you. He put you ahead of—" Cora stopped as abruptly as she'd started.

He'd picked her instead of Cora. The woman was jealous of a dead man's attention. She should've been jealous of Orin. That was who Edward loved most. But Cora wasn't aware of that. And if she wasn't, she had no reason to suspect that Sadie didn't have syphilis.

"I wish he could see how far you've fallen," Cora said. "You have nothing. Not your health. Not a single friend. Not even your precious Texan."

Sadie's heart thrashed like a bird trying to escape a shrinking cage. Her hand squeezed into a trembling fist. Even if she had the strength to hit her target, no good would come from punching Cora...except for maybe silencing the woman's venomous words.

"Let's figure this one out together, shall we?"

Sadie raised her palm between them. "No."

"Yes." Cora seized her wrist, once more shackling them together. "You've been wondering where he went, gazing at the door with lovesick eyes. You won't look farther. The Star ain't the only place in Dodge with women willing to enter-tain a man."

An icy cold lodged in Sadie's veins. Noah wouldn't—

She stopped herself before she could add to her lies. The truth was she wasn't certain what Noah would do. He wasn't here. He hadn't been for two days. He'd whittled away her defenses, made her crave his company, and then deserted her. Again.

She didn't believe that Cora understood Noah any better than she did. That didn't matter. What mattered was that she'd put herself in a position of weakness by opening her heart to Noah. She cared for him. The possibility of him not caring in return and abandoning her hurt. Horribly.

She had only herself to blame. She should've held on to her refusal to have anything to do with him.

A flurry of taffeta and lace approached. "What's going on?" Gertie demanded. "Cora said you asked for more medicine. So drink it and get on stage."

Resignation settled like a yoke on her shoulders. She was back where she had started. This was what happened when one got distracted from their plans. To hell with distractions, whether they were her health or Cora or Noah.

She downed the foul liquid in one bitter swallow and headed for the stage. Whatever came next, even if it was her death, she'd embrace it alone.

NOAH STRODE along the murky corridor of Front Street, his pace increasing with his heartbeat. By the time he reached the bright shaft of light spilling out of the saloon door, he was jogging. He took the steps in a single bound. The moment he entered the Star, Sadie's voice—flowing and ebbing in a sweet, breathless melody—washed over him, soothing him.

She was still here. She was still safe.

He'd been a fool to stay away, though. Even for a couple of days. What if something had happened in his absence? What if her illness had worsened or someone had hurt her?

Giving her a new home was important, but restraining his feelings for her had been useless. All he'd accomplished was to lay a foundation and erect four walls. The roof, and of course Bat's blasted fence, remained unfinished while he charged back into town, and the Star, with all the restraint of a stampeding bull.

He needed the impossible—to be in two places at once. He forced himself to slow down, to walk in controlled, measured steps, to advance midway into the room and then to move no more.

He couldn't control his eyes, though. His gaze clung to Sadie, refusing to budge. And when her beautiful emerald eyes met his, a surge of happiness left him dizzy.

Her wide-eyed look of surprise collapsed into utter sorrow. She missed a word in her song, stumbled on a high note, but kept singing.

His worry propelled him toward her, only to be diverted by an arm twined around his elbow and a soft form plastered against his side. Glancing down, he discovered Cora, her bosom once again overflowing her corset, her lips parted in a breathless, expectant smile.

Mid-sentence, Sadie stopped singing.

He raised his head in time to see her disappear behind the ruby curtains framing the stage. He untangled himself from Cora and shoved his way through the crowd. Ignoring their boos and catcalls, he vaulted onto the stage. When he rounded the swaying drapes and found Sadie in a cramped corridor, he breathed a sigh of relief.

Eyes closed, back pressed to the rough-hewn boards, she stood as if the wall were the one thing keeping her upright. In a hushed, almost inaudible voice, she repeated a single word. "Concentrate...concentrate...concentrate."

His anxiety returned full force. The passageway seemed

to tilt. He swayed along with its walls and reached for her. "Sadie, what's wrong?"

She recoiled from him as if he'd branded her with a red-hot iron. For every step he took toward her, she took one back. She'd done the same thing a year ago on her farm. Her eyes, dark green bruises surrounded by ashen skin, stared at him accusingly before shifting to a point over his shoulder.

Cora's voice, overflowing with rock-candy sweetness, came from behind him. "Sadie darlin', the crowd, your admirers, you mustn't keep them waiting."

He opened his mouth, intending to tell Cora to go to hell.

Sadie spoke before he could. "Don't worry, Cora *darling*. I'll return in a minute. But first I need to speak to Mr. Ballantyne. Alone." Her bloodless lips compressed into a thin line.

Damnation. They were no longer on a first name basis. He didn't waste time looking over his shoulder to gauge Cora's reaction. He kept his attention on what mattered most.

Sadie stared back at him with glittering eyes while Cora muttered something indiscernible under her breath. Finally, her boot heels clicked, fast and furious, fading until a brittle silence hung between him and Sadie.

"Your game, with my farm, I refuse to play it anymore." Her words fell on him like the lash of a drover's whip, swift and stinging.

"What happened while I was away?"

"I came to my senses. I'm better off on my own. Always have been. I should never have accepted your offer. The price we settled on—"

Head spinning, he latched onto her words. "I'll give you whatever you ask. Name your price."

The sadness that flitted across her face made him regret

saying anything. Then she lifted her chin in that all-too-familiar manner. "You misunderstand. It's not my price I'm talking about but *yours*. It's what I have to pay you."

"I've only asked for your time."

"Yes. And that's asking for too much. I have plans that don't include you." She pushed past him, returning to the stage and leaving him alone in a world where darkness pressed in from all sides.

CHAPTER 10

*S*adie surveyed the Northern Star's storeroom and the crates stacked to its ceiling. Crates she'd searched without success before returning them to their tidy rows and columns. Gertie's passion for organization hadn't helped her quest.

But now only a single crate remained. It could be the one. She pried off the lid and peered inside.

Hope gave way to disappointment. Again and again. Always the same. Nothing but whiskey bottles and food tins. No watch. No jewelry box.

Would she ever see them again? Would she ever fulfill Edward's dying request and get out of Dodge?

His jewelry box had been small enough to hold in one hand. It could be anywhere. She'd always assumed it'd be hidden in the saloon. Now, doubt assailed.

Could Gertie have stashed the box elsewhere? Or given it to someone for safekeeping? Neither seemed likely. Gertie wasn't the type to trust anyone or allow anything of value far from her sight. The madam enjoyed being in control too much.

Could she have already sold Edward's heirlooms? With Marshal Masterson and his friends guarding Dodge, the sale of stolen goods would warrant special care. Gertie's best bet would be to take the train east to a city like Chicago, where she could make an anonymous sale and still receive top dollar. That's what Sadie planned to do when she found them. But Gertie hadn't made such a trip.

Edward's treasures had to be in Dodge.

But if they weren't in Gertie's bedroom, her strongbox or her storeroom, what did that leave? It left Sadie's head spinning until she couldn't even remember where she'd started. When she'd found Edward dying in his room at the Great Western Hotel, what had he said?

Find them... Promise me... What if she couldn't keep her promise?

Her eyes watered and her nose twitched, making her sniff. She wasn't crying. It was merely the blasted dust she'd disturbed during her search. She swiped the back of her hand across her eyes. She had to keep looking, but she didn't know where.

And without her search to keep her thoughts occupied, they went where they shouldn't.

Noah.

She hadn't spoken to him since his return last night. He'd approached her repeatedly, but each time she'd forced herself to walk away...when all she'd wanted to do was the opposite.

Dejection made her shoulders slump. She missed talking to him.

Which made her all the more aware that she couldn't waver in her decision to shut him out of her life. She couldn't forget how deeply even his temporary disappearance had hurt. The fact that she'd let down her guard, after all the disappointments she'd endured, should have made her even more determined.

She must be more forceful. She had to solve her problems on her own.

She put the lid back on the crate and straightened it to align with its sisters. There. She was tougher than everyone —including herself—believed. She could continue to rebuff Noah. He'd soon give up and leave Dodge for good.

A wave of misery and exhaustion rocked her on her heels. She sat down on the crate with a thump. Resting her elbows on her knees and her head in her hands, she closed her blurry eyes and cursed the dust again.

A groaning creak made her jerk upright.

Gertie stood in the doorway, eyes narrowed into slits. "I've been searching everywhere for you, and I find you here?"

Dread squeezed the air from Sadie's lungs. She'd finally been caught.

"Well?" Gertie demanded. "What're you doing here?"

"I..."

"Are you hiding?" The outrage raising Gertie's voice suggested she considered that was the worst thing Sadie could be capable of.

She'd admit to hiding if that deflected attention from what she'd really been doing. Her chest expanded, and she could breathe again. Words continued to fail her, though. She could only stare as Gertie stomped into the storeroom.

"I said I was looking for you." Her employer halted in front of her. Planting her hands on her hips, she loomed over Sadie. "Why are you sitting there like a lump on a log? Are you feeling all right?"

Sadie shook her head. She hadn't felt "all right" since she'd come to work for Gertie.

"Christ Almighty, you look like hell," Gertie snapped, examining her with belated concern. "Don't go dying on me, girl. Not when I've found a buyer for you."

Sadie's voice returned, screeching like a rusty gate in a gale. "A buyer?"

Gertie seized her arm and jerked her to her feet and out the storeroom door. "Have no idea what he plans to do with you, what with the shape you're in. But if he's willing to pay, I ain't gonna argue."

She dragged Sadie into the next room, a fancy one for customers willing to pay extra. The room even had a shelf full of eye-opening books, including one about a girl named Fanny. She'd discovered the collection while searching for Edward's possessions.

Gertie shoved her onto an enormous four-poster bed. Wherever she looked, a never-ending rainbow of vibrant colors bedazzled her already spinning senses.

"Now listen up, missy. He's waiting upstairs in your room. I'll escort him down, while you..." She shook her head and threw up her hands. "Just don't pass out while I'm gone. And try to act like you're worth a hundred dollars. I don't want him to take one look at you and demand his money back."

"A hundred dollars?" Sadie gasped. But she was speaking to Gertie's broad backside. The madam had rushed out the open door.

The urge to flee trumped everything. She raced toward her freedom only to be brought up short by John's unexpected appearance in the doorway. She searched his eyes, silently beseeching him to let her pass.

He met her stare. Solid. Unmovable.

Her gaze dropped to the gap between him and the doorframe. She'd slipped through smaller spaces.

"My orders say yer to stay in this room." His tone was somber. "I don't want to hurt you again."

Ugly images from a year ago charged through her mind: John coming after her, finding her all too easily, bringing her back, and then...Gertie ordering him to show Sadie, with his two-tailed leather strap, why it wasn't a good idea to run.

She set her teeth and lifted her chin, glaring at him through stinging eyes.

"Hate me all you want. I've earned it. But don't go askin' me to do somethin' I can't. We're the same in that at least. We both got control over nothin'. Dodge owns me, same as it does you."

Shock made her retreat a stride. He'd never said anything about his reasons for being at the Star. He'd never shared how he got his scars either. She took another step back, so she could better scan his face.

His mood remained indiscernible. "Now, you buck up. You'll get through this, same as you done everythin' else. Yer tiny as a mouse but tougher 'n rawhide." He closed the door, leaving her gaping at nothing but wood.

To hell with that. This mouse is leaving!

She raced to the window. Despite all her heaving, it wouldn't budge. She frowned at the hunk of metal on the sill. Locked and rusted. Lord knew when it'd last been used. It was her one hope. She raked her fingers through her hair in search of a pin. Muffled voices came from behind her and the door, growing louder. She spun to face them.

Hard against her spine, the window mocked her while keeping her upright. She'd wasted too much time trying to convince John to let her go. She was about to pay dearly for that mistake.

The door burst open, and Cora barged into the room.

John's bulk blocked her attempts to shut the door behind her.

"Leave Sadie alone," he growled. "She don't need you revelin' in her misfortune right now."

Cora laughed. "You're the oddest box herder Gertie ever hired. A rich man willing to pay a bundle for a woman ain't a bad thing, an' as you can plainly see—" she held up the yards of silk draped over her arm, "—I'm only here to make Sadie presentable. Why else would I be lugging this dress around?"

John's gaze leapt from Cora to Sadie. He gave her a look full of pity, then closed the door.

As soon as he did, Cora bore down on her with a swift stride. She didn't even pause when she tossed the dress on the bed. Sadie braced herself for a fight.

Instead, Cora folded her arms and leaned against the window frame so they stood face to face. "Bet you wish you could crawl through this window an' run like a rabbit."

Sadie flinched. Cora was definitely here to gloat. She mimicked Cora's stance and scoured her mind for a way to make the woman leave. All she could think was that at any time the door would open again. This time it'd be Gertie and her buyer.

Cora arched a brow at her continued silence. "You pitiful thing. Your heart's hammering so fast you haven't stopped to consider who's chasing your tail."

Frustration made Sadie's mind spin even faster. She didn't have time to ponder who might be coming for her. Or time for Cora. She had to leave this room.

"Well," Cora drawled. "I can't count more than two men who'd want to, an' could afford to, drop a hundred for you."

Sadie shook her head. The price didn't matter. All she cared about was getting far away from this buyer who'd taken a sudden interest in her. Her thoughts ground to a halt. What if the attention wasn't so sudden? Relief swelled inside her as a single name filled her mind and spilled from her lips. "Noah."

Cora snorted a laugh. "Yes, one possibility is your Texan. Lewis told me his friend owned a ranch in Texas. A large one."

Noah couldn't be rich enough to warrant the hungry look in Cora's eyes. Or could he? If he'd gone back to the bank and sold her farm—the land she'd refused to barter her time for— he'd at least have ready cash again. He could pay Gertie. If he had, there wasn't a burning need to run. She'd rather stay and give him a tongue-lashing for discarding her farm so quickly as well as using his hard-earned dollars to feed Gertie's greed.

Cora's gaze roamed her face. "An' what of the other man? The first owns a ranch. The second likes to believe he owns a town."

Fear drained her of all other emotion. "Wardell."

"Not such a witless rabbit after all."

Icy tendrils of panic snaked around her, making her shiver uncontrollably. She'd been lucky to escape Wardell last autumn when Edward outbid him. Now it appeared her luck had left town before she could. If there was even the remotest chance the buyer might be Wardell—

She had to get Cora out of this room so she could then get out the window. She seized her nemesis' arm and strove to pull her toward the door. Like the sturdiest of oaks, Cora remained rooted to the floorboards.

"If you're done gloating, why don't you leave me alone to my fate?" she demanded.

Cora released a breathy laugh as she leaned toward Sadie and said in a conspiratorial whisper, "Because I want to give you this." She slid her fingers into the top of her corset and fished out a tarnished key.

"What's that?"

Cora tapped the key on the window lock. The rust on both matched. "The means to your escape."

Sadie fought the impulse to snatch the offering. "The last thing you'd want is to help me." The woman had admitted she craved a slow, painful death for Sadie.

Cora's glare could've cut the glass on the window. "We don't always get everything we desire. Despite my longing to see you laid low, there's something I need more. You snatched Edward out of my hands, but you won't steal another rich patron who should be mine."

"You don't want Wardell. He's—" She couldn't describe the horrors she'd heard.

"He's a sadistic bastard." Cora arched one brow in challenge. "Aren't they all, to some extent? If he becomes unbearable, I can always slip a little rat poison into his bourbon. But not before I get his money. Lots of it. You stand between me an' that windfall."

Cora and Wardell were a pair of devils. They deserved each other. Sadie would gladly leave and let them torment each other. But doubts still nagged her. "This is a trick. You want me dead."

"I want you gone." Cora's voice grew gruff with impatience. "So take the blasted key and go. I'm not leaving till you do."

Cora left her no choice. She did as commanded. On the plus side, keys were quicker than hairpins, and she needed every second to escape. She'd wasted too many of them talking to Cora and John. The window shot up with a screech of protest.

Both she and Cora glanced at the door and froze. Had John heard?

"So you're saying you won't put on the dress?" Cora demanded in an exaggeratedly loud voice as she eased the window closed.

Sadie raised her voice to match. "Damn the dress and you too. Get out."

"Ungrateful bitch," Cora shot back with a laugh. Then she strode toward the door, scooping up the dress as she went. She paused in the open doorway. Long enough for John to stare over her head and catch a glimpse of Sadie.

"I hope I never see you again," Cora said as she closed the door.

A sense of calm purpose stole over Sadie. This time, she raised the window with care. So it didn't even utter a squeak. She poked her head outside and scanned the alley. Empty. Thank the Lord.

Sitting on the windowsill, she swung one foot through the opening, then the other. She didn't pause. She pushed off.

The hard-packed dirt jarred her bones. She ignored the discomfort and ran. A hasty glance over her shoulder confirmed that, for now, only her guilt followed her. Staying to fulfill her promise to Edward had given way to sheer survival. If there was one chance in a hundred that Wardell was coming for her, she couldn't stay.

Wardell was a fight she couldn't win.

She could only run and pray that this time John and Gertie didn't catch her and drag her back to the Star...and a room she'd gambled everything on escaping.

Nervous as a long-tailed cat in a room full of rocking chairs, Noah followed Madam Garrett through the packed saloon toward the door behind which she'd ensured him Sadie waited. A door John and Cora stood outside of while conversing with irate gestures. When Cora spotted him and the madam approaching, she disappeared into the crowd at a brisk pace.

The men milling around the half-dozen women in the room slowed his pace and continued to delay his efforts to speak with Sadie. The recent arrival of several cattle drives meant Front Street was never empty. He hadn't been able to use the balcony to reach Sadie's room unseen. Nor had he been able to approach Sadie in the saloon without Cora interrupting.

No surprise, then, that as soon as he'd secured a way to be alone with Sadie, he found Cora nearby. This time arguing with John. Had they been discussing Sadie?

His gut warned him that the woman had stoked the trouble between him and Sadie. Exactly what she'd said or done, he hated to contemplate. After Sadie's continued refusal to talk to him, he'd demanded answers from Cora. All she'd offered him was her personal company again.

The resulting impasse had forced his hand. That didn't mean he was comfortable with what he'd done. Not by a long shot.

Once more, his conscience plagued him, like a burr beneath a saddle blanket. But if paying one hundred dollars resulted in Sadie talking to him, then it had to be done. She'd be hard pressed to remain silent all night in a room with him. Especially when she couldn't run away.

He'd pushed her pretty hard, first with his brazen bargain for her land, then with his kisses. What if he'd gone too far this time? Sweat broke out on his forehead as he pictured Sadie inside the room. How angry would she be?

He stopped a stride from the door, not sure he wanted to find out.

Madam Garrett gave him a strained but determined smile. "Come, Mr. Ballantyne. Sadie's waiting for you."

He raised a halting hand. "How'd she take it when you told her?"

"Told her...?"

"That I'd paid you a hundred dollars to speak with her."

"She was...delighted." The madam appeared both relieved and heartened to find the word. "I've put you in the best room in the house. You won't be disturbed. Come," she beckoned, then gestured for John to step aside.

"Delighted's a mite optimistic," John muttered as he complied.

Noah stared at the man, his resolve disintegrating. Half an hour ago, he'd been dead certain this was the right path. The last one left open to him.

As Madam Garrett opened the door, he braced himself for the sight of blazing emerald eyes and the fight of his life. An empty room greeted him. So did an open window.

The madam let out a howl like the cat he'd compared himself to moments ago. He'd set the rocking chairs in motion.

"How dare she run away!" She elbowed Noah aside and sank her nails into John's arm with such ferocity, even the giant blanched. "I assumed she'd learned after last time. Apparently, she needs a *reminder*." She patted John's arm and lowered her voice to a more cajoling tone. "Now, John, I know you felt sorry for her, that you held back. But look what good that did. Find her. And this time, make the lesson stick."

The look that passed between the pair robbed the air from Noah's lungs. "Madam, you'll do no such thing. Not on my account, or ever. I don't want—"

But John was already pushing his way through the crowd toward the back door that led to the alley. Panic threatened to swallow him whole as he chased after John.

He'd once again disturbed a delicate house of cards. Made them come crashing down when he'd inserted himself into the fragile framework of Sadie's life. And, like last year, she'd be the one to pay the price.

THE PEAKED ROOF of the livery stable, high above all the others, beckoned. Sadie left the shelter of the alley and forced herself to stroll down the busy street. *Almost there.* But getting there felt as if it were taking a lifetime, rather than the exact number of seconds she'd carefully counted the morning after Edward died.

Even though she'd planned for this—had almost left after Davenport threatened her life or when she'd believed Doctor Rhodes told Noah she didn't have syphilis—she couldn't stop shaking. So much could go wrong. She flinched at every footfall, every shout, imagining a search party in pursuit.

Until she slipped through the livery door and closed it behind her. But not completely. She left the smallest gap. Enough to peer through and scan the street.

No one looked or pointed her way.

She slumped against the door, shutting out the world, but not her thoughts. Remorse squeezed her chest, solid and unforgiving. She'd failed Edward. Oddly, that wasn't what hurt most. She'd never see Noah again.

She should've waited to learn if he was the buyer. But what if Wardell had walked into that room instead of Noah? She would've waited on a man and lost her one chance to escape. Same as she'd waited on Edward and his promise to take her away from Dodge.

No more waiting.

She ran to the ladder leading to the hayloft. By the time she reached the far corner of the loft, she was panting and praying.

Let it still be here. She dug through the hay. If it's gone—

Her fingers brushed coarse cloth. She hugged the sack to her chest, then stripped to her underclothes and donned the bag's contents. Chosen for their size as well as their dull homespun weight, the coat and pants hung on her and hopefully hid all of her curves. Next came oversized boots and a hat large enough to hide her hair underneath. Reaching up, she swept her palms over a roof beam and rubbed the dirt on her face and hands.

After she covered every inch of her body, she stuffed her harlot garb in the sack, buried it under the hay, and prayed once more.

Please let my old life disappear as easily.

She retraced her steps to the livery floor and out the door. Tramping along the street, she pondered how best to walk like a boy. She didn't know how long she'd have to play this role, so she'd better get it right.

Behind her, galloping hoofbeats froze her feet but sent her heart racing. Her last ounce of good sense propelled her to sit beside two youths playing jacks on the boardwalk.

John urged his mount down the road. A man on a gray horse followed. The silver badge on his vest caught the sunlight, blinding her, making her gaze plummet.

Why was Noah riding with John? Was he here to stop John or help him? What would happen if she ran?

The murmurs of a growing crowd amplified her worries. Their bodies crowded close. Snug as a noose. She wasn't going anywhere.

The horses skidded to a halt in front of the crowd. Their hooves churned up dust as their riders reined the nervous animals in circles, doing their best to keep them in one spot.

"I'm looking for Sadie Sullivan," John shouted. "The prostitute who works at the Northern Star."

She raised her chin. Guilty people looked down.

Noah's mouth was a grim line, his brows dark slashes over narrowed eyes. He scanned the crowd slowly... painstakingly...hunting. When he came to her and the two boys, the nerves along the nape of her neck prickled. She imagined he lingered a mite too long before continuing his search.

"There's a reward for anyone who brings her in." John's gaze swept the townsfolk as well. "And a beatin' for anyone who don't. So if you see her, haul her straight back to the Star."

His audience mumbled their agreement. John understood their desires and their fears. Even worse, he was as persistent as a Virginia coonhound. If she didn't leave town fast, she'd be back in the Star and a world of pain.

John spurred his mount down the street. Noah followed.

On wobbly legs, she rose and continued on the path she'd chosen. Thankfully, that direction led her away from John...and Noah. Her shaking increased. She concentrated on not tripping over her own feet. She was finally leaving Dodge. Nothing was going to stop her. Not even her foolish heart.

Clouds of dust high in the sky, along with a muted thunder, were her beacons. The sound swelled into bellowing cattle, shuffling hooves, and men shouting orders. She'd reached the rail depot. Just in time. A train was loading its final cattle car. It'd leave in a matter of minutes.

She sprinted for the locomotive. A single leap took her over the track and around the cowcatcher. Her feet slipped in the loose dirt. Arms windmilling, she fought to stay upright. She ended up on her hands and knees, crawling behind the engine.

The smokebox with its fluted chimney towered over her. The depot stood on the other side. So did Dodge and the eager eyes of everyone who might drag her back to Gertie.

A mysterious array of pipes and pistons drew her attention down the train. Her gaze halted on a ladder.

The iron rungs, smooth and solid under her hands and feet, made for a quick climb. When she reached the top, a glimpse of the workers trudging back to town sent her ducking as she jumped over the last rung. Her pant leg caught on something. She flipped forward into blackness. She landed hard on her belly and chest.

The air left her lungs. Wouldn't return. She rolled onto her back. The coal for the firebox was an unforgiving bed as she struggled to breathe. One painful gasp at a time.

The bright starbursts obscuring her vision faded. A swathe of blue, broken only by lazy puffs of charcoal smoke, arced above her while the railcar vibrated beneath her. She lay hidden from the men she'd spied returning to town.

Relief rendered her aches and pains insignificant. This part of her plan had worked. She was leaving Dodge and everyone in it. She closed her eyes against the memory of whiskey-colored eyes. Her future lay elsewhere.

All cattle trains leaving Dodge went to Chicago's stock-yards. At the end of the rail line, a new town awaited. From all accounts, it was a bustling rabbit warren of streets where a runaway might hope to disappear. She couldn't hope to go farther. Not without Edward's jewelry box and watch to pave her way.

What should she do when she reached Chicago? Could she keep the boy's garb and find work in the cattle yards? In four days, she'd find out. She'd have new challenges.

All of which she must face alone.

The warmth of the sun vanished. When she opened her eyes, a silhouette the size of a bear descended toward her. Panic sent her rolling sideways and scrambling across the coals. A rough hand seized the back of her collar and hauled her up onto her toes. Then her feet left the coal bed. She dangled in the air, as if she were as light as a child's toy.

"We got another stowaway," a baritone voice announced above her head.

"Toss him down." The high-pitched reply came fast and from far below.

"No!" Her shriek ended when she hit the ground. Pain knifed into her hip, stabbing up her ribs and down her thigh. Her momentum sent her tumbling. Each bounce inflicted another bruising wallop on a new part of her body. She couldn't do anything but curl into a ball—until she crashed into something hard and stopped.

"Jesus H. Christ! When I said to toss him, I didn't mean on me."

Arms wrapped around her aching body, she squinted up at the thin man furiously rubbing his shins. When he lifted his head to glare at her, she recognized the close-set eyes and pointy nose under the short brim of his hat. His soot-covered overalls confirmed her worst nightmare. She'd seen this rat-faced brakeman at the Star.

And if she knew him, he knew Sadie Sullivan.

She scuttled backward on her heels and her butt.

"Oh no you don't." He grabbed the shoulder of her coat and thrust his nose close to hers. "You ain't leaving till you learn not to steal a free ride on our train."

She lowered her chin and hid under her hat. The blur of his arm swinging toward her made her duck even further. The crown of her hat took the brunt of his slap. The cord yanked tight under her chin before it snapped. Released from its tether, her hat flew into the air. Her hair did the same before falling around her shoulders.

A gasp of surprise whistled in her ear, followed by a hushed voice. "You're the whore John's searching fer." He swept off his own hat and used it to beat the dust from her clothing, clouding the air even more. She coughed and winced, his whacks reminding her of every bruise.

"Reckon the boy's taken enough punishment." The deep voice grew louder, coming closer. "When I get done climbing down from this car, you'd better have turned him loose. We gotta get this train moving."

Do as the bear says. Release me, you horrible little rodent.

Her captor yanked her to her knees so that she faced the train. "But look! The *he* you threw off the coal car is a *she*."

Clenching her teeth against the pain she suspected would follow, she lurched to her feet and tried to run. A hand as heavy as an enormous paw grasped her head and forced her face skyward. She glared up at the same massive silhouette that'd thrown her off the train.

A moment of silence stretched her nerves tight.

"She's the escaped whore." Excitement raised the thin man's voice to a squeak. "The one with the French pox."

"I ain't blind," came the answering grumble. "I've eyeballed her at the Star, same as you."

"John said we gotta return her to the madam."

"All in good time."

A cold sweat turned her skin to ice. She needed John right now. "He's offering a reward."

"And I'll take *every* reward in my grasp." The big man's gaze cut to his partner. "Ain't you ever rubbed your dick while listening to her singing out of reach on that stage?" His hand dropped from her head to encircle her arm like a band of iron.

That didn't stop her from fighting to break loose. "Madam Garrett will—"

He hauled her toward the train. "She can do whatever she wants. Same as I'm gonna do what I want—which is stripping you naked beside that train and jerking off while you wriggle beneath me with all of your pale flesh free for my other hand to grope."

His partner jumped between them and the train. "Hey! When do I get my turn?"

"After you stand guard and make sure no one interrupts me."

"I discovered who she was first. So I should go first."

"Too bad yer a bandy-legged runt who'll spend his life being second."

The thin man tugged her toward him. The bigger one jerked her back. She felt like the wishbone on last week's pheasant dinner, pulled in two directions and ready to snap.

The only direction she wanted to go was away from these two men. She needed help. Any help. At the saloon, she'd overheard that brakemen often worked in pairs. Was the other man in the caboose at the end of the train? Or walking along the backs of the cars? If she could get his attention, she might have a chance.

She screamed as loud as she could. Then she bit the palm that descended to cover her mouth. She could do nothing to escape the punch that followed. Pain exploded in her jaw and cracked her head back. Once again she hung from the big man's grasp.

"Hit her again," he said, "and I'm gonna darken yer daylights."

"But she bit me!"

"Remember those rules Garrett likes to harp about? We can do anything we damned well please except leave one of her girls too beat up to work in her saloon."

"We can't stick our pricks in this one."

"There are other ways to get off."

Eager fingers reached up to squeeze her arm. "If I help you *get* her into the engine cab, no one needs to stand guard. We can both be first."

A frustrated grumble swelled above her. "I'm only sayin' yes to shut you up."

She threw the last of her strength into getting away. The two men ignored her. With a determination gained from a single-minded purpose, they pulled her across the dirt toward the train.

CHAPTER 11

*N*oah's heels hovered over his gray's flanks as they followed John's horse like a shadow through the rail depot. With the slightest command, Pepper would turn onto a new course. They'd been together long enough for the horse to sense his decisions a heartbeat after he'd made them. The trouble was he hadn't a clue what to do right now.

Should he stay with John or start his own search?

On their first lap, John halted long enough to bark orders at the townsfolk and workmen. This time they didn't stop. They raced past the caboose, the railcars packed with bellowing cattle, the empty corrals and loading ramps, the locomotive rumbling and puffing black smoke while it waited to leave.

John's attention was riveted on the workmen retreating into town. Noah squelched the urge to abandon the chase. The Star's strongman was riding in circles. But he couldn't take the chance, however slight, of John stumbling onto Sadie without him nearby.

The orders Madam Garrett had given back at the Star made him rigid with worry and anger.

They'd punished Sadie before. They meant to do so again. There'd be a reckoning for those offenses...as soon as he made sure Sadie was safe.

How could she have disappeared so quickly? Why hadn't anyone found her? John was offering enough incentives to make even a by-the-book preacher turn her in.

From the din behind him came a sound, faint as the cry of a bird high overhead. It raised the hair on his neck. He reined Pepper around. On the opposite side of the locomotive he'd sped past, two men dragged a struggling form.

A tangle of brown with a flash of familiar red. Gone behind the locomotive in a blink.

His stomach flipped over, sick with dread. Pepper raced forward and bounded over the tracks straight toward the two men climbing into the engine cab. Long red hair hung from the bundle they were trying to force inside.

With a roar, he jumped to the ground, his revolver cocked and pointed at the biggest man's back. "Bring her down. Or you're both dead."

The pair froze. The smaller man tensed, most likely preparing to jump on him.

He shifted his aim and pressed the trigger. The man's hat flew into the air. He cocked the hammer and swung the barrel back to the first man, who now glared down at him. He raised the gun until he stared straight down the barrel into a pair of black eyes.

The man's gaze dropped to Noah's chest, to the silver star pinned there, then rose to clash with his again. "Ain't it against the law to shoot unarmed men, Deputy?"

"Noah?" Sadie's voice flowed over him, dulling his rage, but only for an instant.

He kept his attention and his gun on the men, but his softly spoken question was only for her. "Did they hurt you?"

"The big one threw me off the top of the coal car. The other one punched me in the jaw."

He bit back his curse.

"She stowed away on our train," the smaller man said in a shrill rush. "She's that escaped whore John wants brought in."

"That why you were forcing her back onto your train?" Noah demanded.

Silence met his question.

He drew in a deep breath, struggling to hold on to his raging emotions. "I killed the last man who tried to take her. Shot him square between the eyes. But you—" He lowered his aim to the man's crotch. "You both deserve a bullet between your legs. Marshal Masterson will understand when I tell him you ignored my direct order to bring her down."

With exaggerated care, the two men climbed down and set Sadie on the ground. Then they raised their hands and retreated as far as the engine would allow.

"Get back on that train," Noah growled, "and out of my sight."

The pair scrambled to obey. As soon as the engine started moving, Noah holstered his revolver and dropped onto his knees beside Sadie. She lay curled in a ball on her side.

"What were you thinking, going anywhere near those men?" His voice came out hoarse, unwilling to speak of the danger she'd exposed herself to because she wanted to run away from him.

"I developed a sudden need to disappear."

The train rattled by, picking up speed. If she'd succeeded in hiding on it, he might have never seen her again.

"Mule-headed little fool," he muttered. He brushed her hair away from her cheek and tucked it behind her ear. "Why is your face streaked with so much dirt?"

She released a long sigh. "So, I failed there as well. I'd hoped to cover all of my face. And my hair...I should've cut it."

You shouldn't *have left. What if I hadn't found you in time?* He gathered her in his arms with all the gentleness he could muster.

She didn't utter a sound, but her pain was evident in the stiffness of her muscles.

"I'm just glad you're safe." He breathed the words into her hair, then forced himself to continue in a firmer voice. "I made you run from the Star. I'm sorry."

"I wasn't running from you," she replied without hesitation. She was telling the truth.

Her truths baffled him as much as her lies. "Then why did you leave?"

"Cora said it'd be either you or Wardell coming. Wardell was a possibility I couldn't face."

Wardell. The name echoed in his mind as the last railcar swept by. Its wake buffeted him and made him stagger. His hold tightened on Sadie as he stared after the receding tail of the train. He should've hauled Sadie onboard himself. He should've left Dodge with her safe and secure in his arms... and never looked back.

"I need you to return her to the Star."

Noah spun from the train to face John, standing opposite him on the other side of the tracks.

His muscles coiled, preparing for a fight. But he couldn't slug or shoot his way clear of John. Not with Sadie in his arms. He'd have to set her down. His arms refused to release her. He strode toward Pepper, who patiently waited a short distance away.

John set a parallel course beside him. "She ain't in no shape to travel."

Noah kept walking. "I'm not leaving her alone with you and Gertie."

"There's a room waiting for you at the Star. For you and Sadie. Or have you forgotten that you paid for a night with her?"

Noah halted beside Pepper. "And in the morning?"

"Sadie will have had time to rest, and the madam will have had time to cool off."

"I need to go back." Sadie's words held a quiet certainty.

"Like hell you do," he bit out.

"If Wardell wasn't coming for me," she continued in the same tone, "then I've no reason to run."

She had no reason to stay either. At least not one she'd shared with him. And she had yet to pay Gertie's price for running away.

Anger whipped him around to face John. "You didn't hear Madam Garrett telling him—" he thrust his chin at the man, "—to punish you as soon as he found you."

"She knows the madam's rules." John widened his stance, with one foot behind the other, braced and ready.

Damnation. He'd have to set Sadie down after all.

"I knew," she said, "and I still climbed out that window." The warmth of her palm on the back of his neck made his pulse jump. With the barest of pressure, she pulled his head down until her lips brushed his ear. "I don't want to return to the saloon, but..." Her halting, soft-spoken words made his heart race even faster. "I must finish what I started."

If he hadn't seen the clearness in her eyes a moment

before, he might've assumed she was so exhausted she was letting her secrets slip. This was no accident. This secret was for him, and him alone.

He turned his back to John and lowered his voice to match hers. "What's so important it's worth risking a beating or worse?"

"A promise made to a friend. Someone who helped me when no one else would. Will you...help me fulfill that promise?"

Finally, she'd asked for his assistance. Without hesitation, he said, "Yes."

SADIE FORCED herself to say the words. "Then take me back to the Star."

As soon as they left her mouth, Noah stiffened in rejection while at the same time his arms tightened around her. He gave a whistle and his horse, and John, followed them toward town.

She relaxed in his arms, wanting to stay there forever and dreading the moment when he must put her down... when she'd be alone again. All too soon, they reached the alley behind the Star. As soon as they did, the back door burst open. Gertie stood in the doorway, hands fisted on her hips, her glare sharp as a blade.

Sadie's anxiety returned full force. She concentrated on remaining still, on not showing her fear. A hefty challenge that kept her well-occupied.

"I'm sorry you've been inconvenienced, Mr. Ballantyne." Gertie's voice was tight with repressed anger. "Rest assured she'll be disciplined for wasting your time."

Noah's embrace couldn't stop the cold from reaching her.

Icy tendrils streaked down her back, reminding her of what was to come—the lash of John's strap.

She tamped down her shivers. She'd chosen this path. *Too late to head down another. Pain is temporary. Fear is fleeting.* Making sure Gertie couldn't savor her triumph over Edward would strengthen her forever. But to get to forever, she had to survive today.

Noah's fingers squeezed her arm with a gentle reassurance. She hadn't hidden her fears after all. He'd felt them. How could he not, when he held her this close?

"My time with Sadie has been well spent, Madam Garrett," he said. "I look forward to enjoying my entire night with her."

She'd forgotten his purpose for coming to the saloon an hour earlier: an entire night alone together. Her jaw sagged along with Gertie's.

The madam recovered first. Her smile didn't reach her eyes, however, and the lines around her mouth remained hard. "Room's where you left it. That much hasn't changed. It hasn't sprouted wings and flown the nest like the ingrate in your arms did when she ran us all ragged in search of her."

Sadie swallowed the urge to comment that Gertie hadn't run anywhere and didn't look in the least bit ragged.

Gertie's gaze cut to John hovering behind them. "You're needed at the bar. Have one of the girls stable your horses." She stepped back to let John pass. "We'll talk in the morning."

Noah blocked John from entering the saloon. "I'd hate to hear of Sadie being punished for this or anything else. When I come to the Star, I bring only my money. I want to leave my duties as a lawman outside."

John looked to Gertie for confirmation.

The madam's lips compressed into a thin line. Finally, she nodded. Then she gave Sadie a crafty-eyed once over. "I reckon you'll want me to add a tub of water to your bill, Mr. Ballantyne."

"And clean clothing for Sadie," he replied.

Gertie nodded again, this time with approval. "I'll send something appropriate, something to match your room."

Noah cleared his throat. "I'll probably need a bottle of whiskey as well." A muscle jumped in his jaw as he carried her through the door and into the chaos of the saloon.

A volley of voices fought to be heard over the strident notes of the piano. Noah's scowl made the crowd fall back as he strode straight to the fancy room and kicked its door closed behind them. The noise on the other side faded to a distant thunder as he carried her to the bed.

The ache inside her returned, coiled tight. She went still around it. Waiting. Wanting.

With infinite care, he set her down on the mattress and sat beside her. His hands moved to her waist. His grip tightened and eased, drawing her back to his warmth. She held her breath, anticipating what he'd do next.

He released her and went to stand by the window.

The loss of him, sturdy as a house of bricks around her, left her shaking. She needed to put an even greater distance between them, so she could rebuild the wall around her heart. She needed to stop lying to herself. From day one, she'd never had a hope of maintaining that wall.

"Where did you go, this time, when you left me?" She regretted her question immediately, the weakness in it and in her. Her hands clutched in her lap seemed the safest place to look.

"Sadie," his voice was gruff, "after we kissed, you had me

tied up six ways till Sunday. It's not wise for me to be near you when I'm in such a state."

She nodded. In this way, they were similar. She stole a look at him from under her lashes.

He leaned heavily against the window frame while he surveyed their surroundings. "This room is...astonishing. It's so colorful it hurts my eyes."

She'd been so wrapped up in Noah that she hadn't given the room a second of her attention as he carried her in. The setting sun made the jewel tones even more vibrant. She fidgeted with the sleeve of her jacket, then stopped, realizing how filthy she was from her fall in the coal car and her tumble from the train. She was covered in dirt and coal dust, but her wretched appearance hadn't seemed to bother Noah.

"You know this is only temporary," he said.

She clenched her teeth. *Pain is temporary. Fear is fleeting. Don't let him distract you.*

He heaved a sigh. "I can't protect you if Madam Garrett believes no further payments can be gained from the arrangement."

"You're in this room because of Gertie?" She sealed her lips, mortified that she'd almost blurted her hope he was here for a whole lot more.

"And because—" He pushed away from the window. When he reached the bed, he leaned down until his lips hovered over hers. "I want—" his voice was low, urgent, "—you." He breathed the last word into her mouth.

She opened to him wholeheartedly. Her pulse raced to an ancient tune. A primal need devoured all coherent thought. All except one. It wasn't enough. She must, some-how, get even closer. She pressed against him and gasped when the pain from her fall reminded her not to move so quickly.

With a muffled curse, Noah stepped out of reach...out of hers and his. "I shouldn't have—" He scrubbed his hand over the back of his neck. "You need to rest and heal. Most of all, we need to talk."

"About what?" She brushed her fingertips over the tingling warmth he'd awakened in her lips before he retreated. Words couldn't describe what she felt, what he made her feel.

"I'm not leaving you again." Despite his reply, he paced the room like a caged wolf.

Another truth fell into her grasp. They were the same in this as well. "Dodge's oppression is eating at you. You crave the open country." Her now fisted hand lowered from her lips to her lap. "You'll leave."

"I won't."

"Yesterday you went..." *Far enough for me to fear you'd never come back.*

He stopped in the middle of the room, halfway between the window and the door. "I went to your farm."

Disbelief made her gasp. "My farm?"

"You could go there as well."

"I can't. I have to—" Her gaze ricocheted around the room, her mind searching beyond the walls for where she might look for Edward's possession. She'd run out of places.

He spun to face her. "Tell me," he urged, "about your friend, the one you promised."

She wanted to tell him. It'd be a relief to share this burden with someone as strong-minded as him. But how much could she say about Edward before Noah unraveled all of her lies? After that, how long before Gertie knew as well?

A knock shattered the brittle silence between them.

He crossed to the door and held it wide. "I'll take that." He lifted a copper bathtub from the straining hands of two of Gertie's girls. He carried it across the room as if it weighed nothing. The women's eyes followed him, frank and admiring.

"I assume there's water coming as well?" He asked over his shoulder.

The women's steps slowed as they left but picked up when they returned with buckets filled to the brim. Each time he met them in the doorway and bid them to bring more. When he declared the tub held sufficient water, they brought a whiskey bottle, two glasses and a chiffon peignoir—red as a sunset before a storm, thin as the steam rising above the tub. The harlot's dress she'd stuffed in the livery loft looked like the garb of a schoolmarm in comparison.

Noah urged the women out and shut the door behind them, leaving her alone with him and her longing.

She stared at the peignoir clutched in her hand. Why did her body crave only him? And her mind as well? The notion of wearing the sheer garment in front of him filled her with excitement, but also an impulse to run again. A fine strumpet she was. She could learn a lot tonight.

"Are you contemplating climbing out that window again?" The closeness of his voice made her start.

Her gaze darted up to meet his. When had he moved to stand opposite her?

He sank down on his heels, so he was the one looking up at her, and she down at him. His amber eyes glowed with a warmth that heated her straight through. Her desire to run went up in smoke.

"Neither of us can leave this room tonight," he said. "We

have a role to play. One that will convince the madam there's
no need to punish you."

Her heart was willing to cooperate. More than willing.
But where was her common sense? Yesterday she'd
convinced herself the wisest option was to have nothing to
do with him. Today her nerves were jumping like fish in a
stream, pulled by an unfamiliar but irresistible force.

He removed his hat and clenched it in both hands,
staring at it as if he fought something inside him as well.
"There's one thing I need from you."

Only one? That didn't sound right. Not when she craved
a hundred things from him. She shook her head.

"Promise me—" his voice deepened with urgency, "—
you'll come get me next time you need to leave Dodge."

She continued shaking her head. She was done making
promises she couldn't keep. His gaze lifted to meet hers. The
worry in his eyes made her shake her head all the harder.
She wanted so much more than his concern.

"How long before someone comes along demanding the
privileges Madam Garrett believes I'm taking tonight?"

The space between them felt as charged as the second
before a lightning strike. She dared not move for fear that a
misplaced gesture or expression might reveal her secrets.
"You said you're the only one the doctor told I wasn't
contagious."

"And nevertheless, those men were forcing you onto
their train."

"I misjudged what others might do despite the risks." A
stupid thing to do, considering how she gambled so reck-
lessly with her own life.

His grip on his hat eased. "I can think of several things
I'd like to do with you that aren't too risky." He played the
brim through his fingers, softly, reverently.

"Show me." The words surprised her as much as him.

He stood in a rush and found the window very interesting to stare at again. "You don't want that."

"What if I did?" She moved between him and the window. If he forbade her to run, then she wouldn't let him either.

"You'd regret it in the morning after the shock of escaping what those men had planned—" He thrust his fingers into his hair and held on tight.

Wanting to ease his distress, she reached for his arm. He shied away from her touch.

"Noah, I'm okay. I feel better than okay." She wasn't about to tell him that tonight wasn't the only time she'd been overwhelmed by her desire for him.

He shook his head. "Folks often feel this way after an ordeal. I did after my parents died. I jumped into everything without a plan or a care for the consequences. Thank the Lord my brother was there to wake me up to what was important. I'm in this for the long run." His eyes widened like he regretted saying so much. He yanked his hand out of his hair and crossed his arms.

She blew out a frustrated breath, wishing she could expel her yearning with it. Then maybe she could focus on her promise to Edward. "You're the most stubborn man I ever met."

"I'm also a man who won't take advantage of you. I promise on all that I hold dear. I'm going to earn your trust. I'm not laying a finger on you tonight."

His declaration only made her crave his touch more. She moved forward till they stood toe to toe. She raised her chin. "I'm not a child. You don't rule my life. I do."

"Not tonight." With a swift step sideways, he yanked a sheet off the bed and then stomped over to the tub. "Your bath's getting cold. I'll rig up a curtain so you can have some privacy."

Damnation. She desired him to the point of madness, and he decided *now* was the time to keep her at arm's length? She couldn't think straight when he was this bull-headed. Nor could she stop her desire from making her daft whenever he was in sight.

Now he'd be in her sight all night long.

Double damn. Didn't men come to the saloon full of lust and then leave without a backward glance? Why couldn't it be the same for a woman?

Life would be much easier if her enthrallment with him ended. Plus, a saloon girl should understand how to seduce a man and walk away in the morning. She wouldn't learn anything if she followed Noah's orders like a lamb.

The swathe of red fabric lay where she'd dropped it at the foot of the bed, a call for bravery or a flag of warning. She wouldn't know until it was too late. She'd gambled on everything else, so why not this?

She picked up the chiffon peignoir and followed him to the tub.

CHAPTER 12

*O*utside the saloon window, darkness had descended. Inside the brightly colored room, candlelight flickered behind the sheets Noah had strung around Sadie's bath. The cloth shone like a scarlet apple, begging to be plucked from where it hung...so he could see and touch and taste the woman on the other side. Temptation. The original sin. He felt Adam's torment keenly.

On his side of the sheet, he paced in the shadows while he clung to every word Sadie sang in her sweet, breathless voice about 'The Yellow Rose of Texas.'

Sadie was his rose, a vibrant red one.

Everything he longed to see was red. Sadie's hair topped the list. Would it be heavy with her bathwater and dark as a glistening garnet? Or would it hold the perfect amount of dampness to make the silky curls coil around his fingers?

And what of the sheer red garment that had arrived for Sadie to wear? Would it hug her every curve? Would it reveal more than it concealed?

He'd learn the answers when she finished her bath. She

couldn't stay in the water forever. At best it'd be lukewarm by now, and she must be tired from today's ordeal.

There was only one bed—on his side of the curtain.

Ribbons of light danced on the sheet, following the rhythm of her song and the movement of her splashing naked in the tub. He fought the urge to tear off his clothing and join her. Then they'd be naked together and he could—

He spun away from the curtain and sank his fingers deep into his hair. He'd certainly be damned if he yielded to this temptation. *You're in this for the long run. You want thousands of nights with her, not just one.*

He'd been a blasted fool to promise not to touch her before embarking on an *entire* night alone with her. Now he'd pay the price. He'd probably have torn out every hair on his head by morning. He'd need to use his hands elsewhere. As soon as Sadie came out from behind the sheet, he'd go behind it and do the only thing that would get him through this night—using his hands to drain his lust.

More pacing ended with his hand somehow reaching for the curtain again. Swallowing his curse, he retreated to the bed. He'd lie down and not get up until Sadie appeared.

He yanked off his boots and vest. With his fingers linked behind his head and his legs crossed at his ankles, he lay flat on his back and stared at the ceiling as he hummed *Amazing Grace* and concentrated on blocking out Sadie's sultry voice.

After a few minutes, he didn't have to. Silence ruled on the other side of the curtain. No singing. No splashing. Not a sound.

Then the floorboards squeaked, and Sadie stood on his side of the curtain. She headed straight for the bed and him. The sheer red fabric showed more than he could've dreamed. Her small, high breasts, her swaying hips, the dark juncture between her legs rendered him immobile and mute.

In a corner of his brain, a niggling thought prodded him. He was supposed to do something...which involved going behind the curtain and—

The mattress shifted as she set one knee and then the other on it. She came toward him on her hands and knees in a slow glide that made him picture a lioness stalking her mate. Mesmerized by her pink cheeks and the smile on her lips, he dared not even blink.

One kiss was all he needed. She could trust him to stop after that. The glaring falsehood sent him scrambling off the bed. He didn't trust himself right now.

Her smile vanished.

Desperate for a way to soften his rejection, he scanned the room. He needed a distraction for her and him. He yanked a random book off a shelf by the headboard and held it between them. "Shall we read something to pass the time?"

That stopped her. Set her back on her heels, too. Her cheeks went red as the cloth failing to cover her sweet body. His mouth went dry as dust.

She raised her chin and her hands and rose on her knees so she could take the book from him. When she opened it, the title faced him: *Memoirs of a Woman of Pleasure*.

His heart skipped a beat. Holy hell, what kind of book had he given her?

She flipped the pages with a swiftness that spoke of familiarity. She searched for something. Maybe the book's contents weren't as salacious as its title. It'd better not be, or he didn't have a hope in hell of making it out of this room without dishonoring himself and her.

Her fingers halted. She drew in a deep breath and held the book up for him to see the page she'd found. "Here's how I'd like to pass the time."

An illustration showed a man standing in front of a woman who knelt on a bed. Just like them. Except in the book, the man's trousers were down and the woman had her hand around his johnson.

He snatched the book from her and returned it to the shelf. "I'm sorry. I shouldn't have..." A dozen apologies flashed through his head. The final one being ripping the book from her hands like a prudish dolt. Instead, he said something even more idiotic, "You've seen the book before."

"I found it while I was searching for—" She shook her head. "I don't want to talk about that. I want to talk about the woman in the book. Fanny Hill. She embraces a new life after finding herself under the care of Mrs. Brown, a London brothel owner. I hoped I might learn from Fanny's experiences, since they appeared similar to mine."

He was more than willing to help her learn, to be the one to teach her. Confusion made his mind swell with questions. She sounded like she'd never done what she'd shown him in the book. How could that be? A full year had passed since she started working at the Star.

"Gertie said the courts banned the book for obscenity. I'm glad it found a home in this room." She leaned toward him. "I'm glad I'm in this room right now with you."

His thoughts narrowed to one. He needed to hold her face in his hands and kiss her senseless. Lord knew he was already in that state. If he dropped his trousers right now, would she put her hands on him as well?

She moved even closer, like she just might. Then she swayed back and nearly toppled over. He reached out to catch her, but halted when he realized she was trembling so violently that the bed shook. Her face had gone pale as moonlight.

Worry doused his lust faster than a head-first tumble into a river. "Sadie, what's wrong?"

"Nothing's wrong. Why do you ask?"

He caught her before she fell flat on the mattress. Her skin was ice cold. It chilled him to the bone and left him shaking as well.

She stared at him with sad eyes. "That didn't go as I'd planned."

He drew the coverlet over her and carefully tucked it around her shoulders and chin. "In the morning, once you've rested and recovered your strength, you can make a new plan." He arranged a pair of chairs by her bedside.

"You'll be gone when I wake up."

He sat down in one chair and propped his feet on the other. "I'll be sitting right here." He pulled her hand from under the coverlet and held it firmly in his.

She stared at his hand enveloping hers. Finally, her smile returned.

He felt his lips curve as well. "Me promising not to lay a finger on you wasn't a well thought out idea. Try to sleep."

"I don't want to close my eyes."

Was she worried she'd have nightmares about the men succeeding in getting her onto their train? He certainly would. He'd never forget that horror. "You're safe. I won't let anyone touch you. Not even me." He winked at her. "My hand won't wander from yours."

"I'm not worried about tonight. It's tomorrow that concerns me."

She feared that Gertie wouldn't heed his warning to forgo her punishment for running away.

He shared her fear. What could he say to ease her mind?

Not much. Not unless he lied. His grip on her hand tightened. He forced himself to relax and stroked his thumb over the back of her hand to make up for squeezing the daylights out of her fingers...and probably making her worry even more.

"I'll be beside you all night," he said. "The only way I'm leaving this room is with you by my side. Hopefully your hand will still be in mine when I do."

"I like the sound of that and holding your hand. I expect I'd like holding other parts of you as well, like Fanny Hill did with the man in her book."

He groaned. He wasn't going to get a second of sleep tonight with that image in his mind. "Go to sleep. There'll be plenty of time to talk in the morning."

Her eyes drifted closed. "Edward told me his parents always greeted each other with a kiss in the morning." Her smile faded. "Mine never did. Will you kiss me in the morning?"

"Sadie..." Her name came out hoarse. He deemed it a miracle that he could utter a single word. "If you're feeling better in the morning, I'd like nothing better than to kiss you."

"You're sure your health's improved this morning?" Noah's voice was so quiet she barely heard him. The fact that a whole room separated them didn't help.

Her fingers stalled on the hooks of her corset. Around the curtain of sheets, she snuck a peek at him sitting on the bed as he pulled on his boots. A minute ago, one of Gertie's girls had woken them both with a knock on the door. A second after that, the door had opened.

Sadie had received new clothing, while Noah got a message from the madam. *Your time's up.*

Now a stream of women flowed in and out of the room. They removed the bathwater by the bucketful, along with any hope of sharing a private conversation...or a good morning kiss.

Noah yanked on his vest as he crossed to join her behind the sheet. Focusing on her corset, she willed her fingers to stop trembling and secure the last clasp.

"Sadie..." Her name on his lips was as soft as a sigh. Or maybe a prayer.

She swept her hands over her ruffled shirt and grimaced at the short length. "Yes?" Her response shot out. Sharp. Scared.

Noah's fingers brushed her cheeks. His gentle touch, so at odds with the brisk movements of the women invading the room, made her jump.

He tucked her hair behind her ears and, holding her face in his palms, slid his thumbs over her cheekbones as if searching for his answer in the chaotic scroll of her freckles. The reverent gesture fortified her with hope. So did the memory of how he'd held her hand all night...and asked for nothing in return.

Dodge bombarded men with opportunities for self-indulgent acts, but Noah appeared fascinated by the simplest of pleasures. Not that there was anything simple about the way he made her feel.

She clutched her skirt to stop herself from grabbing hold of him in return, and never letting go.

"Sadie, you can trust me. How do you feel?"

Loved...and more afraid than ever. She closed her eyes against the admission, even if it was merely a silent one whispered by her heart.

"I feel—" She stopped before saying fine. He wouldn't accept such a blatant lie. "Better than yesterday," she said and forced her gaze to meet his.

He nodded, but his brow remained furrowed. An echoing clank claimed his attention. One of the girls had pushed the copper tub on its side to drain the last of the water.

Noah laughed under his breath. The melancholy sound filled her with her own questions.

"What is it? What's wrong?"

"When my brother was little, he loved playing hide 'n seek. He fooled me only once when he overturned our washtub. Never entered my head to look underneath. Back then, he was half my size." He shrugged one shoulder. The boyish gesture made her chest ache. "Haven't recalled that day in years. Useless to dredge it up now."

"Jacob was lucky to have you as his brother." She'd never been more certain of something.

He released her and drew back, shaking his head as he went. A handful of words wouldn't stop him from blaming himself for his brother's death. A death he wished he'd prevented.

Another similarity they shared.

She reached up and linked them together in the same manner he'd done a moment earlier. Under her palms, his face was a network of unwavering bone and muscle. She was always amazed when he yielded to her uncertain strength. Now was no different.

He leaned into her hands as if she were the only thing keeping him standing.

"You made a life with him." She relaxed her hold, readying herself to release him if he should pull away. "You gave him the greatest gift you could give anyone—your time."

"I wish I'd spent more time with him. But working the ranch kept me busy. And before long, he was dogging my heels and insisting he share the work."

"He sounds stubborn." A sudden urge to tease him made her say, "Must be a family trait."

Noah's lips parted in surprise before curving into a smile. "He was a determined little cuss." He stroked her chin. "When you lift this, you remind me of him."

"I do not—" She bit back the lie and ended up lifting her chin, which immediately made her laugh.

His laughter joined hers. Then his gaze locked on her mouth, and he drew even closer.

Finally, he was going to kiss her.

Behind her, a cough intruded. Then the girl who'd delivered Gertie's message spoke. "Madam said she wants the room emptied to make ready for the next payin' customer."

The next customer... That truth drained the happiness from her soul. She released Noah and faced the door, and the saloon beyond.

"Will you walk me out?" He'd told her last night that the only way he'd leave this room was with her by his side.

She walked with him to the double doors opening onto Front Street. He didn't step through them, though. He stopped in front of her, halting her as well. The determination in his eyes stole the air from her lungs and left only foreboding.

"The promise that holds you here, the one you mentioned at the rail depot, the one you made to a friend— if you tell me your friend's name, I'll be better able to help you both."

"You can't help him," she blurted. "He's dead."

"He's—" He pinched the bridge of his nose. "He's Edward."

Too late, she clamped her palms over her mouth. She'd feared this would happen. She'd said too much.

"How can you call him your friend?" He kept his head lowered as he rubbed his brow and hid his mood from her.

She let her hands fall to her sides. "Because he was." She refused to lie about such a gift.

"He bought you and made you—" Crossing his arms, he stared over her head at the room they'd left. "I'm a fine one to talk."

"Neither you nor Edward are responsible for giving me a whore's life. My father and Gertie, plus a string of bad luck, did that. Edward never forced me to...do anything."

Jealousy twisted his features. "Then he was indeed a good friend. And a better man than me. I'm glad he was here to help you when I wasn't."

She fought the urge to grab hold of him again, to bind him to her, to tell him the whole truth. "You're here now."

"And I'll be here tomorrow, and the next day, and the day after that. I'm stubborn. Remember?" He turned, but stopped short of giving her his back. His profile resembled an impenetrable mask. "I'll be down the street. If anything happens, come get me."

The weight of one promise she might not be able to keep made her reluctant to make any more. She ducked her head. "I can't promise you—"

"I know. Only Edward was worthy of your promises." The saloon doors complained loudly in the sudden void his departure created.

She seized the swinging panels and held tight. Solid under her hands, the wood gave her no comfort. She pushed up on her toes to peer down the street. Head and shoulders above the crowd, Noah continued to walk away from her. Then the throng swallowed him from view and left her alone.

Strident laughter echoed in the room behind her, reminding her that she wasn't completely alone. Cora stood by the piano with the girls who'd helped hasten Noah's departure. Their laughter faded as they cast hesitant looks from her to Cora.

Cora remained silent, her attention fixed on Sadie.

A bitter taste filled her mouth, not unlike the medicine the woman had pressed upon her. She stormed toward her. "If you truly want to kill me, a bullet would be quicker than poison."

The saloon went quiet as a graveyard.

"Sadie darlin', you sound distraught. Or has the pox finally pushed you to the point of insanity?"

A series of gasps followed hot on the heels of Cora's question.

"You're a fine one to cast stones. You're possessed by an evil nature. Edward would've sensed that." The truth came in a rush, raising her voice. "That's why he chose me over you."

Cora glanced at the women hovering behind her. "Leave us."

Only when they'd gone, did Cora face her again—with a glare so sharp it could have sliced the tail off a squirrel at fifty paces. "Edward chose you because he needed an obedient lapdog, not a bed partner."

Sadie's heart clenched tight as a fist. The odds were high that Cora's hands would be in the same state.

"He wanted the world to revolve around him," Cora continued. "If he'd picked me, Orin's attention would've been split between us."

"Your conceit—" she shot back with forced bravado, "—knows no bounds."

"I know you never slept with Edward."

"You know nothing. You weren't there."

"But Orin was." Cora shook with barely restrained anger. "He told me *everything.*"

"Ha! You ooze lies. Orin wasn't the sharing type. He never willingly spoke with me, so don't expect me to believe he'd tell you one single, solitary thing."

"He was my brother."

The revelation left Sadie speechless until another truth hit her. "Gertie found you both at an orphanage." Her voice was no louder than a whisper.

Cora lowered her voice as well, but hers maintained a cutting edge. "We were inseparable until she sold him to Edward. She assured me we'd be reunited—when Edward could pay her fee. But gamblers are unpredictable with their earnings. When Edward's luck returned, mine disappeared. You came careening into Dodge. You stole my place. I wish you had syphilis. I wish I could tell Gertie every one of your lies."

"Why haven't you?"

"She'd announce your miraculous recovery to the entire town, then sell you to the highest bidder again. That wouldn't be your cowboy."

Fear drove the air from her lungs along with one word. "Wardell."

"Not if I have my way. An' I will. His money's mine. You've taken too much from me already." Cora's smile resembled the bared teeth of a dog sensing fear and growing bold. "Everyone believes Orin ran off with Edward's tawdry family trinkets. I know better."

She knows Gertie killed Edward. Like a trap sprung, the pressure around her chest squeezed tight.

"You stole his possessions," Cora said quietly.

Shock made her stumble back. Her vision blurred. A distorted world of gray whipped around her. She groped for something solid. Anything. Her fingers found the piano. She couldn't recall the sound of Edward's music or the exact color of Noah's hair. She was alone in her haze.

"Orin came to me before he fled." Cora's voice drew nearer, close to her ear. "He begged me to help him. Suddenly, after months of ignoring me, I had value again. He babbled about murder and vengeance. I told him he was a fool. I'd take care of him again, like I always had. When I turned my back, he took my money and disappeared. He stole everything I'd saved because he hadn't been able to reach Edward's hotel room before the law showed up, gathered everything of value an' stowed it in the jail. You were the only one in that room between Edward's suicide an' the law's arrival."

"I didn't take—" Her throat closed around the denial, wouldn't open again.

"What you did with them afterward is anyone's guess. But these facts remain certain: I lost my brother and every penny I had saved. I'll take Wardell's wealth in payment, along with your life."

The fog circling her thickened. She couldn't breathe. Only the piano's solid mass under her hands kept her upright. *I need help. I need Noah.*

She lurched in the direction of the door, ready to run to the jail...or crawl if she had to.

A familiar hand shackling her wrist halted her. "Tell your cowboy an' he'll come barging back in here, brandishing his badge an' his holier-than-thou attitude. Waste of my time informing him that you're a thief. He won't believe a word I say. He'll have to die as well."

She shook her head, rejecting Cora's declaration. "Noah's too strong, too vigilant, too quick with a gun."

"When the time's right, the mighty fall as fast as the scrubs. It'll be easy taking him down."

"He's not alone. He's got the law on his side. He'll throw you in jail."

"My challenge is patience. Don't want to give your Texan his medicine too earlier."

"No..." Her world went black.

"Oh yes. In fact, when you failed to leave town yesterday, I was sorely tempted to slip a dollop of arsenic from the rat trap into the whiskey bottle delivered to your room. You'd have been responsible for his death."

From the darkness she dredged up her last ember of strength and blurted, "Leave Noah alone. This is between you and me."

"Finally." Cora's sigh, dripping with satisfaction, filled her ear. "I hold your acceptance to the last nail in your coffin. Couldn't be certain before. Now, I am." Her words snapped with scorn. "Should've known. Love is a weakness, a burden. Never again. Not for me, or for you."

The restraint on her wrist fell away. The satisfied click of boot heels retreated, fading into silence.

She stood alone. Utterly defeated.

Why couldn't she have found Edward's watch and jewelry box? Then she'd be long gone from Dodge. And so would Noah. Now she couldn't even go to the jail to warn him.

The jail... What had Cora said about the jail and Edward's possessions? The jail held the deceased's property.

She sucked in a ragged breath, then another and another until her vision cleared.

What if Edward's watch and box were there as well? What if after Gertie stole them, she'd decided to hide them with his other belongings? So they wouldn't be found at the Star? So she could retrieve them whenever the time was right?

Sadie had to find them first.

CHAPTER 13

*W*hen the storm had provided the distraction required to slip from the saloon unseen, Sadie hadn't hesitated. Now doubt and fear buffeted her, along with the rising wind.

Her absence would not remain unnoticed. This time it would not go unpunished...unless her plan succeeded. Once more she'd gambled everything on leaving the Star.

Lightning illuminated the world beyond—the boy standing on the jailhouse porch talking to Noah and Marshal Masterson. Then darkness returned. Thunder boomed. And once more Front Street stretched before her, an intimidating expanse of murky ground. But tonight, even Dodge's most notorious thoroughfare looked inconsequential compared to the hurdles she needed to cross once she reached the other side.

Get inside the jail, find the watch and box, jump another train for Chicago, run even farther so she wouldn't be caught and hauled back...all so Noah would be free to leave as well without being involved and held accountable.

Repay a friend. Protect the man she loved.

The man now departing the jail alongside the whip-smart lawman...and the messenger she'd sent to make them leave. The boy trotted beside the men, striving to keep up with their long strides. All three moved swiftly down the road in her direction. She pressed her face to the wall, hoping to hide her paleness, praying to become another shadow.

The boy's voice reached her first. Muffled snatches of words, whipped by the wind. "A disagreement between drovers and railroaders...insulting each other's profession.... a brawl...at the rail depot."

He'd embellished the tale she'd asked him to report, but he'd kept the location. Thank the heavens. The depot was the farthest point from the jail. Distance meant time. She needed all the time she could get.

The boy's voice faded, and then vanished, leaving her alone in the gloom and the growing storm, both outside and within. An irrational disappointment that the first part of her plan had succeeded overwhelmed her.

Noah was no longer near.

She gritted her teeth and counted to ten before she faced the street. Directly across stood the mercantile and next to it the jail. Both silent and somber. She'd donned her drabbest dress of faded blue, hoping it'd help her blend into the shadows.

Probably wouldn't do a lick of good.   •

She ran as fast as she could. Behind her, the Star buzzed with its usual music and laughter. When she reached the boardwalk, she flattened her spine against the storefront and strove to catch her breath. To her right waited the jail with its brick walls and barred windows.

The wood creaked under her feet. She concentrated on placing her feet carefully. It didn't help. Finally, she stood outside the jail with a pair of hairpins in her hands. The lock opened surprisingly fast. Her recent practice had paid off.

She slipped inside and secured the door behind her.

Nothing but shadows greeted her. She crept into them, past a chair by a desk. The bars of a cell made her halt. A black hole of a doorway loomed on her left. She went through it. Her knees bumped something hard and soft. A mattress on an iron frame.

She ran her hands over the bed to the low table at its head. Her fingers brushed rough metal and smooth glass. She lit the lantern's wick, then turned it down so it'd be less visible from the street.

Around the bed, and her, loomed a jumble of haphazardly stacked trunks and cases.

She searched for Edward's leather-bound and brass-studded steamer trunks. When she found the matching pair, she dropped to her knees and rifled through their contents. She didn't bother to return the items to their proper order.

Despair riddled her heart when she reached the bottom of the second trunk. Why hadn't she found his watch and box? She scanned the room for her answer. Could they have gotten mixed up with the other baggage?

Too many. Too little time. She raised her chin. No time to lose. She couldn't leave until she checked every one.

She scrambled to complete her quest. On and on. Faster and faster. Until her head throbbed and her chest grew tight. She paused to focus on drawing in air. The dizziness would pass. It always did. But tonight she couldn't wait for it to even recede.

Hurry. You can't leave empty-handed.

She stood to move to the next trunk. Her blood roared in

her ears. An inky circle swallowed the edges of her vision, closing in...until all went black.

NOAH'S STEPS faltered as he slogged through the mud. He rubbed his eyes and gave his head a shake. Water sloshed from his hat onto his shoulders and down his back. Adding to the soaking he was receiving from the heavens.

Lord, he was tired. He hadn't slept at all last night. It'd been worth it. Every minute Sadie had trusted him to hold her hand and keep her safe, while she slept and regained her strength had been time well spent.

Tonight's activities hadn't been worth a plug nickel. First, the false alarm at the depot. Then, as he and Bat walked back into town, a real fight. This one between two girls at the Crystal Palace over a customer who'd offered his wages to both but only had sufficient for one.

Now, all he wanted was to collapse on his bed.

The instant he glimpsed the Northern Star through the downpour, his fatigue faded and his pace quickened. What was Sadie doing? Was she safe? Would she trust him to help her again?

He halted with one boot on the saloon's bottom step. The wind picked up, howling around him in rebuke. *You can trust me,* he'd told her. Trust him to act the jealous idiot... and not ask what she'd promised Edward.

He bounded up the steps. Why hadn't he asked? Behind him, a sudden gust roared over his shoulder. The wind hit the saloon doors before he could. They whipped inward and slammed back against his outstretched hand.

Son-of-a— Pain shot up his arm and spun him sideways,

away from the light blazing within toward a fainter one down the street. Something flickered in the jail's window.

His stinging palm went immediately to his revolver. He hadn't left any lanterns lit.

Was Bat inside? When they'd parted ways, the marshal claimed he had an errand to run before heading to his own bed at the Dodge House Hotel.

He squinted through the rain. The illumination wasn't coming from the jail's main room. Why would Bat, or anyone, go into the other room? The only thing in there besides his bed and worn trail gear was that god-awful clutter of abandoned baggage.

With his hand on his revolver, he jogged, and slipped and slid, through the muck to the jail. The door wouldn't open. Bat never locked it when he was inside.

He drew his gun first and the brass key ring from his vest pocket second.

Inside, across an expanse of black, a glow filled the doorway leading to his sleeping quarters. The light flared, fed by the air he'd let in. Careful not to make a sound, he shut the door behind him. He kept his footsteps silent as well. He couldn't stop the water from dripping off him and pattering on the floor.

Hopefully, whoever was in the other room would only hear the rain drumming on the roof.

He lunged the last two strides and braced himself in the doorway. His revolver swept the room. Trunks and cases lay open. Their contents strewn on the floor around a heap of faded blue and bright red.

Dread sucked the air from his lungs as he scrambled through the chaos to reach Sadie. Her face was as white as the daisies blanketing the graveyard he'd followed her to on his second day in town.

On his knees beside her, he struggled to speak. Failed. Tried again. Her name came out no better than a croak. "Sadie?"

She didn't answer, didn't move.

He shut his eyes against her stillness, rejecting it. His entire body shook as he leaned down to hold his ear over her lips...to feel her breath. Warm. Alive.

His own breath left him in a whoosh, leaving space for questions to form. What had happened at the Star to bring her here? Was she running away again?

When he opened his eyes, the nearest trunk filled his vision: lid raised, contents hanging out, more scattered on the floor. The rest of the room was in a similar state. She hadn't been fleeing; she'd been searching for something. What?

He shoved his revolver back in its holster, so he could use both hands to brush back her hair and turn her face to his. No answers lay there.

"You can't go on like this. You're going to kill yourself."

Her skin was hot against his palms. A wave of anxiety rolled his gut into a knot. Not just hot. Burning up. He had to lower her temperature. Fast.

Scooping her into his arms, he stood in the middle of the room. Where could he take her? Not the Star. Never there again. This time Madam Garrett's anger would burn as hot as the woman in his arms. He couldn't take her to the doctor or even to Bat across the street. The second he stepped out onto Front Street, too many eyes could be watching.

He'd promised to keep her safe. He couldn't expose her to the storm brewing in the Star or the one raging outside. The rain continued to pummel the roof. It'd pour down the walls and turn the surrounding mud into a lake of ice-cold molasses.

A cold Sadie needed.

Outside the rear door, a barrel collected water from the roof. When he reached it, he pressed his lips to her ear and whispered, "I'm sorry."

Then he plunged her in up to her neck. She writhed in his grip, struggling to get out. He made sure she didn't. That didn't stop her from trying. The suffering contorting her face stabbed his heart. Luckily, her eyes remained closed. He wouldn't have had the strength to withstand the hurt in them.

Only when her fever receded did he give in. Under the overhang of the roof, with his back sheltering her from the storm, he cradled her in his arms and prayed again. Unsuccessfully.

The heat under her skin returned.

She'd have to go back into the water. Probably many times. Each time she came out it'd be best if she were dried and made comfortable enough to rest.

Her dress had to come off. He carried her inside and laid her on his bed. Then he went back for the barrel and wrestled it inside.

Undressing a woman while focusing only on her face was slow work. He refused to look elsewhere. Last night, he'd seen her as close to naked as a person could get. He'd be damned if, while she was sick and unconscious, he looked at anything below her chin.

His fingers fumbled with the top button near her collarbone. He didn't grow any steadier as he finished the job. He wrung out the garment, spread it on a trunk to dry, and froze with his fingertips hovering over the fabric.

The checked pattern of blue gingham had faded. That didn't matter. He'd never forget this dress, or the day he first saw it. Sadie had been wearing it when his herd demolished her farm. He'd come back searching for the girl in this dress. The confounding creature who'd snared him with her grit and then humbled him with her tears.

The weight of that day, packed with regrets, bowed his head. He swayed forward. The dress' warmth stopped him. Heated by Sadie's fever, it yanked him back to the present. Danger circled her again, closing in. He couldn't let her die.

"Noah." The raspy murmur spun him around to find Sadie's eyes open. "I'm sorry I broke into your jail and—" she glanced at the room before she met his gaze again, "—made a mess of things."

"Your presence is an improvement." His fingers found her cheek, wanting to reassure her, to soothe her worry.

She turned her head away. "I won't get you in trouble. I must leave."

His heart skipped a beat, but he kept his voice even. "I can't let you go. I have to put you back in the water barrel."

With wide eyes, she faced him again. "Don't you mean the bathtub? Are we going back to the Star after all?"

"No, you're staying here and...you've already been in the water once, but you need to go in again."

Her eyes flared even wider. Whatever was in them wasn't fear or even worry. "To do that, wouldn't I have to undress first?"

His gaze disobeyed and swept down her body. The linen of her shift clung to every swell and valley. He glanced up in time to see her gaze go where his had been a moment before.

"Oh," she said in a hushed voice.

He held his breath, dreading what she'd say next.

"Aren't we going to take off my underclothes as well?"

He bit back his groan. The thin garment didn't need to come off, and continuing this particular discussion wouldn't help lower her fever. "We'll put you in as you are." He leaned down to gather her in his arms. "I'm sorry. It must be done."

"Noah, stop." Her hands captured his face.

Her gentle grasp held him immobile, every part of him except for his fingers clenching the mattress on either side of her. "Your illness has worsened. We need to—"

"Stop." She pressed her forehead against his lips. "Stop trying to save me. It'll be your downfall. What can I say to make you listen?" She slumped back against the bed, and her gaze slid over his face, drifting, slipping back toward oblivion...but her hold on him remained tenacious. "You think I'm ill, but it's merely a temporary weakness that came with the medicine."

He fought not to rip holes in the mattress. "I suspected it wasn't helping. You won't swallow another drop."

"Listen to me. It's not that simple."

"It is. The most important thing is that you get better, which is why you have to stay and go back in the water."

"Everyone assumed I'd become sick. Foolish to correct them. An easy lie." She released him and covered her face with her hands. "The rest was harder."

"Sadie—"

Her fingers curled into fists over her eyes. "Why won't you listen?"

He was trying to, but his worry made it difficult. She was trying as well—trying to tell him the truth. He couldn't understand any of it. And if he didn't, he'd lose her. The increasing likelihood of that outcome left him short of breath and courage. "There's no reason worth taking that blue swill."

"Not in your world." Her laugh came out sad and tired.

"But in mine? If I wanted to thwart Gertie, I couldn't waste any gift, even if it had a sharp edge."

"Too sharp," he said through gritted teeth.

"Not at first. In the beginning, the medicine promised protection along with Edward's other gifts."

An uncontrollable anger flared in his chest. "Tell me what your *friend* ever gave you besides illness?"

"He taught me to play cards, when to gamble, and how to lie when all else fails. It didn't surprise me that his final gift would be a lie." Her voice faded like the dying wind, sighing around the rafters. "The shock is how painful it's been to hold the truth."

What did you promise him, Sadie? Why can't I earn the trust you gave him so freely? Why can't you love me as well? "Tell me the truth."

"I have, but you can't hear me, can you?" Her hands fell onto the bed, limp with defeat. Her eyes remained closed. "You can't hear me telling you that I don't have the French pox. I never did."

CHAPTER 14

*S*he never had syphilis. The truth toppled the weight off Noah's shoulders and onto his heart.

Lies. It all came back to lies.

That's why she kept taking the medicine. Not to cure a disease everyone assumed she had, but to support the lie that she did. She'd cobbled together what little she could from the tragedy of her friend's life and death, and built the only wall she could between her and every grasping hand in Dodge.

By the time he'd ridden into town hell-bent on rescuing her, she'd already pulled off a feat more daring than any he could've imagined. More perilous, as well.

She'd gambled one too many times. Her blasted stubbornness had run out. Now there was only fever and death.

He picked her up and put her back in the barrel. This time she didn't struggle. Above the water, her head lolled against his arm. Without him, she would've slipped under.

The seconds dragged by as he waited, then minutes too many to count. Finally, her skin cooled. He lifted her out, wrapped her in a sheet, and sat on the floor to better cradle her in his arms. A shell of her former self, her shivers nonetheless rocked him.

You must get better.

And when she did, he couldn't let her lies go unchallenged. Not about her health, the so-called medicine, or what she'd promised Edward. Not about anything.

No more lies.

The dreaded heat returned, burning them both. He immersed her in the water until she cooled, drew her out and held her until she grew hot. The endless routine filled the night. He clung to it and her...until the room lightened with the coming dawn and he realized the storm had retreated along with Sadie's fever.

Once again looking nowhere but her face, he swapped her sodden shift for a dry sheet. Only after he'd bundled her up, did he set her on his narrow bed...and let go. He sank to the floor. Adrift. Lost.

He latched onto her hand. Her fever might return. He needed to know if it did.

Exhaustion clawed him, deep to the bone. With her hand in his, he stretched out on his side on the floor. The second the stiffness in his muscles eased, he'd get up.

He wanted to be awake when Sadie opened her eyes.

EVEN IN SLEEP, Noah held her captive. Not just his hand, engulfing hers. Or his arm, solid with muscles that continued across his bare shoulders and chest. But his face. Relaxed in slumber and free of its usual furrows of concern, he appeared...content. The angle of his jaw remained resolute, though, marking him as a man who got what he wanted.

When he'd proposed his deal for her farm, he'd said he wanted her company. A day ago in the saloon's fancy room, he'd been blunter. He'd said he wanted her. Last night, he'd found her in his jail, in the room where he slept. Now he slept on the floor while she lay on his bed. He wore only his trousers, and she was wrapped in a...

She glanced down. A sheet?

He'd seen her completely naked. He got her naked. That undeniable truth made her skin tingle as if his gaze and his hands were touching her right now.

What had they done? Good God, what had she *said?* Her last memory was being in her chemise, wanting it off, and not only because she'd been unbearably hot. He'd said something about a fever and a bathtub. But the room only held a water barrel.

Once again he'd played nursemaid with the limited resources at hand. He'd undressed her to look after her health.

If she cared for him even a little bit, she'd leave. Gertie would be hollering for her return. Cora would be itching for vengeance. John would've searched the entire town, questioned everyone...except Noah. Her heart pounded. Was John already crossing the street, heading their way?

She had to go back. Willingly, so there wouldn't be a fight. Without Noah by her side, so he wouldn't be hurt. Or killed.

She stared at the ceiling, trying to banish an image of him, like Edward, lying lifeless in a sea of blood. She steeled herself for what she must do: retrieve her dress draped over the trunk on the other side of Noah and somehow free her hand from his hold—which had suddenly tightened.

Her breath caught in her throat. His breathing had

changed as well. Silent. Held. Waiting for whatever she did next. He wasn't going to let her go.

She bolted upright. On the floor beside her, Noah sat up as well. Reaching for her dress, her hand landed on his chest. He didn't budge. But the bed did. It tipped and tossed her onto him.

Without letting go of her hand, his free arm lassoed her waist as he fell back onto the floor with her held securely on top of him. They both groaned. Her body was still sore from her tussle with the men at the rail depot. And Noah...? He couldn't appreciate her landing so hard on him.

He didn't complain, but he did scan her face. Finally, he sighed. The tension in his expression, as well as his tightly coiled muscles under her, eased...until his gaze dipped to the sheet she wore, then shot back up to lock with hers.

He let go of her. All of her, including her hand.

Even stunned by the feel of him, warm and solid beneath her, she regretted the loss of his hand deeply.

"I'm glad you're feeling better." His deep voice lowered even further, vibrating in his chest, heavy with fatigue and something more. Energy, held in check, pulsed underneath her.

He snatched her dress off the nearby trunk and offered it to her. "Your shift is—" he swallowed roughly, "—around here somewhere as well. Once you get up, I'll help you find it."

"Last night, did I...?"

He stared at her dress bunched in his fist, the one she hadn't moved to take. "Your fever's gone. That's all that matters."

"Surely there's more." *So much more matters to me. I don't want to lose you.*

"You're right. We have a lot to discuss." Despite his

agreement, uncertainty flashed in his eyes. "First of all, you can't go back to the Star."

She went rigid with rebellion. "Then why should I get dressed?"

"So you don't distract me while we talk." His growl of frustration rocked her against him and sent a thrill coursing through her veins.

Instinctively, she pressed closer, seeking more.

With a curse, he lifted her off him, placing his hands only where the sheet touched her, making sure the thin fabric stayed around her. He set her on the bed and rose to sit beside her. He'd done this before—when they'd first entered the fancy room together. Afterward, he'd moved as far away from her as the room would allow.

He didn't now. He sat very close. Between her and the door. He offered the dress to her again. "Are you ready to talk?"

Not if it meant putting him in danger. She had to leave, and she couldn't do that naked. She grabbed the dress.

His grip on the garment remained firm. "As soon as you're clothed, you're going to run away again, aren't you?"

I don't want to. I have to. Gritting her teeth, she tried to tug her dress free.

"Who else knows you don't have syphilis?"

Shock dropped her jaw with the force of a sledgehammer. "What? Who said—?"

"You told me. Last night."

In horrified silence, she gaped at him, waiting for him to say more. He didn't, which meant *she* hadn't said more. Or so she hoped. She released the breath she hadn't realized she'd been holding and prodded her brain to function.

If she told him everything, he'd confront Gertie. Maybe even arrest her. With nothing more than Sadie's word, he wouldn't be able to hold the madam. Gertie would go free. When she did, she'd know Sadie's secrets as well. She'd hold all the cards. She might do to Noah what she'd done to Edward. And if she didn't kill Noah, Cora would.

Noah's continued silence along with his steely-eyed perusal sent her gaze skittering until it landed on the water barrel. "You can't trust what someone says when they have a fever." She cringed at the weakness of her bluff.

"I probably shouldn't trust what you say at any time. But —" He exhaled a weary breath. "I want to believe that taking the medicine was a temporary measure to shore up the illusion that you had syphilis. What will make you stop taking it?"

She refused to look at him. Another of his lengthy silences stretched her control—until it broke.

When she turned back to him, he no longer assessed her but the room instead. "If you'd found what you came hunting for, would you stop?" He shook his head. "No, you'd have your promise to Edward to fulfill." He froze. "You're here because of him."

The walls pressed in on her. She had to leave this room. She yanked the dress they now both clutched in a white-knuckled grip.

"Your luck won't last forever. You beat the odds surviving Edward's illness and keeping away from all the men who wanted you afterward." His breath hissed between his teeth as his gaze shot back to her. "No one came after Edward. Maybe not even before him. That's why you said what you did about that book. That's why your kisses—"

She seized the dress with both hands and heaved on it as hard as she could. "Let go."

His eyes widened. "Edward was your first lover, your

only lover. Everything you've done, you've done because you loved him."

She shook her head, denying his words.

"What did you promise him you'd find?"

"No more questions." She clamped her hand over his mouth.

He pushed her palm sideways and pressed it against his cheek. "Why didn't you come to the jail sooner?"

"Stop." A growing panic squeezed her chest. She fought to free both her dress and her hand from his hold. "Stop talking."

"Someone told you about the deceased's unclaimed baggage. You came as soon as you knew, searching for—" He scanned the room again. "Not money. Nothing so simple. Not when you wouldn't take my money for your farm."

She released the dress. Surging up onto her knees, she clasped his face in both hands and forced his eyes to meet hers. "I don't want to talk about—"

"Of course!" His eyes shone like molten rivers of gold as he closed in on the truth. "It's not what you want, but what Edward wanted. What did he hold dear? What did he lose?"

Too close. And yet not close enough. She was done with talking.

"What—?"

She kissed him, drawing his words into her mouth along with any protests he might make. He didn't protest. Not even when the urge to be closer to him had her straddling his lap.

His hands landed on her hips. Hot against her bare skin. That was her first clue that the sheet had slipped away in her haste to silence him. His, as well, judging by the way he inhaled sharply. His hold on her tightened, but he didn't pull her closer.

Questions were forming inside him again. They vibrated

in the small gap still separating them. Soon he'd continue seeking answers. Or worse, he'd push her away.

She couldn't let him.

For months— No, for an entire year, she'd pretended to be a woman of experience. She'd done what the men of Dodge, and women like Gertie and Cora, had expected. She'd said what they wanted to hear, shown them what they wanted to see. The willingness to act on what she'd learned while playing her role had carried her through every challenge.

She'd done it all alone. By her own hand. Wasn't that the definition of strength?

Or was it another lie? She'd never been alone. Nor did she want to be, she realized. Not when the world held someone like Noah.

Using every technique he'd taught her, she kissed him. Then she improvised several new ways. Instinct filled in the blanks.

His breathing, racing along with hers, gave her courage.

She made her mouth as persuasive as she could. He did the same. Her lips, her skin, the ache building inside her, craved his touch. She could almost forget this was another act of insane desperation. With so many lies between them, she couldn't hold him forever. But she could have this one moment.

His hands traveled up to grasp her waist. The stroke of his work-roughened palms over her skin left her shaking. She grabbed one of his wrists to steady herself.

With his mouth hovering over hers, he froze again. Did he believe she meant to push him away?

She lifted his palm to her breast.

He groaned his pleasure against her cheek, down her neck, and lower. How could such a simple sound enthrall her so completely? And his kisses as well? They fell like summer rain, soft and sweet on her skin. Then his tongue joined the dance.

A spark of sinful yearning made her arch toward him. She wrapped her arms around his neck and let her head fall back. Sure in the belief he held her safe, she gave herself up to him, to the fire he so deftly coaxed to life inside her.

His fingers skimmed down to where the heat flamed the hottest. He lifted his head and studied her with an intensity that made her heart race. His eyes never left hers as he stoked her desire until she blazed with need.

"Noah." His name slipped from her lips in a husky voice she didn't recognize as her own.

"Are you asking me to stop?" His question shot out with the force of a growl, but his touch remained gentle.

"I need—" she struggled for air, for words, "—to be closer to you."

Despite her reply, he drew back. She gasped with disappointment, then surprise when he flipped her sideways to lie on the bed. A second later, he'd shucked his trousers and hovered over her on his elbows.

With patience at odds with his labored breathing, he pressed the hard length of his desire against her. "In a second, we'll be as close as a man and woman can get. Is that what you want?"

"Yes." She wrapped her arms and legs around him. "No more questions. No holding back."

He complied. The resulting pleasure was intoxicating.

A rumble of satisfaction escaped his lips...until an unbearable tightness halted his advance. His eyes widened, and his palm rose to her cheek. He stopped short of touching her, as if he were afraid.

"What's wrong?" she asked.

He shook his head. "This can't be your first time."

"You say that like it's a bad thing."

"It isn't. But it is unexpected." He swore, fast and low. "Utterly unexpected. I thought you and Edward—"

"I needed to keep you at a distance."

"And now you don't?" The weight of his body against her, and inside her, was nothing compared to that of his scrutiny.

She tried not to squirm. She couldn't stop her huff of frustration. "Now I can't bring you close enough." She stared at his hand that remained out of reach.

Finally, he cupped her cheek with a strength and tenderness that was uniquely Noah. With a sigh, she leaned into his touch.

"Sadie, why are you doing this with...me?"

Hadn't she done this to escape his questions? And now she lay under him with her body and her soul open to him. She searched for a lie and ended up with only the truth. *Because I want a lifetime with you, but I might only have this moment.*

"You're hiding from me again. Why?"

"Because you ask too many questions." She tried to move beneath him and couldn't. "When all I want is something I cannot reach."

Noah released a low groan. "I'm going to hurt you."

"You won't. You've had a hundred chances to harm me since you returned to Dodge. You never have."

"This is different. Out of my control." He thrust into her with a need that wouldn't be denied.

She stiffened as pain intermingled with pleasure.

His muscles bunched whipcord tight in response. "You've every right to tell me to go to hell, but will you give me one chance to show you what you desired a second ago?"

Whatever she'd craved, it still coiled deep inside her. Before she could speak, he drew back.

She caught him before he left her fully. "Show me."

His hand moved between them, stroking her, distracting her, until he once again rested deep inside her without any pain at all, with a pleasure that curled her toes and her lips.

"When I found you in the Star, I feared I'd wounded you so gravely I'd never see you smile." He scanned her face as he moved inside her with a rhythm she instinctively matched. His lips parted on a gasp that intermingled with hers. The grin he gave her made hers grow. "I love making you smile."

Love. The word, sudden and unexpected, made her flinch. His happiness vanished in a blink, replaced by his familiar look of concern.

"Keep making love to me," she urged. "Keep making me smile."

He obeyed, moving faster and faster until her desire and her happiness became one.

She'd wanted to be closer to him, but nothing could have prepared her for the intimacy of him inside her, making her part of him. She rose to meet him, chasing waves of desire until they formed a single crest that propelled her over the edge into bliss.

He came into her one last time. Hard and fast. Then he collapsed, whispering her name. The only sound that followed was their ragged breathing. Entwined. Like their bodies. She didn't move. She wanted to stay like this forever.

But with every heartbeat, the world beyond Noah's embrace, and the walls of her temporary sanctuary, wormed its way back into her thoughts.

She couldn't stay with him. Not with John coming for her. Not with Gertie and Cora willing to commit murder.

One could only lie to one's self for so long. Clinging to Noah's strength and goodness, even for a minute longer, was selfish.

She surveyed the chaos around them, seeking the least cluttered path for her departure. A fine mess she'd created. At least she hadn't opened every trunk.

Disbelief settled like a stone on her chest. She'd gotten it wrong. All wrong. She couldn't leave the jail. She had to make Noah leave. Again. This time far enough for her to search—she counted the closed lids—four trunks.

The weight on her chest centered on her heart. Relentless. Her stolen moment of happiness with Noah was over.

He must've sensed the change in her, because he rolled them both so they lay on their sides, facing each other. He gave her a lopsided grin. "Sorry. I must've been heavy."

"You weren't, at least not in an uncomfortable way. What I'm trying to say is I'm—" She clenched her teeth as a shiver of regret rocked her.

His smile vanished. "You're cold? Next time tell me sooner. You can't afford to become ill again." He retrieved the fallen sheet and tucked it around her with hands so gentle it made what she must do next all the more difficult.

It was time to lie again. "I'm never going to be able to tell you what you want to hear." Her fingers knotted in the sheet. "So you might as well let me go."

His eyelids shuttered, hiding his expression as he bowed his head until his forehead touched hers. "Without a word you've told me far more than I could've ever hoped for. Your body can't lie. Not when we're this close."

The certainty, and reverence, in his voice made her stiffen. What more had he guessed? That she loved him to the point of distraction, to the edge of madness?

Above the sheet, his fingers traced her collarbone.

"Every inch of your skin continues speaking to me, whispering secrets." His voice lowered, rumbling deep inside him with restrained emotion. "I'm sorry for assuming the worst. And grateful to be proven wrong. And humbled that you gifted me with this particular truth."

She shoved away from him, breaking the fragile bond he'd spun between them. She would not tie his life to hers and destroy him in the process.

The loss of his touch, and soon his affection, made her throat tight with unshed tears. "I can't stay here." Ignoring her own words, she remained sitting beside him on the bed. Her departure hinged on him leaving first, but she had no idea how to make him go. She hugged her knees to her chest. "John will arrive soon."

In one swift movement, Noah sat up to form a formidable wall between her and the door. "I won't let him take you back to the Star."

She couldn't allow herself to be deterred by his strength or his determination. "What if John hurts you and takes me back, anyway?"

The bed shifted, and the comforting heat of Noah's body moved closer. "I'd come after you. There'd be hell to pay."

He'd be the one to pay. Weighted with defeat, her chin dropped to rest on her knees. "I refuse to gamble with your life."

"But you'll wager yours? Repeatedly?"

She shrugged. "Right now, it's the only card I'm willing to play."

A long silence elapsed before Noah asked, "What about Marshal Masterson?"

"What about him?"

"He'll help." Conviction rang in his voice.

She snorted. "Deger, the lawman in charge while Masterson was occupied elsewhere, didn't help."

"Bat's different. If he'd been in town when you went from frying pan to fire, things would've been different."

Masterson also wasn't here in this jailhouse. Recent talk said if he couldn't be found at the jail, the next place to go was the Dodge House Hotel...across the street. She swung her legs over the side of the bed. The cold floor on the soles of her feet stopped her from moving any further.

You can't leave, she reminded herself. *Not yet.*

But if Noah departed to fetch Masterson, she might have time to finish her search. With four trunks remaining, she didn't need long. She stole a peek at him from the corner of her eye.

Once again his scrutiny had shifted from her to the room. "Bat could prove helpful in many ways. He might shed light on what you're trying to find. This is his jail after all."

Her stomach knotted. Masterson would've heard about Edward's missing possessions, but he'd also protect his deputy. Securing Noah's safety was what mattered most.

Trying not to appear too eager, she chose her next words carefully. "Are you expecting him soon?"

His jaw went rigid as he shook his head.

"Then the odds are John will arrive before the marshal does."

"Not if we move fast." He did just that. He dressed in a flurry, but when he knelt beside her with her shift and her dress in his hands, his movements slowed. "I need to know you'll be here when I return." He released a sigh of resignation. "I'm sorry."

Alarm skittered up her spine. "For what?"

His grip on her clothing tightened as if he doubted the

wisdom of returning them to her and for what came afterward. "As soon as you're dressed, I'm going to have to lock
you in a cell."

Coldhearted bastard. That's what Sadie's wide-eyed
expression told him. It's what his conscience said as well.
Loudly. Only the cruelest of men incarcerated a woman
minutes after bedding her. Once again, he scoured his brain
for an alternative. And found none.

He dropped her clothes on her lap and stood. "I can't
take you with me. Not when you're already in the safest
place in town. A locked jailhouse will keep John and
Madam Garrett out, but it won't keep you in. Only a cell
will."

One of her hands rose to fidget with her hair. Her unfet-
tered red mane, without a single pin to tame it, made his
fingers itch to caress the silky locks as well.

Under his continued scrutiny, her eyes flared even wider.
Then her hand fell to her lap, where it joined the other one
clutching her dress and shift. Her gaze dropped as well.
Then promptly shot up again to clash with his.

No wonder. He was hovering over her like a wolf ready
to pounce. He fought the urge to lay his hands on her. Not to
drag her into a cell, but to entice her to lie down on his bed
again. With him. For a second round of lovemaking.

Only her second time ever. That truth kept him reeling.
His farm girl turned strumpet had been a virgin until she'd
kissed him with an ardor that had finally brought them
together, body and soul.

He couldn't imagine his life without her. He wasn't
letting her go.

But he shouldn't be fixated on bedding her again so soon. Not when she must be tender from their first encounter. And not with so many lies still between them. Beneath her guarded expression, he glimpsed her usual determination...and a flash of impatience. She was chomping at the bit to head down a new path while he mooned over her without a plan in sight.

"Could I have some privacy to dress?" Her chin rose to an obstinate angle, warning him she'd begun her campaign.

Flummoxed as to what it might be, he'd nevertheless honor her request, to a degree. He moved to stand in the doorway with his back to her.

"You've got to the count of thirty. When I turn around, your dress had better be on and you'd better be ready to go in a cell, or—" He bit back his groan. Or what? He doubted he had the willpower to tow her anywhere. Or carry her wrapped only in a sheet, for that matter. But if he didn't—

The whisper of the sheet falling made him tense with longing. She was naked, barely two strides away. He gritted his teeth and started counting. He dreaded reaching thirty and having to lock her up. The possibility of John arriving before he could retrieve Bat, drove him to finish.

"Ready?" he called over his shoulder.

"As I'll ever be. You can turn around."

When he did, she stood fully clothed, her hands on her hair. Probably attempting to smooth it into some semblance of order. She soon gave up and swiped her palms down her skirt, attacking the wrinkles next. "Shouldn't you be fetching the key to my prison?" Her question shot out, brisk as her movements. "Or have you changed your mind?"

With a heavy heart, he headed for the brass key ring hanging on a nail in the other room. Her footsteps followed him, neither rushed nor hesitant. Had she come to the same inevitable conclusion as him?

The sooner he put her in a cell; the sooner he could take her out.

Now he was lying to himself. In spite of her acceptance of the current situation, he knew he was in for a fight. Sooner rather than later.

On the other side of the door leading onto Front Street, muffled footsteps approached. Growing louder. Faster. They pounded up the jailhouse steps. Was it John?

His heart missed a beat, failing him for an instant. His gun hand didn't.

Sadie latched onto the back of his shirt at the same time as he leveled his revolver at the door. Neither of them moved after that. The tension on his shirt told him she wasn't going to let him rush whoever was outside.

In the following silence, the door handle rattled. It didn't open. Their visitor wasn't getting in without a— Something scraped the lock. *Hellfire and brimstone.* He cocked his revolver and prepared to press the trigger.

Bat burst in. He skidded to a halt with his hands raised. One of them held a ring of keys similar to the one hanging on the wall. Noah's own hands shook with relief as he lowered his weapon.

The marshal's gaze followed his gun down and then lower, to the swathe of blue gingham that'd be plainly visible behind Noah. Despite laboring to catch his breath, Bat's curse rivaled anything he'd heard.

He holstered his weapon. "I was coming to find you. We need your help."

"Miss Sullivan shouldn't be here."

Sadie stepped around Noah, angling for the door. "I'd be happy to leave."

"No." Bat barked the word at the same time as Noah.

The marshal slammed shut the door and moved to look out the window. "You're a bigger pair of fools than I could've imagined. Why is she here?"

"She came looking for something she promised Edward she'd find. Any idea what that might be?"

Bat continued staring out the window. "I ain't inclined to hazard a guess right now."

"What the hell does that mean?" He rubbed the back of his neck, struggling to ease the frustration building inside him again. "Are you saying you don't know?"

"I'm saying you need time to cool off. Remember *where* you went last time to do that?"

Bat wanted him to go to Sadie's farm, to leave— "I'm not abandoning her."

"Well you can't take her with you, or stay with her in this jail. Not without making things worse." Bat spun to face them again. "If you had a secure place for her to hole up in, then things might be different."

Damn. Bat was right. If he'd finished the roof on Sadie's house, he could've hidden her there.

Sadie hadn't lifted a foot or a finger since they'd both rejected her offer to leave. But her gaze jumped between them, following their conversation, watching them like a rabbit waiting for something, or someone, to swoop down and swallow her whole.

He wanted to assure her she was safe. Even if he stayed by her side, that'd be a lie. They needed Bat's assistance, but his entire body rebelled against Bat's suggestion for helping her. "You go, and I'll stay and—"

"Shoot someone?" Bat snapped. "Or get yourself shot? Right now, you can help the most by being elsewhere. I'll keep her safe. You have my word."

Sadie's gaze swung back to his, and held. The truth he read in her eyes deprived him of speech. She wasn't afraid. She was confused and very determined to change that. Maybe he needed to change as well.

"What if Madam Garrett comes for her while I'm gone?" His throat seized before he could add, *And I lose the one person I love most. Again.*

"I imagine Gertie will send over John first," Bat replied without a drop of his usual humor. "When she does, I don't want you so edgy you blast a hole in him. Despite all his faults, John doesn't deserve that." His words whipped out, faster and faster. "Go work off some steam. Do something productive. That's an order." He paused to haul in a breath. "I promise Miss Sullivan will be here when you return. Jus' don't come back until tonight when you can't lift a pistol or a hammer."

A HAMMER? Sadie strove to make sense of Noah and the marshal's conversation. At least they weren't talking about Edward's belongings. Or so she hoped. It was hard to tell.

"Time's a wastin'." Masterson's voice was unusually curt, as if he struggled as well. Not for clarity but patience.

Noah continued staring at her. A storm of emotions too complex to define raged in his eyes.

"Deputy," Masterson's growl yanked Noah's attention away from her. "Leave now. Don't let anyone see you. Use the back door."

Without a farewell glance in her direction, Noah finally left.

His absence made her lightheaded, like the air had been sucked out of the room with him.

Masterson tossed his ring of keys on his desk as he swung to face the other door, the one leading onto Front Street. "My apologies, Miss Sullivan, for what comes next. Didn't want anyone killed."

Killed? Why did he—? A pounding on the front door made her jump.

When the marshal opened it, John stood on the porch. His familiar scowl deepened when he looked over the marshal's shoulder and spotted her.

"Assume yer here to collect Miss Sullivan."

John's reply came fast and hard. "Yes."

It knocked the remaining air from her lungs, turned her body heavy as lead. She wanted to lie down and never get up. She'd gambled and lost everything. She wouldn't be completing her search. Noah was gone. Noah—

She drew herself up. Noah was safe. And the marshal had yet to hand her over. He remained in the doorway between her and John.

"Where's the good madam?" Masterson's voice had resumed its unhurried drawl.

"You know where," John shot back in a slightly winded and very disgruntled voice. "You watched us come out of the Star together. Ain't looking forward to the earful she'll be giving me for losing our footrace."

Masterson chuckled. "Inform her that the odds were in my favor. I had a shorter distance to travel. The Star's close but the hotel's closer. Now back to the question at hand: where's the madam—right now?"

"Waiting. On the Star's veranda."

"Well, that won't do." Masterson beckoned her forward. "Shall we go meet her?"

Disbelief made her lurch away from him. She ended up

facing the bedroom, with its trunks, with the four she hadn't yet searched.

"Whatever yer pondering—" Masterson drawled, "— it can wait."

With sluggish steps, she followed him onto the porch. Across the street, Gertie's stout figure stopped pacing the Star's veranda.

Masterson held up his hand, halting Sadie as well. "No need to go any farther. You neither, John." He folded his arms and propped his shoulder against a porch post.

John mirrored his pose by the other post. "How long we gonna stand here?"

"That's entirely up to the madam."

A stride behind them, Sadie hovered in the doorway, her mind and body buzzing with nerves and questions. Could she dash back inside, bolt the door from within and finish her search?

"Time to stand our ground." Masterson's back remained a taut line. His profile shared a similar rigidity as he tracked Gertie's progress down the Star's steps and across the street. "Time to look the devil in the eye."

When the madam reached the foot of the jail's stairs, Masterson faced her dead on, his expression now hidden.

He raised his hand again. "To what do I owe the pleasure, Madam?"

"Stop delaying." Gertie thrust her finger at Sadie. "I want her back at the Star. She works for me."

"That's why I'm arresting her."

"What?" Gertie screeched before Sadie could.

"I found *your* employee with *my* employee. Found 'em coming out of my deputy's bedroom, to put things bluntly."

Sadie's face burned with the implication and the truth.

In the opinion of many, she was now a fallen woman for real.

Gertie's glare sliced her. "Tell the marshal that his deputy forced you."

"He did not! He'd never force me to do anything." Outrage balled her hands into fists. She inhaled deeply, struggling to regain control. Noah would not be blamed for her crimes. She'd have to admit she'd broken in to search the jail. "I came here of my own accord. I—"

"Well, there you have it," Masterson said. "Nailed herself to the counter with her own words, she has. Nothing I can do but arrest her."

"This is preposterous." Gertie threw up her hands. "She's got the pox. The only man who'd bed her is a crazy one."

"My deputy fits that description at times."

"If what you're sayin' is true—" Gertie growled from between clenched teeth, "—your deputy's broken the law as much as her."

"What law?" *What was going on? What was Masterson up to?* She moved to the edge of the porch, so she could see his face, and read her answers there. But it was John's expression that claimed her attention.

His glower had vanished. "The law that's always cast a blind eye on certain activities inside Dodge's saloons and brothels."

Masterson nodded. "But when those *activities* spill into my jail, I'm entitled to break tradition. Especially since on paper, prostitution's illegal in Dodge."

"That law's hogwash," Gertie shot back. "No one's ever enforced it."

"Until now." Masterson hands moved to rest on his pistols. "Time for you to step off this porch, John."

A chill rocked Sadie's body. Had she exchanged one prison for another?

"Your jailbird don't look so good," John remarked as he complied.

"Why don't you go back inside 'n sit down, Miss Sullivan?"

She rubbed the ache building between her brows. "You're arresting me for being a prostitute? Where were you when I needed you a year ago?"

"Unfortunately on an errand outside of Dodge."

"And your deputy? Where is he?" Gertie demanded.

"His duties took him out of town as well. Until he returns, Miss Sullivan remains in my custody."

"For how long?" The madam's voice had gone deathly quiet.

"Hard to say. Could be a day. Or a week."

A day or a week, did it matter? She barely stifled her gasp. She couldn't stop the excitement coursing through her, though. She only needed a few minutes to finish searching the jail.

Masterson took her firmly but gently by the elbow. His other hand never left his pistol, nor did his attention leave the madam, as he steered her back inside the jail.

At the bottom of the steps, John stood behind Gertie, his stance oddly relaxed.

In contrast, Gertie bristled with rage. "That girl owes me a debt. A growing one. She'd best not forget." Her words pricked Sadie's conscience, but the warning that followed cut her to the core. "The moment Mr. Ballantyne sets foot back in Dodge he'll answer for her folly."

Masterson closed the door, shutting out the madam but not her threat. It rang in her head. She couldn't let Noah be harmed because of her.

"Well," the marshal said on a sigh as he released her and locked the door. "At least we now have some time. Not much, but more than when I found you in here with Noah." He gestured to the chair by the desk. "Have a seat 'n catch your breath. We've lots to discuss before his return."

She stared at the bedroom. She didn't want to talk. She wanted to continue her search.

"Did you hear what I said, Miss Sullivan?"

"I don't feel well," she lied. Or did she? The throbbing in her head only rivaled her compulsion to complete her search. "I might better concentrate on our conversation if I rested for a few minutes in the other room."

"You still hunting for what you promised Edward you'd find? Might that be the watch 'n jewelry box that went missing after his suicide?"

She spun to face him. "You said—"

"That I didn't want to *hazard a guess*. And there were plenty of hazards with John barreling down on the jail, 'n Noah ready to shoot him in yer defense."

"You lied."

"I did what was necessary to grease Noah's departure."

Noah had been right. Masterson was different. Her respect for the man grew. So did her wariness.

Masterson's nose wrinkled like he'd smelled something offensive. "Marshal Deger, the witless whale who was too often left in charge of Dodge, including when you came to town 'n when your friend died, blathered on about Edward's lost treasures." He gestured to the bedroom. "Did you find what you came looking for in there?"

A blush burned her cheeks. She'd found more than she could've ever dreamed of with Noah in that room. And now Gertie had vowed to hold him accountable for her wanton recklessness. "My search was interrupted."

"If I let you finish, will you stop wasting yer energy arguing with me?"

Relief robbed her of words. She nodded. Vigorously.

"Good, 'cause I suspect that even though you use yer poor health to get yer way, you ain't feeling top dollar. You ought to lie down. But when you do, it'll be on the cot in my jail cell."

This time her nod was curt. Escaping a cell was a gamble but, same as when Noah had resolved to lock her up, she was betting on her hairpins to free her before his return.

Whether she found Edward's possessions or not, Noah's well-being depended on her reaching Gertie before Noah returned to Dodge.

CHAPTER 15

*N*oah urged Pepper across the dusky prairie toward Dodge's lights. He'd worked hard, hammering away even in the last seconds of twilight to finish the roof on Sadie's house. He could barely lift his reins, let alone a gun. He released a long sigh.

Bat should be happy. Hell, he was happy to have Bat on his side.

But even though the marshal had vowed to watch over Sadie, unease gripped him as strongly as his exhaustion. He had to get back to Sadie as fast as possible.

When he entered town, he straightened in his saddle, every sense on alert. The alleyways on either side of him were thick with shadows.

One of them bounded toward the street and him. He drew his revolver. On a dog. Without a glance in his direction, the mutt trotted across the street in front of his horse and joined the gloom on the other side.

Feeling foolish now, as well as tired and sore, he urged Pepper forward again. He didn't holster his gun, though.

He'd end up drawing it at the next shadow, and that'd slow him down. He'd relax when he was with Sadie again.

Until then, he was no better off than that lone cotton-wood in the gully he'd seen on the way to their picnic. He had everything he needed to survive: a revolver, a trusty horse, and a fine home waiting for him in Texas. It wasn't enough.

A fiercer need churned inside him. Now, more than ever, he felt driven to protect Sadie. That compulsion had become as important to him as breathing. But if he was honest with himself, he craved more. He ached to hold her again—tonight, tomorrow, and every day after.

No amount of distance or bruising labor could dull that longing.

Sadie desired him as well. That truth quickened his blood. What would it take to make her feelings grow into love? He imagined riding side by side with her to her farm, showing her the house he'd built for her, and hearing her say she wanted him to stay with her inside. He'd carry her across the threshold like a husband and make love to her for days in a fervor reserved for newlyweds.

Bat was right. She made a man eager to visit the preacher.

If he thought she'd say yes, he'd already have proposed. A wedding had solved many a woman's problems...and made others worse. After living with her father and the townsfolk of Dodge, he didn't blame Sadie for being leery of hitching her life to another's.

He wanted her to join with him wholeheartedly. Same as she had this morning. A marriage of convenience reminded him too much of her position at the Star. Whatever she felt for him wouldn't grow if he didn't play his cards carefully. Her affection would wither and die.

Someone ran down the center of the street, heading toward him.

His grip on his revolver tightened. Short and thin, the man racing toward him didn't look very threatening. He squinted for a better view. Not a man, but a boy. The boy who'd delivered the news about the disturbance at the rail depot the other evening.

In the nearest alley, the shadows were moving again. They took the shape of a hulking giant. Or a familiar saloon barkeep.

Noah kneed Pepper forward, cantering the final distance required to put himself between the boy and the threat. His hand came to rest on his thigh, where the boy wouldn't see his revolver now cocked and pointed at the alley and its shadow. He pinned his gaze there as well.

"Marshal Masterson sent me to warn you." The boy halted to gulp air.

Don't look at him. Don't even blink. As soon as you do, whoever's watching will—

The boy's voice dropped to a whisper. "Madam Garrett's made threats."

The hushed words hit him like cannon fire. When had she done that? Noah's stomach turned hard and cold. The madam had visited the jail.

The hefty shadow grew smaller, retreating. Not a murderer then, but a messenger similar to the one hovering by his horse. What would the madam do when John informed her of his return?

Nothing good.

He swung down from his saddle. "Will you deliver my horse to the stable and see to his care?"

The boy's gaze had found the revolver in his hand. Despite his wide eyes, he nodded.

Noah tossed him the reins and several coins. Then he sprinted toward the shadows and became one of them.

SADIE SHIFTED POSITION, struggling to get comfortable. The mattress on the prison cot wasn't friendly to the flesh of her backside. She missed the bed in the other room. She missed Noah. It'd long since gone dark outside. Why hadn't he returned?

She glared between her cell's bars at Marshal Masterson sitting on the other side, at ease in his chair. He showed no sign of leaving. "Your move," she reminded him. *Why don't you move outside on the porch for a few minutes...and leave me alone with my hairpins?*

He continued contemplating the cards in his hands. "Hold yer horses, I ain't done thinking."

Which made her even more agitated. He couldn't only be pondering this useless poker game he'd suggested, could he? The marshal had proved much too cunning for that.

"The boy you sent to warn Noah has been gone a long time. Shouldn't you go check on him?" *And Noah too?*

"Won't break my word. I stay with you till Noah returns."

She exhaled a long breath, struggling to expel her growing irritation with it. A useless endeavor. Leaving this jail was turning into a herculean feat.

"Relax, Miss Sullivan. Ain't that one of the tricks to gambling? If you don't mind me saying, considering all the times you dealt cards at the Star, you don't appear to know much about playing games."

"I know this. In blackjack, you track the cards, count what's been played, and estimate the odds of what might come next. In poker, you study your opponent, analyze his mood and mannerisms, and link them to his hand." *Look at me, so I can figure out what you're planning.*

"I'll keep that in mind for the future." Masterson stretched his legs out in front of him and crossed them at his ankles. "Although I think I might be more partial to faro."

"Marshal, none of this helps Noah." Her curt words made her cringe. Maybe the lawman wouldn't notice.

Masterson's gaze finally rose to meet hers. A flicker of satisfaction flared inside her with this one victory.

"Feel free to call me Bat." The corners of his eyes crinkled as he smiled. "Yer concern for my deputy is noted 'n appreciated. I see why he likes you. I hope you care for him as much in return."

She glanced down, feigning interest in her own cards. How swiftly he'd spun the table in his favor. "*Marshal Masterson*, are you asking me about my intentions toward your deputy?"

"I'm praying whatever happened in that other room, before I came in, wasn't a calculated move. You ought to recognize a man's heart can be broken as easily as a woman's."

Her cheeks grew uncomfortably hot.

"There you go again," he drawled. "And now I'm definitely not thinking about our game. I'm thinking the moment Noah returns he should escort you to the church 'n—"

A muted knock rapped the back door. Lightning fast, Bat was out of his chair with one pistol drawn. He pressed his index finger against his lips and crossed on silent feet to open the door.

Noah shoved past him and his weapon. Sadie's heart swelled with happiness for his safe return, then squeezed tight when he slammed to a halt with his wide eyes fixed on her.

Bat closed the door and reclaimed his chair. His cards lay discarded under his feet. "Glad you returned safe 'n sound, Deputy. Yer woman was concerned."

"You locked her in a cell?" Noah demanded as he spun to face Bat. "Why?"

She scoffed. "You're a fine one to ask that question."

His gaze dropped to his boots. "I was worried about Madam Garrett."

"So was I." Bat's words snapped Noah's attention back to him.

"She came here?" he asked.

"Of course," the lawman replied with a shrug. "And that's when I chose Miss Sullivan's new accommodations. I was concerned for her safety as much as she was for yours." He raised an eyebrow in her direction, one full of challenge. "Ain't that right?"

"You arrested me!"

Noah drew in a startled breath. "For what?"

She angled her face away from both men and raised her chin. "For prostitution—with you."

Noah's silence stretched her nerves. She studied him closely. Or as close as one could from the corner of one's eye...so he wouldn't guess the importance of his response.

He opened his mouth, then shut it. He didn't refute her crude statement.

She struggled to be indifferent, but she couldn't stop the heat overflowing her cheeks and scorching her entire body. "In the eyes of Dodge, I'm a criminal."

Bat waved her declaration away. "No charges will be laid. By the way, Deputy, while you were gone, I let her finish her search. We didn't find anything. I looked as well when I had to put everything back...as best as I could." He sent her a disapproving look that dissolved into a grin. "Be warned, Deputy, when you two finally set up house, yer woman ain't a tidy person."

Noah drew back as if he'd been slapped, then he shot her a glance. "You wouldn't tell me what you were looking for, but you'd tell him?"

"I guessed," Bat drawled. "Had to be Edward's jewelry box 'n watch that went missing after his suicide."

"How convenient for you to guess *after* I left," Noah muttered. "So," he exhaled the word on a long-suffering sigh. "If this box and watch aren't here, where are they?"

"Hell if I know. Suspect she don't know either."

Noah grumbled a curse and looked everywhere but at her. "Seeing her behind bars doesn't sit well with me."

"Then let me out," she said. *I'm not getting you killed.* "No good can come of keeping me here now."

"I disagree." Bat studied her. "Yer free from the madam's grasp, for a while at least. Ain't that a good thing?"

Noah's attention finally settled on her as well. She squirmed beneath his scrutiny, her nerves twitching. Unbearably. This time she refused to look away while she awaited his reply.

"The last thing I ever wanted was to force you to stay in my company."

"Better that than letting her face her troubles alone."

"Still doesn't feel right." Noah rubbed his eyes. "Maybe we could keep her here without locking her up."

Disbelief made her stomach flip. He wasn't actually considering the absurd idea, was he? He wouldn't. The Noah she knew bargained. He coaxed and cajoled.

Bat stared at the window and the deepening gloom beyond. "Madam Garrett wants her back. Bars keep people out as well as in." He canted his head in her direction. "How long will she stay here if we don't incarcerate her? She finished her search 'n came up empty-handed."

The reminder made her shoulders slump. She failed Edward. Completely. She couldn't let the same thing happen with Noah. "I want to leave Dodge," she blurted. "Right now."

The surprise on his face clashed with the certainty in her heart. Protecting Noah was all that mattered.

"Take me away." *Tonight. Together. Just you and me.*

He yanked off his hat and raked his fingers through his hair. "You once told me if I removed you from Dodge, you'd find a way to come back—without me."

"I won't. Not now."

"Is that a promise?"

"Yes." She'd never meant anything so strongly.

Noah's brow furrowed. "You also said you couldn't promise me anything."

She opened her mouth. Nothing came out. What could she say when he challenged her with the truth?

The marshal broke the silence. "She's yer woman, so whatever happens next is yer decision."

Noah tossed his hat onto the desk and crossed his arms. "How long can we keep her here?"

Real alarm, not merely uncertainty, made her scramble to her feet and grab the bars. "You can't *keep me here* a minute longer. It's too dangerous."

Bat grunted. "She's right. This is damned dangerous. She's also wrong. We have a week."

Noah's frown deepened. "Someone who looked like John was waiting for me on the edge of town."

A growing pressure squeezed her chest.

"Don't worry 'bout John," Bat said. "I had a word with him."

"When?" The surprise in Noah's voice matched what she felt.

"After our summons to that false alarm at the rail depot."

"*That* was your errand?"

"I called in a couple of favors. The first was John letting me win a race this morning."

Frustration made her shake the bars until they rattled. Her gaze clung to Noah. "Listen to me. You need to leave Dodge. If you don't, they'll kill you."

"Who will?" both men demanded.

How could she tell them about Gertie when there'd never be any proof? She didn't even have Edward's missing possessions. Noah would be even more determined to stay in Dodge and bring the madam to justice. And then there was Cora. "You can't let your guard down around anyone at the Star."

"No, you can't. But John..." Bat shook his head. "He ain't a saint, but he's no murderer either."

"I believed the same of Cora." Her lips parted with surprise, then dismay. Damn her loose tongue!

Noah's hands tightened into fists. "She threatened you?"

If she shared this one truth, would they stop asking questions? "Not me, you. She said if I went to you for help, she'd end your life with poison. Your honest strength can't win against her evil. Every moment I stay in this jail makes the target on your back bigger. That's why you have to let me go."

Noah glanced at the marshal. "Can we arrest Cora?"

"Need more than a threat."

Noah crossed to stand close to the bars separating them. "Why does Cora want to punish you?"

"Edward's partner was Cora's brother. The one way she could stay close to Orin was to become Edward's paid companion. But he chose me instead and ruined her plans."

"It always comes back to Edward." Noah pinned her with an unwavering stare. "There's more to his story than you're telling us, isn't there?"

"What did you plan to do with his lost possessions?" Bat asked. "Give them to Cora? So she could stop the rumors about her brother stealing them?"

They remained determined to pry every last drop of truth from her. She'd told them too much. She wouldn't utter another word about the past. Only the future mattered. "We need to leave Dodge." She stared at Noah, willing him with all her heart to do as she said. "Everything depends on it. Release me."

He shook his head. "Fulfilling your promise to your friend once mattered more than your own life. What's changed?"

I won't watch someone be killed again. She almost screamed the words. They echoed in her head. She spun away from the bars, from Noah, and paced her cell. She stopped as soon as she faced him again. She couldn't escape him or her fear for his safety.

He was going to die. Because of her. Because she'd let him get too close.

"Tell us everything," Noah said. Both he and the marshal regarded her expectantly.

She longed to reach through the bars and pull Noah close enough to kiss. That had stopped him before. For a while. She pressed her hand to the ache building in her forehead and was startled to find she still held the cards from her poker game with the marshal.

"Tell us what you saw." Noah's voice was quiet but determined.

She blinked in disbelief. "What I—? What are you talking about? I never said—"

"You said you wouldn't watch someone be killed. *Again*."

Dear God, she'd said that aloud? She squeezed the cards in her hand, crumpling them. *You fool,* she berated herself. *You loose-lipped, addle-headed fool.*

Noah reached through the bars, reaching for her. "You never mentioned witnessing your father's death, and Edward's was a suicide. Or was it?"

Damn him and his resolve to learn the truth. Frustration and fear propelled her toward him. She hurled her cards through the bars. They struck his chest, making him flinch, before they fell with a harsh patter to the floor.

His hurt expression made her cringe.

He stood his ground, though. He didn't retreat. He waited for her to take his hand.

A wave of weariness made her grope for the cot behind her instead. Her bottom hit the mattress hard. "Stop playing with me."

"I only want to keep you safe."

That was the problem. Her well-being would cost him his own. "I'm tired. Is there an end to your constant badgering? Or do you intend to keep me up all night with these useless questions?" She wrapped her arms around her waist. She didn't have to fake her exhaustion. It settled on her like a yoke, hunching her shoulders. Her chin drooped to her chest.

An uncomfortable silence descended on the other side of the bars.

"I understand you're worn out," Noah said softly. "But I'm not leaving. I won't let you face your troubles alone."

"Neither will I." Bat's chair squeaked, then his footsteps came closer until he halted beside Noah. "Trust us to do what's best."

"What's best? You're both holding me against my will." She couldn't stop her tone from growing increasingly strident. "A jail is a jail. How different is this from the Star?"

"I can think of one large difference," Noah replied.

"What?" she snapped.

"Cora."

The woman's name made her recoil. Uncertainty leached her voice of any strength. "What about her?"

"For the next week, she can't continue forcing you to take that vile swill masquerading as medicine. That's why she threatened to kill me and not you." His tone turned as harsh as hers had been earlier. "She was already killing you. And you both knew it. If I ever see her again, I'll—" He spun to glare at the front door like he wanted to kick it down and storm across the street to the saloon.

Damn her foolish mouth a hundred times. She'd been so worried about him going after Gertie she'd forgotten his need for justice would double if he discovered the scope of Cora's malice.

Her carelessness had pushed Noah one step closer to the grave.

SADIE SWIPED her hand across her forehead. Her fingers came away damp. Hades must feel like this—hot and stifling and impossible to escape. The air hung in her cell, trapped like her by jailers who wouldn't open a window enough for a draft to slip in…let alone turn their backs long enough for her to slip out.

She stopped pacing her cell, so she could better glare at the marshal who once again lounged in his chair. This time his feet were on his desk while his attention alternated between a copy of the *Dodge City Times* and a pocket watch. At ease, but on guard.

Curse him for being so consistent.

After a final glance at his timepiece, he folded the paper and rose to his feet. "It's time," he called as he moved to the front door.

She fought the compulsion to stare at the bedroom. The creak of the floorboards told her Noah now occupied its doorway, after being summoned from his rest in the other room. A room with a bed they'd recently shared.

Bat opened the door leading onto Front Street. The breeze was short-lived. So was the glimpse of the boy, the one both she and the marshal had employed to deliver their messages.

Bat took a tray covered in a red-checkered cloth from the boy. "You watched the cook prepare the entire meal, like I asked?"

When the boy nodded, Bat tossed him a coin and told him to light out.

As soon as the door closed, Noah invaded her line of sight. His bed-tousled hair stole her breath as easily as he claimed the tray from the marshal, so the man could relock the door.

"See you tomorrow, Deputy." Bat collected his ring of keys from the nail where both sets hung. Then he tipped his hat to Sadie as he crossed to the back door. "You too, Miss Sullivan. Hope you get a good night's sleep." The door closed behind him.

The faint click of the lock came next. Then only stillness...if one didn't count the uncertainty churning inside her.

Sleep? What was that? Last night, she hadn't slept at all after Noah had agreed to keep her here against her will.

She snuck a glance at him. He stared at her openly. Other than his untamed hair and unshaven jaw, he looked utterly composed. Not a trace remained of the unrestrained man who'd made love to her a day ago. But her skin still tingled where he'd touched her, aching for him to do so again.

The heat rose in her cheeks. He'd left his mark on her. She hadn't done the same. He wouldn't leave Dodge with her. He'd rather keep her in this cell. Was extracting her from the saloon all that mattered to him? That and his quest to gain justice on her behalf?

A frown tightened her brow. Was she so different? Hadn't she sought the same for Edward without regard to her own welfare? She shook her head. That was different. Edward had begged her to help him, and she'd vowed she would.

If she hadn't lied so many times, could she have persuaded Noah to leave with her? She turned her back on him and her useless questions. She couldn't change the past, and maybe not even the future.

A wall of red brick filled her vision. Solid. Unmovable. It didn't matter. The wall didn't need to move. Just one stubborn drover who'd become a lawman, and now her jailer.

Behind her, the tread of his boots approached. Then the metal door squeaked open. She clung to her refusal to acknowledge the man opening it.

"Time to eat," he said.

The hearty aroma of roast beef and potatoes broke her

resolve. It wasn't the entreaty in his voice. She added the lie to the others pestering her conscience.

Noah balanced a plate in each hand. When he held one out for her to take, she accepted the offering without hesitation.

He retrieved a chair from the desk and sat in her cell's open doorway. "Time to talk as well."

She sat down with a thump. Her prison cot was as firm and unforgiving as ever. She couldn't escape it or the truth. Talking had made things worse. She pursed her lips and glared at the plate on her lap.

He heaved a sigh. "I wish I could let you rest longer, that I didn't have to force this conversation. But I must. Our week together will end too fast."

Yes, it would. If she pretended interest in eating, could she delay everything?

She managed three spoonfuls before her stomach heaved and bile burned her throat. She scrambled to her feet. Her gaze ricocheted around the cell.

"Sadie?" Noah's deep voice resonated with his familiar worry, but also with something she couldn't pinpoint. Something that made her want to run.

"I need to get out of here."

"Will you please listen to me?"

Her hands, one clutching the spoon and the other the plate, trembled. She fought to steady them along with her stomach.

"We need to talk about yesterday. I'd never heard of that law Bat enforced. That's no excuse though. I've now compromised your reputation along with your—" His words were muffled by a gravelly tone that had invaded his voice. Or was it in her ears?

"We cannot continue—" The rasping continued to rise

and fall, along with the heat under her skin. "At the church we—"

Her body flared hot as an inferno, and the room spun. She staggered sideways against the bars.

"Sadie! What's wrong?"

Disbelief then anger roared in her ears, feeding the heat raging inside her. What was *wrong*? He'd touched every part of her. He'd made her love him. Then he agreed to lock her up like a criminal and besieged her with questions that hurt more than they helped.

She shoved away from the bars, from him. She hurled her plate at the wall. It fell with a clatter reminiscent of mocking laughter. She stabbed the wall with her spoon. Once. Twice. She didn't stop. Shards of mortar and lime-stone rained down, pelting the toes of her shoes.

Noah pried the spoon from her fingers. "What're you doing?"

"I'm—" Her vision narrowed, black edging in. The room only stopped moving when her palms found the wall. She sagged against its cool roughness. Within seconds, the brick flamed hot under her touch.

Large hands covered her shoulders. "Sadie, you're scaring me."

His admission snuffed out her anger, but not the heat. The illness building inside her swelled stronger and swifter than anything she'd endured before. Her insides coiled and her skin itched, begging to be scratched, while her head hurt as if pressed in an ever-tightening vise.

"I don't know what's happening to me. But it's not good." Her legs dropped out from under her. Strong arms caught her and held her secure.

As if from a long distance away, Noah said, "You've had

hot spells and chills before. You got through them. This will be the same. You'll see."

He sounded so certain. She wanted to believe him.

"This feels..." The darkness around her became complete, "...different."

Muffled footsteps disturbed the silence, followed by the murmur of someone talking. The voice grew increasingly muddled until it reminded her of wasps droning high in a nest.

"Noah?"

He didn't answer her, but the buzzing continued. Muffled then brusque, rising then falling, but always growing louder until it howled in her ears and blocked everything out.

"Noah, I'm scared too."

CHAPTER 16

*N*oah knelt beside the bed, held a damp cloth to Sadie's brow, and watched helplessly as she rolled her head in delirium. It hadn't taken long before her body started rebelling against the loss of the blue mass syrup.

At first, he'd failed to notice her decline, hidden as it was under a growing restlessness and irritability. When he and Bat had agreed to keep her locked up, he hadn't blamed her for being cross. Afterward, he'd been distracted by his guilt. Putting Sadie behind bars wasn't right, but the opportunity to better protect her had been an irresistible lure.

Now her deterioration had snowballed, laid her out like a landslide, left her incoherent and once again burning with fever. When he'd found her passed out amid the trunks she'd been searching, he'd been afraid. That medical emergency was minor compared to what she now endured. This wasn't an illness one recovered from in a day.

"Noah?" Her voice, hushed and hesitant, made his heart race with hope, then dread.

She hadn't spoken since she'd collapsed, and her last

words haunted him. *I'm scared too.* The confession, coming from a woman who never admitted to fear or weakness, terrified him.

"What can I get you?" He strove to keep his tone even. He needed to be strong for her sake. "How about some water?"

She didn't open her eyes. A peeved expression wrinkled her nose as she muttered, "When this is over, I'm going to make you pay." She sounded coherent again.

He exhaled a sigh of relief. "You deserve whatever payment you choose, and I'll gladly give you whatever you ask for." He brushed her damp hair away from her face. "Until then, is there anything else you need?"

"Water will do for now."

When he held the cup to her lips, she raised her head and opened her eyes. She managed a sip before collapsing back onto the bed. Her face was pale and pinched. But her eyes worried him most. They glittered much too brightly.

"You'll feel better soon," he said, striving to believe his words.

She stared at the wall. A single tear ran down her cheek.

He instinctively reached out to comfort her but halted midway. "Don't worry. I'm not going to let anything, or anyone, hurt you again." *Not even me.* He grasped his knees to prevent himself from touching her. "This illness will pass."

"That isn't why I'm crying."

"If you're worried about Gertie and Cora, don't be. They can't reach us inside this jail."

Finally, she faced him again. The tears brimming in her eyes made them sharp as shattered emeralds. Her distress cut him to the quick, slammed him back on his heels, until she said, "More than anything, I'm confused."

He had to clear his throat before he could speak. "About what?"

"I used to know what needed to be done. I had everything mapped out." Her tears fell unchecked. "I had a plan."

He clutched his knees tighter. "Tell me what you need done, and I'll do it for you."

Her gaze drifted to a point over his shoulder. "I can't."

"Why not?"

"I can't trust you."

His heart sank. She was right. He'd destroyed whatever trust he'd hoped to build between them when he'd forced her to stay with him in this jail.

"I can't trust you not to get yourself killed trying to save me." The brilliance in her eyes faded to the color of sludge at the bottom of a well.

He recognized the look. She was slipping back into delirium. His hope, along with his heart, plummeted to a depth akin to hell.

"You shouldn't trust me either," she whispered. "I've lied too many times. I can't leave Dodge."

So the other day—when she'd finally said she wanted to leave town, when she'd asked him to take her away—it'd been a lie. He cursed himself for a fool. He'd warned himself not to get his hopes up, but he hadn't had the strength to listen.

"But I want to go." She shifted onto her side, drew her legs up, and hugged them tight to her chest. "I want to go far, far away. And never look back." She pressed her face against her knees, hiding from him.

He released his death grip on his own legs and stroked her hair as gently as he could, wanting to soothe her. He needed to do more. He had to find—

"I can't leave you, Noah." Her hushed words penetrated his chaotic thoughts.

Him? She couldn't leave him? His heart took off at a gallop. He reined in his excitement. He couldn't have heard her right. She was rambling. She'd admitted to being confused. She—

"Stubborn Texan. I can't go if you stay. I won't abandon you to pay for my sins." She exhaled a quick breath. "Not when you're the most honorable person I know."

Her words blasted a gigantic hole in his conscience. He hadn't shown her what true honor looked like. When her fever finally broke, it'd be time that he did.

And maybe after he accomplished that feat and helped her be truly free to do whatever she wanted, then maybe she might once again ask him to leave Dodge with her, and spend every day after that by her side. All of his nights too.

He grasped his knees again. With that yearning constantly resurfacing, it was going to be damned difficult to be honorable.

FOUR DAYS after Noah had agreed to take away her freedom, she sat in his bedroom. This time on a chair he'd carried in from the office. She stared mesmerized by the play of muscles along his arms, revealed after he'd rolled his shirt-sleeves to his elbows and bent to change the bedsheets... an arm's length away...if she had the strength to reach for him.

Fatigue and doubt, a hundred times heavier than the woolen blanket he'd wrapped around her, held her prisoner. She watched. She waited. She who'd once gambled so brazenly, now too timid to turn over the next card and discover what it held.

Finally, he padded toward her on bare feet. Dressed so casually, his hair wild and uncombed, he looked like a diligent husband eager to embrace his new wife.

That recurring wish wouldn't die. Better for them both if it did.

After being bedridden for days, what more could he see in her than a bedraggled waif spat up from hell? But at least her flesh no longer pained her to the point of madness. Her illness had retreated. It might be gone for good. It was hard to tell now that she was well enough to once more appreciate his proximity...and be overwhelmed by it instead.

"The bed's made." He stared at the object in question and scrubbed his hand over his face. Several days' growth of beard darkened his jaw. Deep lines framed his eyes. How much sleep had he gotten since she'd taken ill?

He reached for her but paused midway.

The hesitant gesture made her grimace. "Don't worry. I can walk."

"No. I'll carry you." He swallowed roughly. "If you'll agree to let me."

Why was he behaving so strangely around her? Like she was made of glass and he was afraid to touch her. She longed for him to touch her.

When she nodded her consent, he picked her up. Her head found the perfect spot to rest against his shoulder. The distance to the bed wasn't long enough. Too soon, he set her on the mattress and let go to draw the top sheet over her legs. A floral scent curled around her, along with a wave of longing.

Ask him to lie down beside you, a voice inside her begged.

Leaning against the headboard, she stared at his hands, straightening the bedding, tucking in the edges. Her own fingers ached to touch him, to explore the man beneath the clothes. *Ask him to take them off.*

When she opened her mouth, the most mundane words came out. "The laundry pulled out all the stops."

"The laundry?"

"They added lilac water."

His hands stilled on the sheet. "I asked them to." His gaze met hers with a heat that left her mouth dry, unable to utter a word.

"I should let you rest. You can't afford a relapse." He spun toward the door. Ready to leave her.

She grabbed his hand. He didn't pull away. Nor did he clasp her hand in return.

"Noah..." She stared at her hand clutching his much larger one, at his strong fingers that wouldn't hold hers in return.

"What's wrong?" The familiar worry had crept back into his voice.

More than ever she wanted to leave town with him. But he didn't believe she'd stay with him, and she'd lied too many times for him to trust her if she tried to convince him otherwise. "Now that I'm getting better..."

"You can no longer use your illness to keep everyone at a distance." His fingers closed around hers. Then he dropped to his knees beside her.

Her heart took off at a gallop, while the rest of her went still as stone. Waiting. He was close now. So very close.

"I hadn't planned for this," she whispered. *I hadn't planned to fall in love with you.*

"What had you planned?" His voice was equally hushed.

"I wanted to leave Dodge a free woman."

"I'll do whatever it takes to make that happen. You have my word." His hand turned in hers as if to seal his pledge with a handshake. But when his thumb grazed the sensitive skin along the inside of her wrist, he stopped.

Had he felt her pulse leap at his touch? Like it jumped again, along with her every nerve and sinew quivering under his thumb now stroking its way higher and higher up her arm?

She swayed toward him.

"Sadie." Her name came out hoarse. "From now on, I'm doing what's best for you. You need time to heal." He released her and drew back.

Before she could protest, a knock came from the other room. It rattled the door that opened onto Front Street.

Her heart thundered in her chest as she watched Noah grab his revolver from his holster slung over a nearby trunk.

The knock came again. Louder. More insistent.

"Don't say a word," Noah ordered in a low voice. "Or move from this bed."

When he disappeared through the doorway into the adjoining room, she scanned the bedroom for a weapon of her own. She'd be damned if she'd hide and let whoever was outside harm him.

Noah's muted curse made her freeze.

"If you've come for Marshal Masterson," he said in a raised voice, "you'll find him at the Dodge House across the street." His tone sounded more wary than angry.

She leaned toward the door, straining to hear more.

"I'm here to see Miss Sullivan," a muffled voice replied.

"She doesn't need a doctor," Noah shot back.

Doctor Rhodes was outside? Why? Had Gertie sent him?

"I'd like to ascertain her condition for myself," Rhodes said. "My visit will be short."

"You're not needed here, Doctor."

"Yes he is!" The words shot out before she had time to reconsider. She had to learn why he'd come.

This time Noah's curse resonated loud and clear. It made her ears burn. The door clicked open and closed.

"Follow me." When he returned to the bedroom, his attention stayed on the doctor who followed a stride behind until they both stopped—the doctor in the doorway and Noah at the foot of her bed.

Rhodes studied her closely. His frown relaxed, but his shoulder remained hunched and his hands restless. He twisted the handle of his case until it creaked. "How are you, Miss Sullivan?"

"I'm—"

"She's still recovering," Noah said from between clenched teeth. "She needs to rest."

"Noah's taking excellent care of me, Doctor Rhodes. So you needn't worry. It was kind of you to visit, but you didn't have to."

"No, I had to come. I have to—" He stepped forward.

"That's far enough." Noah raised his hand in warning. "You've seen her. You can go."

Rhodes came even closer. Noah moved between them and seized the doctor's arm. When she grabbed Noah's arm in return, he finally looked at her.

She shook her head. "Let the doctor finish."

"Madam Garrett confronted me," the doctor said in a rush, "demanding why I'd helped you fake your symptoms. She said she'd learned you never had syphilis. Is that true?"

So, Cora had finally told Gertie the truth. And now the doctor was suffering for Sadie's sins.

"I'm sorry that I had to lie to you."

"*Good God.*" Rhodes' voice rasped with horror. "I had no idea that medicine was capable of causing such extreme reactions. I believed the good outweighed the bad. My oath to do no harm—" He clutched his case so hard his knuckles turned white. "I could've killed you."

She grabbed his arm. "This wasn't your fault. You did the best you could when faced with my falsehoods."

"And now the best thing you can do is leave," Noah grumbled.

The doctor's arm remained stiff under her hand as his troubled gaze darted between her and Noah's hold on him. Then he blinked as if he'd unearthed a great secret. His tension vanished, replaced by an easy smile. "You're lucky to have found each other."

She shook her head again. She was lucky. Noah wasn't. If it weren't for her, he'd be safe at home in Texas.

Rhodes' gaze rose to meet Noah's. "I'm glad to see you're still committed to safeguarding Miss Sullivan."

"I won't stop." He glared at her hand on the man's arm. The flash of jealously in his eyes startled her.

She released both men. "Thank you for your visit, Doctor Rhodes. We appreciate it." She certainly did, and she hoped Noah would eventually as well. "I would consider myself a fortunate woman if one day we all greeted each other as friends, but first I need to know: did Gertie send you to check up on me?"

Rhodes straightened his shoulders and faced her. When the man claimed his full height, he stood as tall as Noah. "I cannot lie to you if I'm to be worthy of your friendship. Yes, the madam demanded that I do her bidding."

Dread churned in her stomach. "What's she planning?"

"She didn't say. Was too busy demanding I gather information for her, but I won't. I'm only sharing my knowledge with you. I came to warn you." He glanced at Noah. "Both of you. Gertie's hissing like a powder keg ready to explode.

Even John's steering clear of her. No one's seen him at the Star for days. But there's more." He stared over his shoulder as if recalling the past. "After Madam Garrett, I received another troubling visitor."

"Cora," Sadie said, shaking her head, wanting to deny the fact that the woman still searched for a means to make good on her threat to kill Noah.

"I'll handle her," he assured her.

"I hope you can handle Wardell as well," Rhodes said, "because he was my visitor."

Her dread turned to panic and tormented her heart as well as her stomach. How had she forgotten about Wardell?

"What did the puffed-up partridge want?" Noah's voice rang with anger, clear as a church bell.

"He said he'd followed the madam to my doorstep. Said she wouldn't answer his questions about Miss Sullivan's health. When I said I couldn't either, he vowed that we'd all regret deceiving him, but that you—" his gaze finally met hers, "—would regret it most of all."

$\mathcal{N}$oah sat behind the jail's desk, focusing on cleaning his revolver rather than staring at Sadie. She stood by the window, a few short strides away. Her freckles no longer lay stark against skin as pale as death. The dark circles under her eyes had faded.

She could use more rest, but her health didn't consume his every thought. Nevertheless, his mind was under siege. He longed to kiss her again...along with a dozen other sinful activities.

The light of the midday sun caught the highlights in her hair, making her red mane glow more beckoningly than he'd ever remembered. Lord, she was pretty.

But her spirit captivated him strongest of all. Her grit and determination were worth more than every dollar in Dodge. He grimaced when he recalled trying to buy her company for a meager hundred.

She stole a look at him before she went back to scanning Front Street—for threats, she'd informed him earlier. "You're not still stewing about the doctor's visit yesterday, are you?"

"Haven't considered him all day." That was the truth. He'd been trying to figure out how to get her out of Dodge in an honorable way. No luck there.

"He wants to help. He's not like Gertie or Cora." A frown pinched her brow. "Or even John. That man I can't figure out in the least. But I'm certain the doctor means well."

He stifled his sigh. He'd forgotten the downside of that determination he admired. He respected Rhodes' attempt to make amends, but he hadn't been able to set aside his anger over the magnitude of Sadie's suffering during her withdrawal from a medicine the doctor had supplied.

He couldn't forgive the doctor or himself for putting her in danger.

"Good intentions aren't enough," he muttered.

She folded her arms. "Are you saying you believe he'll betray us?"

"Not knowingly. I agree that he means well, but I'll require a helluva lot more than that before I trust him with your life."

She cast another glance at him. "Sometimes it takes time to accept that you can trust someone." Her lips remained parted as if she wanted to say more.

His blood surged in his veins, urging him to get up and kiss those lips. He forced himself to stay in his chair. He'd vowed to show her what true honor meant.

She'd confessed that she wanted to leave Dodge a free woman. He'd make that happen. He hadn't figured out how, but he would.

He'd prove to her that he was honest and trustworthy and dependable. He swiped the rag along the barrel of his revolver, punctuating each quality he needed to show her he was the man she wanted to stay with...once she was free to make such a choice.

As if propelled by her own demons, she pivoted and made a beeline for the side room. After a brief disappearance that still felt way too long, she returned only to halt in the cell's open doorway. Trailing her fingers over the bars, she stared at the empty interior for a lengthy moment. Then her gaze came back to him. And so did she.

She perched on the corner of the desk. Head tilted to one side, a tentative smile curved her mouth. Not the false smile he'd remarked on when he first met her, but a genuine one, however small.

If he didn't put some distance between them, and soon, he'd scoop her up and haul her straight to his bed again. He holstered his gun and crossed to the potbelly stove to pick up the coffee pot instead. "Can I pour you a cup?"

"Remember what I said when I was ill?"

Sweet Jesus, he recalled so many things. The memories weren't helping him keep his vow to act honorably, to not hike up her skirt like some randy son of a gun after only one thing.

He wanted more.

"Do you remember when I told you I'd make you pay?"

That part he had forgotten. What could he give her? What could she possibly want from him? His shoulders slumped. What she'd wanted from the start. Her farm. The acres he'd proposed they barter for her time.

"I remember." He finally faced her. "I—"

The brilliance of her smile brought him to an abrupt halt. That and the fact she'd followed him and now stood a hand's-breadth away. Smiling again. No, more like beaming. At him.

He cleared his throat. "I remember." He winced. She had him repeating himself like an awestruck schoolboy.

The arch of her brows suggested she doubted if he did

remember. She lifted her hand between them and tapped her index finger on his chest. "And you said?"

"You deserved whatever payment you wanted for the hell you were enduring."

"Yes." Her finger settled on his chest, finding a home. Even that light touch sent shock waves through his body, making parts of him respond that were hard to ignore.

"And?" she prompted.

He wrenched his attention from her hand. Her smile enthralled him again, along with her lips parted in expectation. He leaned toward her. Sweet Jesus, he wanted to—

"You said you'd *gladly* give me whatever I asked for," she reminded him.

Finally, he understood what lay beneath her questions. "You're wondering if I'll keep my word."

She nodded. She'd handed him his opportunity, his chance to show her he was an honorable man.

"I pay my debts."

Her smile faded. "Debts." She said the word with a profound graveness as her gaze cut to the window, the one that had held her attention until she'd approached him. "In this we are once more the same. Time to clear all of our accounts, I think." She withdrew her finger from his chest. "Will you do what I ask?"

He exhaled a long, reluctant breath before he could speak. "I will."

He should've returned her farm long ago. He'd used the excuse of the absence of a house on the land to hold on to her. His gift stood waiting, and Sadie was well enough to go see it. She was right. It was time. But he still couldn't move.

She did. She stepped around him, heading toward the other room. "Come with me."

He found he could move after all. In fact, his feet were already in motion, following her.

She halted by the bed. Her eyes remained downcast, almost shyly so. But her tone, though quiet, held a note of command when she said, "Lie down."

That was the last thing he'd expected her to say. "Lie down?" he echoed in utter confusion.

"You agreed you'd do as I asked."

His bewilderment knew no bounds. He hadn't a clue what to say. So he did as she bid him. The simple act of lying on his bed while she stood nearby made his heart race with anticipation—and more doubts.

This couldn't be happening. He must have misheard her request.

"Sadie, I'll give you back your farm. I should've done so long ago. Let me fetch the deed. It's in the desk in the other room."

She dropped to her knees beside him. Her gaze swept the length of him, making his blood thud in his veins. "Twice now I've been laid out on this bed with fever and illness."

She'd omitted the other time she'd been "laid out" on his bed, provoking a twitch in the rapidly swelling area below his belt buckle. He shifted restlessly, remembering her lying on the bed beneath him, wanting her there again.

A bloom of pink colored her cheeks. "You were always the one in control."

The truth was he'd lost every speck of self-restraint when he'd finally bedded her. She was like the sweet, crisp air on the open prairie. He couldn't get enough of her.

"Have you ever known what that feels like?" she asked. "To be so completely under someone else's power?"

He knew, but he could do little more than nod.

Suddenly, he grasped another truth. Despite recovering from her illness, she didn't feel strong. He made her feel weak with his need to shelter her from harm. He couldn't mute his compulsion to protect her, but he could do whatever else she asked.

"Tell me what you want."

"I'd rather show you." Her fingertips brushed his shirtfront, glided down his stomach to the waistband of his trousers.

Every muscle in his body snapped to attention as if he'd received the shock of his life, or the greatest gift. He lurched into a sitting position and captured her wrist. "You're contemplating your book again."

Beneath her sinfully soft skin, her wrist went rigid as she balled her hand into a fist. "And you're refusing me *again*."

"Yes. No." His reply came out gruffer than he intended.

A flash of sorrow widened her eyes, then her lids shuttered, hiding her thoughts. None of them could be good.

"I'm not sure what I'm doing. I wanted to act—" He swallowed the word honorably. The only disgrace here was him squashing her wish to spread her wings and fly...if that was truly what she wanted to do. "You don't have to do this."

"No, I don't." Her gaze drifted to the doorway. "But just once, I want to do something entirely for me before I must face the inevitable."

I WANT to live before I die. She wanted to soar with no restraints, no holding back. Then maybe she could do more than stare out a window looking for threats. Then she could cross Front Street one last time and tackle Gertie head-on.

As if he could read her mind, Noah said, "If you're

asking me to let you return to the Star, I can't. Nor can I let you leave Dodge alone. It's too dangerous. I can't let you go." Despite his words, he released her wrist and slumped back onto the mattress. "I'll gladly give you your farm, though. And as far as the rest..." His eyes glowed like molten gold. "I'm yours to command."

Her heart pounded with a hundred different requests. Where to start? "Will you take off your clothes? All of them?"

He undressed quickly and lay down even faster. Mesmerized by his hard, lean body and the powerful length of his arousal, she could only stare...until she recalled the picture of Fanny Hill holding that power in her hand.

With the stroke of one finger, she made his strength swell. His hands moved to clutch the mattress while hers wrapped around him.

His hips rose off the mattress. Startled, she loosened her hold. He slid through her grasp, on the way up and down. His deep rumble of appreciation encouraged her to repeat the action. Many times.

"I adore watching you move."

"Then you'd better stop." His breathing grew ragged, as if he might shatter at any moment.

She'd felt that way when he'd been inside her. "What happens if I don't?"

"I find release," he said through gritted teeth. "Doubt if an earthquake could move me after that."

Her best odds of escaping the jail would be then. She didn't want to think about leaving him. She wanted to be even closer to him than she was now.

"Can you keep a firm hold on the mattress for a moment?"

Without waiting for his answer, she released him. His

growl of disappointment shook her as she laid her palms flat on his chest. Then she set one knee on the mattress beside his hips and swung her other leg over to straddle him.

He went dead still. His heat nestled against her naked core.

"Merciful heaven. When did you remove your under-clothes?" His words rumbled, like the purr of a big cat.

"After I left the window."

"You came in here."

"I hoped you'd agree to my request."

"I'm eager for your next command." He held himself still, waiting.

A burning need to be one with him swept over her. The wish to control him in any way went up in smoke. "Do whatever you want, and I'll do the same."

He moved inside her with incredible patience, giving her every opportunity to tell him to stop. When she quickened the pace, he followed readily until they both cried out. She soared with him over the highest precipice. When they came down, he cradled her in the haven of his arms.

She'd won the jackpot, a love more precious than her own life.

The only way she could continue winning was to return to the Star and kill Gertie, and Cora too. Then she'd have repaid Edward and guaranteed Noah's safety. She'd also have ensured her departure from Dodge...courtesy of the hangman's noose.

But first she had to leave Noah's embrace.

∾

ON TOP OF HIM, Sadie tensed, then relaxed again, still struggling to trust him. She wore her dress, while his clothes lay strewn about the floor. But he was far from naked.

He didn't move. He wanted to hold on to her forever.

Underneath him, the bed vibrated. Tiny tremors that swelled until the trunks, the floor, the entire room rattled around them. His world in upheaval. Familiarly so.

Fear tightened his arms around Sadie as she raised her head to scan the room. Her puzzled gaze sought his. "What's happening?"

His brother hadn't even been able to voice those words before he'd been swept away.

"Stampede." He set her on the bed, then scrambled to don his clothing and gun belt. By the time he had, the bellowing of the cattle had joined the chaos.

"Why would a herd be loose in town?"

"Only one way to find out." He headed for the other room.

She jumped to block his way. Her face had lost all color. "You can't go out there. I won't let you."

"I can't stand back and let someone die."

She jabbed her finger toward the street on the other side of the wall. "Those people wouldn't raise a hand to save you. They aren't your brother."

His breath left him in a hiss.

"Going out there won't bring him back," she added.

"You're right."

Her lips parted in surprise. "Then you're staying?"

"No."

"But you agreed!"

"What about Bat?"

Worry for the marshal flashed in her eyes before she ducked her head to hide her expression.

"When Bat hired me, he asked me to help him stay alive. He'll be out there protecting the townsfolk. If I can save him or someone else, I have to go."

She shook her head. "And who'll save you?"

Capturing her face in his palms, he pulled her close and kissed her hard. "You will," he vowed against her lips. Then he folded her into his embrace and held her tight, praying it wouldn't be the last time. "You'll save me," he repeated. "By promising you'll stay here, safe inside these walls, until I return."

"To hell with that." Her words came out hoarse. "I'm going with you."

An image of her chasing after him only to be crushed by the herd flashed in his mind. The pain that stabbed his heart was a hundred times sharper than when he'd watched her try to shoot him and spooked his herd instead. He'd barely reached her before she'd been killed.

Any other time, he'd welcome her by his side. Not now.

"Come with me." Taking her by the hand, he led her into the other room.

That she followed him without question, clasping his hand without reservation, filled him with a joyous wonder —until he stopped to lift the brass key ring from the nail on the wall.

Her hand went rigid. She fought him every step of the way back to the cell, struggling to break free and cursing a blue streak when he wouldn't let her.

He couldn't look her in the eye as he put her in the cell and locked its door to keep her there. Her sudden silence spurred him to run. He raced across the room to join the runaway herd and whatever else awaited him in their midst, leaving behind everything he loved.

CHAPTER 18

*T*hrough the bars, across the room—so very near but impossible for her to reach and halt—Noah yanked open the door onto Front Street. The thunder of hundreds of hooves knocked Sadie back on her heels. The bawling of the panicked beasts held her there. For a split second, Noah paused with his back to her, silhouetted against the surge of hide and horn racing by...then he slammed the door behind him.

The loss of the sight of him made her cry out. She pressed against the bars. She couldn't hear him lock the door, but she knew he would. He'd taken the blasted keys with him.

A silent chant rose in her mind. *Come back. Come back.* A useless plea. The fastest way she'd see him again was by using not her voice but her hands.

She yanked a pair of pins from her hair.

Pressing against the bars, she strained for a glimpse of the keyhole her fingers found by touch on the other side. Turning the pins from the opposite direction proved time consuming. So did remembering to do everything in reverse.

Outside the jail, the din ebbed. Her fear receded with it, then came crashing back. If by some miracle Noah had lingered on the relative safety of the boardwalk, the lull in the stampede wouldn't keep him there. He'd make his move to help the townsfolk now.

Every step he took away from her exposed him to more of Dodge's dangers, both beast and man. She wouldn't let him tackle this battle alone.

That she couldn't even see him made her tremble, fumble, and almost drop one pin. If she never saw him again — If he died—

The lock beneath her fingertips clicked open. She made a beeline for the door. A flash of movement in the window captured her attention and halted her there instead. Across the street, with only a few stray cattle loping between them, Noah stood, tall and unbowed.

Unhurt as far as she could determine. And not alone. Thank the Lord.

Bat helped him guide several men who staggered, either dazed or injured, into the Dodge House Hotel. Intent on following him, she moved to the door, then stopped.

For the moment, Noah was safe, and she was the one who was alone. That hadn't happened since she'd dashed across the street, shrouded by the night and a storm. This was her one chance to ensure Noah stayed alive by returning to the Star and killing both Gertie and Cora.

Her mind balked at taking a life. Could she do it? She had little time to decide, but whatever came next she'd do better armed.

On the other side of the desk, a cabinet full of long, gleaming rifles drew her attention. She wouldn't get anywhere near Gertie or Cora carrying a weapon that big and brash. Her hand went to the pocket sewn into her skirt. Perfect for concealing a palm pistol.

The trunks in the bedroom might— Her shoulders sagged. She'd finished her search. She hadn't found any derringers. A rifle would have to do.

As she rounded the desk to collect one, she tried to ignore the knot in her gut. It grew in direct proportion to her dwindling odds of success. Leaving behind the last of her secrets might help Noah.

She paused when she reached the guns. She must do everything she could to increase the chances of his survival. The truth of Edward's death could not be buried with her. It must be committed to paper and left in her stead. In search of pen and paper, she opened the nearest desk drawer.

The derringer atop a pile of paper took her breath like an arm around her throat.

The floral scroll engraved on the barrel was unmistakable. Not so long ago, this miniature gun had threatened to finish her life when a card cheat's luck had ended. No different from Dodge's other ill-fated souls, Davenport's belongings had come to rest in the jail. The possibility that this tiny weapon might've been his only possession when he'd entered the Star made her limbs heavy as lead.

A life squandered. She straightened her spine. She would not waste what remained of hers.

She shoved the derringer into her pocket and dug through the drawer's contents. A plethora of wanted posters and notices passed through her fingers. Useless without pen and ink. She found the deed to her farm, didn't care, didn't stop. She tossed a spare set of jail keys on the desk. Useless as well, now that she was out of the cell. Her hand reached the bottom of the drawer and a dainty, smooth-sided box with a metal handle.

She lifted it out and blinked in disbelief. In her hand hung an object even more familiar than the derringer in her pocket.

The tortoiseshell writing case was most memorable for its push-button release mechanism that had hindered the majority of attempts to open it. Sometimes the most effective lock wasn't a lock at all, but a fussy fastener, that even after one learned its idiosyncrasies, must be approached with care. Like the case's owner, Orin.

Had Masterson or one of Dodge's other lawmen needed writing materials as well? Had they attempted to open the case, failed and deposited it in the desk to try again later? Only for it to be buried under a growing heap of paper and forgotten?

A shiver crept up her spine. This desk held the ghosts of too many who'd departed Dodge, both dead and alive. She shook her head, casting out the somber memories, so she might focus her mind and her fingers on the fastener.

When it opened, a folded slip of paper tumbled off the inkwells inside. Across its surface two words had been scrawled with a hurried but familiar flair: *My friends.*

She groped for the chair behind her and collapsed onto it. But her vision and hands, free of the illness that had previously plagued her, remained steady as she unfolded the paper and read.

> *Gertie forces me to pen a vile tale. Unaware, for every lie on one letter, I scribble a truth here. Gertie means to kill me. She has my father's watch, my mother's box. Says she'll hide them in her piano, think of me every time it's played, and laugh. Cannot bear the idea.*
>
> *Find them. Steal them back.*

Orin, Sadie—my friends whom I cherish more than any possession—I'm betting on you. Don't let Gertie win.
      Edward

Her stomach did a slow roll. All this time, Edward's beloved heirlooms had been in the Star—under her fingers, never far from her thoughts. How many times had she listened to someone playing that piano and wished it were Edward? Or reached for the piano's sturdy frame while struggling to find the strength to honor her promise to him?

She'd never had the notion to look inside.

A strength of purpose swelled inside her, making her heart beat strong and steady. Finally, she'd learned the location of Edward's watch and jewelry box...and she had his letter. The letter he'd mentioned when she found him dying. She'd assumed he referred to the suicide note he'd held. She hadn't paid close enough attention.

This time she did. She reread what he'd written, searching out one line in particular: *Gertie means to kill me.*

Edward had named his murderer, written it down for all to see.

She leaped to her feet. She must show the letter to Noah. It'd buy both their freedom and their futures. Then no one else need die. She didn't have to kill Gertie or Cora.

Clutching the letter to her heart, she ran to the window in search of him. She found him embarking on his return journey across the road. Never had the sight of him brought her more joy.

Not once had he let her down—a woman for sale in a saloon. His herd trampling her farm was a thing of the past. She'd forgiven him days ago. He hadn't meant for it to happen. He truly regretted the loss and pain he'd caused.

She couldn't even rail at him for her more recent gripes:

his bargain with her farm or him locking her so many times in the cell behind her that every corner and cranny had become as familiar as those at the Star.

In the end, he helped her regain her health. He'd made her smile. He was honest and protective to a fault and...she loved him for it.

Her heart skipped a beat. She loved him for more than that, so much more. Dear Lord, how she loved him. And now he wasn't more than a dozen strides away, while she held the means to get them both safely out of Dodge.

A lanky man, collar turned up, hat pulled low, passed her window in a blur. He stopped on the other side of the door.

She jerked back and forgot how to breathe.

The locked door latch shook but held. Then footsteps echoed down the boardwalk. Running away. Fast.

Exhaling in relief, she pressed her cheek to the glass and peered outside along the wall. The man darted into the nearest alley. His long coat billowed behind him before he vanished. Who was he? Why had he attempted to get inside the jail in plain sight of Noah returning across the street?

More footsteps pounded up the steps onto the board-walk. Noah stood outside the door, scowling at the alley where the man had disappeared—while two others closed in on him from behind.

A cry of warning rose on her lips.

One of them struck Noah on the head. He fell to his knees. The men dragged him down the boardwalk and into the alley where the first had gone.

Fear and anger made her reach for the nearest weapon. Her hand halted on her skirt pocket. Three men required three bullets. Davenport's derringer was only a double barrel. She scrambled around the desk, picked the padlock on the cabinet and yanked the closest rifle from inside.

Muffled voices came from the back alley. Rough voices taunting someone. And laughing. Her chest squeezed tight as a steel trap. Noah was out there. He needed rescuing. What if she botched her attempt? She hadn't shot a gun since she'd left her farm. Noah needed a hard-nosed gunfighter like Bat.

But what would happen to Noah in the time it took her to sprint across the street and fetch the marshal?

Her gaze dropped to the rifle in her hands, and Edward's letter as well. She'd forgotten she held it. Edward's words guaranteed her and Noah's futures. But what good was any future if Noah died before she could use the letter?

Hide it. Use the rifle and derringer to save Noah.

But if she failed with force, she'd need the letter. She could only use it once. Unlike the many weapons in the cabinet, there was only one letter.

A solution rose in her mind, loud and clear. So did the rapid thumps and grunts of men fighting. Or men hitting Noah, hurting him.

The chances of them both surviving what lay ahead were slim. The breath she released was quick and full of acceptance. Once again, she must make the most of a losing hand. Time to gamble and bluff and lie.

The truth must remain in the jail. Damned if she let it die with her. On the nearest piece of paper, she wrote the best of her truths. Then she gathered what she needed, left behind what she must—and opened the back door.

CHAPTER 19

*N*oah's head thudded like a caved-in water well. Clapboard walls, plus one of brick, spun overhead. In the farthest heavens, the midday sun made stars flash in his eyes. Or was it the devil punching him in the gut? Or the fiend's cohort choking him from behind with an arm tight as a noose? The stranglehold vanished.

He plummeted to the earth like a dead man.

A booted foot connected with his side. Razor-sharp pain lanced his ribs, reminding him he was still alive. He struggled just to breathe.

"Reckon you broke a few ribs with that kick, Vince." The voice came from a tall, thin silhouette in a long coat—the man who'd tried to open the jailhouse door. Accompanied by two broader shadows, the man circled him. "If not, don't worry. We've got time to bust all of the deputy's bones."

The trio continued discussing how they'd make him hurt. He'd been a fool to let them get the jump on him. Intent only on reaching Sadie, he'd rushed forward without thinking. He hadn't seen his attackers coming.

"He ain't always been a deputy. Not so high 'n mighty now, are you, Ballantyne?"

Recognition lifted his head. He knew this voice. His vision cleared enough to make out the cowhand named Miller who'd manhandled Sadie at the Star the day of his return. Thank God, she was locked safe inside the jail. Getting beaten in an alley he could accept. Seeing Sadie in the hands of these ruffians would've been more than he could take.

Miller lifted his foot.

To hell with taking anything.

He dodged the kick and seized the man's ankle. Employing all of his weight, he twisted sideways.

"Sonuva—!" Miller crashed to the ground, where he curled into a whimpering ball around his knee. "You—broke—my leg."

Noah grunted. He doubted he'd be so lucky. At best, he'd torn muscle, and the coward wouldn't be able to kick someone on the ground again.

That didn't stop one of his cohorts from snaring Noah around the neck and yanking him onto his knees. The man named Vince stepped into his line of view and drew back his fist.

"Wait." Seething like a hornet's nest, Miller levered himself up and hobbled toward them. Amazing what anger could do. "Get outta my way, Vince." He shoved his friend aside and backhanded Noah across the face.

Without the force to remove him from the lanky man's chokehold, more incentive was required. He spat in Miller's face. The right hook that followed did the trick. Pretending he couldn't move as he sprawled on the ground wasn't difficult.

Shuffling footsteps neared. "Hope I shattered your friggin' jaw."

He lashed out with both feet and struck a pair of nearby shins. A body landed beside him, and the whimpering started again.

"My jaw's fine." Although the part of him in question hurt like the blazes, he was thankful it functioned well enough to let him speak. "How's your leg?"

Miller writhed on the ground. "You're dead," he vowed as he fumbled to draw a revolver tucked under his belt.

Noah groped for his holster. Found it empty. The revolver Miller intended to use on him was his own.

Vince halted Miller with a hand on his arm. "The madam said we can't kill him. Not until—"

"I don't give a fuck what she said." Despite his declaration, Miller released his revolver. "But you and Hank better do as I say." He jabbed his finger at Noah. "Break his legs. Break his head. Break all of him!"

"Raise another hand, or foot, against him and you'll lose it." The voice, followed by the scrape of a gun being cocked, came from the direction of the jail.

From its doorway, Sadie aimed a Winchester at the closest man looming over Noah. The long-barreled rifle made her appear small. But her stance was rock steady as she stared down the weapon's formidable length. Unblinking. Determined.

The sight stole the air from Noah's lungs. "Who released you?" His voice came out no louder than a squawk.

"I did. I don't require a key, but you may. Everything you need is inside."

"You're not." Gritting his teeth against the pain, he rolled onto his hands and knees. "Go back. Now."

"We'll go together, after they leave."

"She—" Vince's tone rose with disbelief, "—ain't the one we're meant to collect, is she?"

"See any other whores coming out of that jail," Miller shot back.

Vince beckoned her forward. "Hand over that buffalo shooter before you hurt yourself."

Noah pushed himself up. Getting even one foot under him left him puffing like a freight train. He paused to gather his strength.

Sadie had yet to move. "Only ones I'm gonna hurt are you and your friends."

"Yer bluffin'." The man named Hank edged closer to her.

Vince did the same. "Yeah, you don't look meaner than a songbird with her feathers ruffled."

Noah braced himself to tackle the men.

"A year ago, I nearly put a bullet in the lawman you've been beating. He hadn't riled me a tenth as much as you lot."

If the situation hadn't been so dire, Noah might have smiled. Instead, he focused on channeling all of his energy into the impending brawl.

"Ain't you full of vinegar." Miller's glare raked her. "The madam said you was better. From where I stand, I agree. You look ready to tumble."

"*Never*." Noah surged to his feet.

Hank spun toward him, fist raised. "Time for you to go down 'n *never* get up."

The gun blast roared in Noah's ears. Then the retort ricocheted off the walls. Hank's gangly frame folded up and sank to the ground. Blood seeped through the fingers he clutched to his shoulder.

Sadie cocked the Winchester and swung the barrel toward Vince. "Your friend should've heeded my warning."

Her voice was hard as flint. "You gonna gather him and Miller and leave, or should I unload this rifle in you?"

A blur of crimson taffeta and powdered flesh jumped toward Sadie. Noah's shout of warning turned into a howl when he glimpsed a flash of silver in the madam's hand. Fury and disbelief and horror pummeled him in waves.

Gertie's blade came to rest against Sadie's throat. "Drop the rifle."

Sadie did as told. Her hands drifted downward.

"Keep your hands up." Gertie fished a derringer out of Sadie's skirt and pocketed it in her own. "Even when hidden, a Double Ace creates an unmistakable outline. Or at least it does for me. But you pack of imbeciles..." She surveyed her men.

Miller lay on the ground, cradling his knees. Hank had transferred a neckerchief from his throat to his shoulder wound. Vince stood unaffected as long as one didn't count his red-faced and guilty expression.

"Blind, brainless and next to useless," Gertie muttered. "John's gonna answer for disappearing and making me turn to you lot." She thrust her chin at the last man standing. "Tell me your name again."

"Vince."

"Well, Vince? What're you waiting for? Show me your mettle. Pick up that rifle."

The man scooped up the weapon.

"Shoot him," Sadie yelled, "and I'll make sure you're hanged for two murders—Noah's and Edward's."

Gertie's breath hissed between her teeth like she'd been the one to get shot.

The Winchester wobbled in Vince's grasp. "I don't know anyone named Edward."

"But the madam does." Sadie drew a folded paper from

her other pocket. She held it up for Gertie to see. "Before Edward died, he wrote how he caught you stealing."

Sadie's face was unreadable, but Noah felt his eyes grow as wide as Gertie's.

"You orchestrated a tragedy," Sadie continued in a voice that matched her impassive expression, "that the townsfolk would gobble up—a gambler faced with the stigma of a notorious and painful death ends his own life. But for every lie you forced from him, he wrote a truth."

"You're the one who's lying." Despite the madam's adamant tone, a frown marred her brow. "Edward's death was a suicide. The entire town of Dodge knows that, including you. You found him."

"I found him lying in a pool of blood," her voice finally broke, "holding a suicide note and a pistol. He wasn't dead. He asked me to take back what his murderer had stolen. On that account, I've spent months failing him until today when I found this letter in a writing set made of tortoiseshell."

Gertie's gaze locked on the letter.

"You remember the set," Sadie continued in a hushed voice. "You watched Edward use it to pen his suicide note. What you didn't do was watch him close enough. He often remarked that the best gamblers excelled at sleight of hand. Shall I read the part detailing where you planned to stash your plunder?"

Gertie continued staring at the letter. Noah couldn't look away either.

Sadie's grip on the paper tightened. "He wrote: *Gertie has my father's watch, my mother's jewelry box. She says she'll hide them in her piano and—*"

"Enough!" The madam's order was more of a high-pitched howl than a word. It raised the hair on the back of

Noah's neck. Gertie's mouth opened and closed, whether searching for air or for words, he wasn't sure.

Vince kept the Winchester on Noah, but he edged away from Gertie. "You all right, ma'am?"

"The girl's lies die in this alley," Gertie growled. "Shoot them both."

"What about Marshal Masterson?" Sadie blurted.

Noah's stomach heaved with self-reproach. Sadie hoped Bat was coming, that Noah had organized a fallback plan to save her. She was unaware that when he'd left the Dodge House, Bat had said he was going for reinforcements. He wouldn't return in time.

"Masterson can't help you." Gertie's words echoed his thoughts. "When he finds you gone from his jail, he'll hope you fled town together. He'll never be certain, but he—" Gertie gasped as if she'd been struck. "He's seen that letter?"

Bat hadn't. There hadn't been time. Hopefully, the madam would remain too distracted shepherding John's replacements to realize her error.

Sadie wore her most unreadable poker face. "Bat said he'd search your piano as soon as he fetched a man named Earp to cover his back."

So, she'd heard about Bat's connection to Wyatt Earp. Bless her talent for shoring up lies with nuggets of truth.

It was his turn to do the same. "Better hightail it back to your saloon and rid your piano of any incriminating evidence before Bat gets there."

Gertie cast him a withering glare before gesturing to the letter in Sadie's hand. "I'm not leaving until that letter's destroyed. Hand it over."

"Let me quicken your departure." Sadie ripped the letter into tiny pieces and tossed them into the air. They fluttered like early snow, unexpected and disconcerting. Then the wind caught them and blew them away. "Leave now and you've won."

The tilt of Gertie's head turned pensive. "Have I?"

"Without the letter and Edward's possession, it's my word against yours. I won't say anything if you let us go."

"Your yap ain't my major concern. You were easy to control." Gertie thrust her chin in Noah's direction. "Until you came along. One sure way to guarantee both your silences. The girl stays with me until I've put my affairs in order."

"The hell she will," he hollered.

Gertie's glare swept her men. "Why aren't you beating him unconscious so we, and everyone else in Dodge, can't hear him bellowing like a bull elk in rut?"

Clutching his injured shoulder, Hank scrambled to his feet. Noah widened his stance, preparing for the man to charge.

"No!" Sadie reached for Noah. The madam's grip on her arm kept her from going anywhere. "Isn't it quicker to lock him in the jail?"

Astonishment made his jaw drop.

Her outstretched hand fell to her side. "You'll find the keys on him."

"Sadie." Her name left his lips like a plea. "I can't let you go with her."

She raised her chin. "You can. It's for the best. You'll understand when I'm gone."

"You won't be gone for long."

"And I won't be far." Her voice wavered, then firmed again. "Just across the street at the Star."

The need to keep her by his side coiled his muscles tight. *Patience. Now's not the time to attack. Not with a cutthroat madam and three hired thugs hovering so close to Sadie.*

"Gentleman," Gertie addressed her men. "Disappointing though it is, Deputy Ballantyne must live. As the girl suggests, lock him in his own jail. Kill him and you won't be paid. But if either of them resists—" the madam's gaze slid to Sadie, "—you have my permission to continue her lover's beating."

SADIE SWALLOWED her cry of protest. As soon as the men left Noah locked inside the jail, he'd be safe. When his focus veered from fighting to escaping, she hoped he'd once again question how she'd got out. If he searched his cell for the answer, he'd find what she'd hidden.

His glare made her heart ache with new misgivings. It might be best if he stayed in jail until Bat returned and released him. At least then Noah wouldn't be alone when he raced into the Star in search of her.

Here she had no doubts. Noah would not abandon her. He'd come after her. She wanted to give him every advantage when he did.

All of her cards were on the table, either overturned like the last of Edward's secrets or soon to be revealed. She'd played the letter with as much sleight of hand as she could wield. Edward would've applauded her all-in attitude. But all she cared about was protecting Noah.

The next moments would determine if her gamble paid off.

Vince kept the Winchester trained on Noah while Hank bent his lanky body to help Miller to his feet.

"Prop me against the wall," Miller instructed. "I'll need yer help getting back to the Star after you secure the bastard inside."

Hank did as told. Then he accepted the revolver Miller pulled from his belt and offered him.

Noah ignored the weapons Vince and Hank pointed at him. He stared at her for a heartbeat longer before disappearing through the jail's door. He took the warmth of the day with him.

The desolation made her wrap her arms around herself.

Gertie pushed her down the alley leading onto Front Street. The street's lively, everyday bustle pierced the chill numbing her. The crowd might offer a chance to escape—as soon as they were an adequate distance from Noah and the jail.

She scrutinized Gertie from the corner of her eye. The madam didn't break stride as she ushered Sadie across the street on the shortest path to the Star.

"Unbelievable, him writing that letter." Gertie's free hand, the one that didn't shackle Sadie's arm, remained hidden from view in the crimson fall of her skirt.

Odds were high she held her knife there, at the ready.

"Should've watched him closer," the madam muttered. "Remember a disturbance in the hall. Stole my attention for a few seconds. Stupid to give a cardsharp even one. Played me like a fiddle." Gertie huffed and shook her head. "Won't happen again."

Despite the madam's vow, Sadie's hopes clung to the letter, and the salvation it might bring. Back in the jail, if the men had incarcerated Noah and left—

"Well, if it isn't Madam Garrett and her cosseted ward," a man proclaimed loudly from behind them.

Gertie spun around, jerking Sadie with her.

Robert Wardell stood before them, arms folded over his tailored jacket and waistcoat. "Imagine my surprise to witness you crossing the thoroughfare. The vigor of your pace is what I find most remarkable, though." Beneath his lofty top hat, his frown deepened into a scowl. "When applied to the subject of Miss Sadie's health, it confirms my every suspicion of deceit."

Sadie's entire body went stiff, begging her to put as much distance between her and the cattle baron as she could. Gertie's hold on her arm prevented her from obeying.

A wicked gleam lit the madam's eyes. She lifted her hand from her skirt and, minus the knife, laid her palm over her heart. "Fear no falsehoods when I say the girl is now fit for service. Why else would I be returning her to the Star with such enthusiasm? You can have her tonight."

Wardell's usually insipid stare pierced her, cruel as the devil's pitchfork. He took a step closer. "I'll have her now."

When she shrank back, he smirked. Curse him for taking pleasure in her vulnerability. She drew herself up as tall as she could stand.

"You shall have all you desire. But first grant me a moment to—" Gertie gestured to Sadie's hair and dress, "—prepare the girl for your attentions." She urged Sadie toward the Star again. "We look forward to seeing you later."

Sadie's alarm receded. She didn't plan on being at the Star for Wardell's return. But instead of leaving, Wardell followed them. Her unease came crashing back.

The tension in her pursuer grew as well. He thrust out his chin. The usually deficient part of his countenance didn't waver when he raised it even higher. "I'm not waiting."

Gertie's lips pressed so tight they went white, but only for a moment. She gave Wardell her best smile. "I'm delighted, as always, by your eager patronage. Rest assured, the delay will be brief. I must attend to a small matter first."

Wardell spat out a curse. "You have another buyer

waiting in your saloon. You intend for me to return to a bidding war exactly like last year with Edward."

Sadie hoped Gertie had something similar in mind. Any delay added to the distraction of moving Edward's possessions would work in Sadie's favor. She needed time. She needed to stall Gertie until Noah arrived at the Star, hopefully with reinforcements.

She glanced over her shoulder in search of him.

Gertie jerked her to face forward and quickened their pace. "You are mistaken, Mr. Wardell. The matter I refer to is a personal one. Nevertheless, it cannot wait."

"Then I'll *wait* inside," Wardell snapped.

Gertie halted at the base of the saloon steps. "What of payment? You're fully aware I never hand over any girl without funds up front. No bidding war awaits, but my price will be steep. Visit your bank. I'm sure you won't be gone long."

Just long enough for Gertie to empty her piano. Sadie's search was at an end...as soon as Wardell departed. Instead, he reached into a pocket sewn into the silk lining of his jacket and extracted a wad of money.

The sight wrenched a gasp from deep inside her.

"I've come from the bank securing funds for new hired hands." Wardell waved the bills. "Three hundred should more than cover her cost."

Gertie's eyes narrowed. "For one night."

"Agreed, if I can take her to my hotel where I won't be interrupted."

Sadie leaned toward the Star. She must stay at the saloon. If she didn't, Noah wouldn't know where to look for her.

Wardell held the money out to Gertie. "Do we have a deal?"

The instant Gertie released her to take the bills, Sadie bolted up the saloon steps. Gertie wouldn't let Wardell follow her inside. She had to reach—

Something snared her skirt and yanked hard. She toppled backward. The street struck a bruising blow on her backside.

"You ain't going inside, girl." Money clutched in her fist, the madam stared down at her from the Star's top step.

Wardell's open hand descended toward Sadie's head.

"Return her too roughed up to work," Gertie growled, "and I'll require double the funds. If she dies—"

"She won't." Wardell's hand landed in her hair and hauled her to her feet. "At least not before I've slaked my needs."

Ignoring the pain knifing her scalp, she gritted her teeth and focused on breaking free. Only the crowded street offered salvation now. When she lost her tether again, she must lose its owner as well—in the throng. Finally, the townsfolk would help her.

Gertie cleared her throat. "Last year while chasing your needs, you nearly planted two of my girls in the boneyard."

Sadie couldn't stop the tremors that invaded her entire body.

Wardell pulled her head back so he could scan her face. "A single night won't be adequate. Not with this one. So she'll be alive come morning."

"Better be." Gertie shook her head. "But jawin' about it won't help. Take her away."

Holding her hair tight, Wardell pushed her ahead of him along the street. She dug her heels into the dirt. He twisted his grip until she couldn't see past the tears clouding her eyes. When she stumbled into a walk, his hold eased along with the pain. Wardell's laughter warned that her reprieve would be short-lived.

Not a soul on the street moved to help her. No one even glanced her way.

She scoured her brain for a new escape plan.

Wardell drew her closer to his side. His breath, hot and fast, assaulted her ear and annihilated her ability to think. "You and I are in uncharted territory." His voice buzzed with excitement. "But there is only one path before us. Bend or I'll break you. Either way, I win."

CHAPTER 20

*N*oah halted two strides inside the jail's door. *Not a chance in hell I'll let Sadie go back to the Star,* he vowed.

He needed his jailers close for what came next. Strike fast. Don't stop. Not until—

Vince's pilfered Winchester poked his back. The door clicked shut. He spun, elbowed past the rifle, and punched. Vince's nose crumpled under his fist with a satisfying crunch. Arms and Winchester flailing, the man toppled backward onto Hank.

"My shoulder," Hank yelped, struggling to shield his injury.

Using the rifle in Vince's grasp, Noah pinned both men against the door. In Hank's hand, the revolver he'd received from Miller—after Miller had taken it from Noah—cleared Vince's shoulder. The barrel pointed at Noah's face.

He seized Hank's wrist and yanked upward. Together they pistol-whipped Vince. The man slumped unconscious between them. Noah fought Hank for possession of the pistol. He also strove to keep Vince's dead-weight between them.

Hank lurched forward. His head struck Noah's with a walloping crack. Shards of piercing light stabbed his eyes and skull. His opponents' combined bulk bore down on him. They all crashed to the floor. As they did, Noah rolled, battling to break free of the tangle of limbs. He came out on top.

Victory roared in his veins. He drew back his fist to knock out the last man keeping him from Sadie.

Behind him, the door squeaked open. Instinct sent him leaping sideways. Not soon enough. Pain exploded in the back of his head. The room spun out of focus. He hit the floor.

A silhouette limped past him and reached down to help Hank to his feet. "Good thing I waited outside."

"What took you so long?" Hank demanded. "He almost killed us."

"Count yourself lucky I chose to hobble in to save yer hides."

Several ringing slaps came from nearby. "Wake up, Vince."

"Yeah," Miller growled. "We need to leave before I give in to temptation 'n knock this bastard's head off his shoulders."

"Don't," Vince rasped. "I wanna get paid."

"Then get the hell up and help us put him in his cell."

Noah's pulse thudded in his ears along with the foot-steps approaching him. He blinked away the blood trickling down his face, straining to see. Rough hands seized him by the arms and lugged him a short distance before dumping him on the floor again.

"The girl said he had the keys on him."

He couldn't let them lock him in. He lurched up only to

have them shove him down, and hold him there while they searched his pockets. Then their hands retreated, and so did their footsteps. The cell door clanged shut, and a key grated in the lock.

Noah found the strength to scramble to his feet. Too late.

On the other side of the bars, Miller tossed the ring of keys in the air. The jangle of brass grated on his nerves. "You want these? Too bad. I'm keeping them. Let's go, boys."

Clutching various body parts, the trio filed out the back door and closed it behind them. The turn of another lock warned that any help wouldn't reach him without the spare set of keys. Of which there was only one. Bat had it.

He seized the bars and shook them. By now Gertie would've crossed the street and hauled Sadie back inside the Star. He couldn't stop the madam. He couldn't reach Sadie. Not unless he could tear down a metal cage.

He did his best to do that. When he failed, he slumped against the bars—solid and unforgiving as the keys the men had taken from him. No victory, no escape, no redemption. Not without those keys. But Sadie hadn't needed them.

He raised his head. She'd got out. She'd said she'd released herself. How?

He pivoted in a slow circle. The only thing inside was the cot. He ran his hands over the frame and the mattress. Nothing looked out of the ordinary. No springs or parts missing. Nothing that might pry open a door or a lock.

What else had Sadie said? *Everything you need is inside.*

He surveyed his cell again. Flakes of limestone and brick dusted the floor by the back wall, reminders of Sadie's angry assault with her spoon after he and Bat had imprisoned her, before her withdrawal symptoms caused her collapse.

He traced the bricks she'd gouged. One shifted under his fingers. He pried part of it loose and found a roll of paper with surprising weight. A ring of keys slid out onto his palm. Keys identical to the ones Gertie's men had taken from him.

Where had Sadie found it? Why wrap it in ink-smudged paper? His blood raced. She'd left him a note? He unrolled the paper and found the words: *My friends.*

Disappointment riddled his heart. Silly to wish any letter Sadie had left would be addressed to him. He flipped over the paper.

His lips parted in astonishment. This was the letter Sadie had mentioned in the alley, Edward's last words detailing Gertie's sins. Sadie hadn't destroyed the letter after all. She'd pulled off a masterful bluff. A dangerous one as well.

He stared at the lines above Edward's signature: *I'm betting on you. Don't let Gertie win.*

Sadie was betting on him as well. That's why she'd suggested his incarceration in this cell. So he'd find this letter. She'd said everything he'd need was inside. He still disagreed. She wasn't here by his side, safe and smiling. He hauled in a deep breath. She soon would be.

When he moved to return the letter to its hiding place, more writing below Edward's name caught his attention. Lines written with a different hand. The script was equally messy, probably scrawled as hurriedly and smeared from being folded before the ink could dry. In fact, the ink was still damp.

He squinted at the first word: *Noah.*

A jolt of disbelief made him flinch. So did the clatter of the keys as they fell from his fingers onto the floor. He clutched the letter with both hands. Sadie had written to him like he'd hoped. With his heart in his throat, he read her words.

Noah. For too long I've thought only of revenge and freedom. Now I hold Edward's letter with the lie he wanted revealed. But all I can think of is the truth I've hidden in my heart—for too long as well. In case something happens, I need to leave these words behind. I won't let the best truth I've ever known die with me. I will always love you.

Sadie.

Her revelation left him reeling. She loved him? Could it be true? Could he be that lucky? Carefully, he folded the letter and put it in his pocket. He wasn't leaving behind something so precious.

Then he snatched the keys from the floor. He couldn't get out fast enough.

Finally, the cell door swung opened. It banged against the steel cage like a starter's pistol. He leaped forward, didn't break stride even as he snatched a rifle from the open cabinet. He raced for the front door, and for Sadie waiting for him across the street.

CHAPTER 21

ardell pushed Sadie inside the Great Western Hotel and across its lobby. She hadn't been there since the day Edward had died—another day when Gertie had come to take her back to the Star.

For five months, she'd lived with Edward in his private rooms upstairs, lulled into a false security. Today, the lobby's warm walnut paneling, serene landscape paintings, and glowing brass lamps did nothing to calm her fears. Wardell's relentless hold reminded her how swiftly one's plans, and one's life, could be derailed.

If Noah found the keys and Edward's letter, he'd be free and have the means to protect them both from Gertie. He'd also have her confession of love.

How would he react? She couldn't guess the answer to that question, but she had no doubt he'd come after her. Unfortunately, he'd look for her at the Star, not here at the Great Western.

He couldn't help her.

Her pulse pounded with no small amount of dread. No

good would come from cowering in the shadows. She must fight her way back into the light, back to the Star and Noah.

But how? She scanned the lobby. The one occupant, the clerk behind the front desk, ducked his head and pretended an immense interest in his ledger. Wardell jerked her to a halt at the bottom of the stairs.

Midway up, Cora blocked their way. The woman's glare skewered her. "What's she doing here?"

"Replacing you," Wardell replied. "You can leave. Go back to the Star."

A winning hand lay in Sadie's grasp if she dared to gamble again. "Tell No—" She sealed her lips. If she asked Cora to inform Noah of her whereabouts, the woman would do the opposite to spite her. "Tell no one you saw me here."

Towing Sadie behind him, Wardell climbed the stairs. "Get out of my way. I don't need you anymore."

Cora swore under her breath. If she went back to the Star, cursing Sadie's name, Noah might overhear.

"Looks like you're no longer anyone's favorite," Sadie said as Wardell pushed past Cora. "Not even Gertie's."

"I don't give a damn about her." Cora's tone was clipped, but not nearly angry enough.

She needed Cora as livid as she'd been during their last conversation, the one where Cora lost control when she'd talked about— "Orin."

Cora's eyes flashed. So did her hand. She grabbed Sadie's wrist, halting her ascent and Wardell's as well. "What about him?"

"Gertie stole Edward's possessions and hid them in her piano after she staged his suicide. I wonder if Orin left town fearing he'd be next."

Cora's grip on her wrist tightened, making her gasp.

"Stop damaging my property." Wardell pried open Cora's fingers. "That's my privilege, not yours. Return to the Star." He shoved Cora in the direction he'd instructed.

Cora rocked back on her heels and latched onto the railing to keep from falling. Her attention, however, remained riveted on Sadie as Wardell yanked her up the remaining steps toward the long corridor of the hall.

Sadie craned her neck, trying to keep sight of Cora. The woman continued staring at Sadie. She hadn't moved. But she clutched the railing as if her whole world were crumbling beneath her feet. And still, she didn't move.

In comparison, Wardell was a locomotive at full steam. He hauled Sadie down the hallway. Her last hope that Noah might learn her whereabouts vanished along with the sight of Cora.

She was alone with Wardell. Soon she'd be alone with him in a locked room.

CLUTCHING the rifle in one hand, Noah reached for the jailhouse door with the other. He froze with his palm hovering over the handle. The last time he'd rushed to Sadie's rescue, he'd made a muck of things. He'd been hauled into an alley, beaten until his head and ribs ached, then locked in his own jail cell. He'd failed Sadie.

If their enemies planned to ambush him outside, he'd fail her again.

He sidestepped to the window and scanned the street. His gaze halted on the Star, hoping for a glimpse of Sadie there. Two saloon girls pushed through the swinging doors and stationed themselves in front of the entrance. Neither woman was Sadie.

A cowboy strutting down the street paused to converse with them. Their postures remained stiff and uninviting. Probably the first time they'd acted this way in the face of an interested customer. The man's swagger deflated. Several abrupt words, and hand gestures, were exchanged before he moved on.

If Gertie's hired thugs weren't on the street, then more than likely they were inside the Star. Anyone with injuries like theirs couldn't stand guard without attracting unwanted attention. They'd need a doctor.

He searched the street again. Sure enough, Doctor Rhodes strode toward the Star with his familiar rolling pace that consumed the distance between him and his destination.

Noah sprinted out the back door and down the alley. His head pounded like the recent cattle stampede, like the one from his nightmares. His brother's face flashed in his mind. Falling. Fast. He stumbled the final steps without seeing his surroundings.

Using the nearest wall to prop himself up, he sucked in a deep breath. The twinge in his side helped clear the throbbing in his head. He had to stay focused if he wanted to save Sadie.

He also had to hurry.

Flattening his spine against the wall, he scuttled sideways until he stood an arm's reach from Front Street. A continuous stream of people flowed by, but not the one he needed. Not until a hunched man carrying a beat-up case appeared.

Noah grabbed his arm and yanked him into the alley.

"What in tarnation—?"

Ignoring his aches and pains, Noah pressed the struggling man against the wall. "Now's not the time to raise a ruckus and draw attention our way, Doc. I need your help."

Every part of Rhodes froze, except for his eyes, which assessed Noah's face before narrowing. "What happened to you, Deputy?"

So, he looked as rough as he felt. "I had a run-in with a trio of Gertie's men."

Even though they were out of sight of the Star, the doctor glanced in the saloon's direction. His eyebrows arched questioningly.

Noah nodded. "I'd bet my ranch that they're the same ones you've been summoned to patch up."

Rhodes snorted a laugh. "What'd you do to get them so riled?"

"They wanted Sadie to return to the Star. I said no."

"Was she injured as well?" Rhodes' voice dropped along with his jaw.

"Not when I last saw her." Worry that she might've been hurt since then made Noah's gut twist. "Doc, I need a favor. Can you—"

"*Last saw her?* They succeeded in taking her?"

Frustration and guilt added to the storm brewing inside Noah. "She went with them."

"That can't be right," Rhodes shot back, shaking his head. "Not now. Miss Sullivan wouldn't—"

"They threatened to put a bullet in me if she didn't cooperate." When Rhodes opened his mouth to comment again, Noah cut him off. "Let me finish. I'm short on time and resources. Sadie's at the Star, and Gertie's got a couple of her girls standing guard outside. I need someone to create a diversion while I cross the street and sneak in. After that, I could use that same someone's help inside as well."

Rhodes drew himself up. Without his customary hunch, he looked Noah straight in the eye. "Tell me what to do."

After he did, Rhodes headed toward Front Street, only pausing to call over his shoulder in a low voice, "Better clean yourself up. Otherwise, you aren't sneaking anywhere."

Ignoring the pain in his side, Noah shrugged out of his vest and wiped the garment over his face until it didn't come away with blood. Then he tossed the vest in the alley behind him and focused on the man continuing his journey up the street with a stride even swifter and more purposeful than before.

Rhodes drew even with the Star and the two women on its veranda. He kept going. The pair called out to him. He didn't stop. The women chased after him. They each grabbed an arm and tugged him toward the saloon. He resisted. The women pulled harder, their attention fixed on him, their backs to Noah.

Keeping his head down, he crossed the street. When he reached the boardwalk on the other side, he stayed close to the shop fronts as he approached the Star. The doctor continued to resist the two women, who continued to keep their backs to the Star and him.

Almost there, Doc. Just keep them busy a moment longer.

He stepped down into the alley beside the saloon—and came face to face with a towering stranger with eyes sharp as blue ice. The sun reflected off the pair of .45s the man held between them, glinting as deadly as his eyes.

Bat appeared by the man's side, his Colts drawn as well. "We were coming to get you."

Noah's relief turned to frustration when Bat gestured for them to follow him into the alley where they'd be out of sight. He did so reluctantly. He could use the law's help, but Sadie needed him now. He had to explain the situation fast.

Bat spoke before he could even open his mouth. "What on God's green earth did you do to your face?"

Noah waved his hand dismissively. "What happened to me isn't important." What Sadie had written at the bottom of Edward's letter was important. *In case something happens, I need to leave these words behind.* His hands tightened into fists. Nothing was going to happen to her.

"Noah, this here's Wyatt Earp." Bat inclined his head toward the man studying him with an unwavering intensity.

Wyatt holstered one .45. Keeping the other drawn and ready, he shook Noah's hand. "Glad we finally meet. Heard a lot about you."

"People in this town talk too much." Noah's frustration consumed every drop of his relief over finding Bat. He strode back toward Front Street.

"The trick is to only listen to half of what Bat says." Wyatt's voice came close behind him.

Noah glanced over his shoulder. Wyatt's blue eyes were steady, without a trace of the mischievous amusement that often beset Bat.

Noah nodded. "Wish I'd met you sooner. That tip would've come in handy during the last few weeks." He stopped short of Front Street and peered around the corner of the saloon. Bat and Wyatt did the same.

The women had linked arms with the doctor and were steering him toward the saloon.

Noah reevaluated his plan, adding Bat and Wyatt to the mix. "Bat, have you seen Sadie?"

"No." Bat gestured toward Rhodes. "What's the doc doing?"

"Creating a diversion."

Rhodes and his escort disappeared through the saloon doors.

"And what's he doing now?" Bat asked.

"He's our inside man. Gertie has—"

"Didn't know the doc had it in him." Bat snorted. "Happy to have him onboard, but what's our destination? We can't prove Madam Garrett started that stampede. We didn't witness her committing a crime."

"I watched her take Sadie."

The marshal's gaze cut to the jail. His jaw went hard as granite. "How many men did it *take* for her to remove Miss Sullivan from your care?"

"Three."

"Well, neither she nor her minions will have her for long." Bat glared at the saloon. "We'll arrest the madam for assault and kidnapping. The charges won't stick, but they'll gain Miss Sullivan's freedom."

"There's more." He told them about Edward's letter.

Bat released a low whistle.

Wyatt drew the .45 he'd holstered a minute ago. "She's gonna be mad as a badger when we barge in and ruin her plans."

"Odds are she'll have moved her loot, but she can't have taken it far." Bat set his foot on the Star's veranda, then paused and looked over his shoulder. "Wyatt, why don't you go in the back while me 'n Noah take the front?"

The lawman sprinted off.

Before Bat could turn back to the veranda, Noah laid a halting hand on his arm. "Best I go a different route, but first I need a favor."

Bat cocked an eyebrow. "What kind?"

"Sadie might be in her room upstairs. I took some hits to my ribs and need some help climbing. Can you give me a boost onto the balcony?"

Bat did as requested.

Ignoring his body's numerous complaints, Noah heaved himself over the balcony's railing, then crept toward Sadie's window. "Hold on. You'll be safe soon," he promised under his breath. But he couldn't shake the icy hand of fear that had hounded him since he'd allowed Gertie to take Sadie from his side.

What if he didn't reach her before the fears she'd expressed in her letter came true?

WARDELL HAULED Sadie down the Great Western's hall, only halting when they reached the last door at the far end of the corridor. It led into the best suite in the hotel, Edward's old residence. Keeping a tight hold on her, Wardell slipped a small but ornate key out of his waistcoat pocket.

She glanced over her shoulder. An insurmountable stretch of hallway stood between her and the stairs, and salvation. Any sounds coming from below were muffled.

Would anyone hear her when Wardell finally made her scream? Would anyone care?

The scrape of Wardell's key turning the lock shattered the quiet. A shiver of alarm unbalanced her, making it all too easy for Wardell to shove her inside the room. The door banged shut behind them with the finality of a death sentence.

Edward's former home remained unchanged, filled with heavy, masculine furniture in the finest polished wood, framed on two sides by tall windows draped in burgundy and gold brocade. Seeing the room again elicited a bone-chilling horror.

Don't look, she warned herself as Wardell pulled her across the room. But she couldn't stop her gaze from gravitating toward the desk, and the floorboards to its left. Someone had worked hard to scrub out the stain. Only a faint circle of reddish brown remained, marking the spot where she'd found Edward, his blood draining out of him along with his life.

Bile burned her throat. She lurched back only to have Wardell jerk her forward again. His mouth came down on hers.

She bit him. Hard. He released her with a shove that sent her sprawling onto the bed. She scrambled off the other side and retreated. She could do little more as Wardell herded her into a corner.

He laughed as he ran his thumb over his bloody lip with slow deliberation. "You'll pay extra for that."

Rigid with fear, she retreated as far from him as possible. A wall ended her flight.

Wardell removed his hat and tossed it aside. His jacket and waistcoat followed quickly. "It's time I showed you what your life should've been like for the past year." He dropped his trousers. His hand went to his erection. "After a couple of rounds on your back, you'll be docile enough to put even your mouth here." He released himself and reached for her instead.

Bracing her spine against the wall, she kicked him—exactly where he'd talked about her touching him, and with as much force as she could muster. His eyes bulged and his lips parted in a silent cry. She astounded herself as much as Wardell. She'd become increasingly stronger since she'd stopped taking her medicine.

He dropped like a thief when the hangman's trapdoor disappeared beneath his feet. Then he curled up in a whimpering ball, clutching his crotch.

She sprinted for the door. Elation gave her speed. Her

heart pounded with the joy of her impending freedom. She wrenched open the door.

Her chest squeezed tight, and she shuddered, feeling as if her blood were being drained from her.

The one thing that remained constant was the figure in the doorway. Handsome John stood between her and the hall. His giant frame blocked her escape, bleeding all hope dry.

CHAPTER 22

*C*rouched on the Star's balcony, Noah paused outside Sadie's yellow curtains and listened. All was silent behind the frayed but cheerful fabric. He parted the curtains with the barrel of his rifle.

The late afternoon light couldn't chase the shadows from the bedroom, but the furnishings remained so sparse that only a cursory glance was required to determine that no one was inside. It was the same room as before, but without Sadie present, he was swamped by a heavy sense of loss.

He climbed through the window. The first time he'd done so, he'd brought her breakfast. She'd been asleep with her red hair streaming across her pillow in wild disarray. Lord, he'd wanted to kiss her. Only her jitters had stopped him, that and his excuse that he was only there to help.

When had it all changed? When had he begun to love her?

Probably from the moment he'd found her singing on the Star's stage. He'd felt the same way as when he'd discovered her standing in the middle of his herd. *Hellfire.* She'd stolen his heart from the beginning. Why else had he come back to Dodge and refused to leave?

He had to find her.

Sighting down the barrel of his rifle, he cracked open the door. The hallway was empty. Muted conversation came from the far end, drifting up from the main floor. He crept toward the sound, and the words became clearer.

"Hold still," a disgruntled voice commanded.

"Yeow! You tryin' to kill me?"

Feminine laughter followed.

"You've fractured your tibia," the first man replied. Noah recognized the dry tone as Doc Rhodes'. "The best I can do is splint the bone and wrap it. Complaining won't help."

"Yeah, it ain't dignified to carry on so," a new voice added. "Yer overreacting."

"Shut yer hole! Or I'll bust one of yer legs 'n we'll see who's overreacting."

"Vince is right. He's got a broken nose and a lump on his head the size of a turkey egg. I got a bullet in my shoulder. But we ain't bellyaching like ol' biddies."

Adjusting his grip on his rifle, Noah stopped short of the landing's railing and peered down through the posts. Two saloon girls stood giggling behind their hands, while Hank and Vince crowded around Miller. He sat on a card table with his leg stretched out in front of him. The doctor wrapped the limb in white cloth.

"You callin' me a woman?" Miller reached for the revolver he'd stolen from Noah. "Maybe a bullet in yer other shoulder would shut yer trap."

"For the love of God, stop squirming and let me finish." Doctor Rhodes yanked on the bandages.

His patient complied amid a barrage of cursing.

Colts drawn, Bat burst through the front door. The

instant he cleared the landing above him, he fired a shot at the roof. The saloon girls screamed and scattered like a flock of sparrows. Wyatt raced in from the back, one .45 leveled at Hank, the other at Vince. The two men raised their hands in surrender.

Miller, still sitting on the table, did not. He drew his gun.

Noah sprinted across the landing to the top of the stairs. "Drop your weapon," he shouted.

The glare Miller leveled at him didn't bode well.

Noah's finger tightened on the trigger. "I said, drop it."

Miller hesitated.

Rhodes plucked the revolver from Miller's hand and aimed it at the man's heart. "I would advise against any sudden movements. I'm a doctor and know exactly where to put a bullet."

Noah scanned the room below, zeroing in on the corners and the shadows. Sadie wasn't here. Neither was Gertie. While the commotion below faded, the turmoil inside him flourished. A door on his left leading out onto the landing opened a hand's-breadth. Gertie peered out. When she saw him, she jumped back and shut the door.

Noah sprinted after her. The door's latch held fast. Stepping back, he kicked with all his might. The door exploded inward to hang splintered on its frame.

Gertie crouched by an iron safe. She tossed a small canvas bag inside, closed the door, and spun the lock. Then she rose to face him. Crossing her arms, she stared at him without blinking...but her eyes were wide.

The emptiness of the room sucked the hope from him again. "Where's Sadie?"

The madam's eyes narrowed and her brows drew together.

"Nothin' to say, Madam Garrett?" Bat asked from beside

Noah. "Better reconsider 'n cooperate. Tell us Miss Sullivan's location."

"You're both here because of *her*?" Gertie's tone rose high with incredulity.

"Don't worry. We'll discuss yer other crimes later. Right now, we're only interested in Miss Sullivan's whereabouts."

She grimaced. "Well, ain't that precious."

"Tell us where she is," Noah snapped.

"What if I don't feel like sayin'?"

He leveled his rifle at her.

Bat's hand gripped his forearm. "Hold up, Deputy. Killing her won't help us find Miss Sullivan."

"That's right." Gertie laughed. "I'm untouchable. But Sadie? She won't be so lucky."

Like a scavenger used to preying on weaknesses, the madam knew where to strike. Her words cut Noah to his core, shredding the fragile hope he'd been sheltering deep inside. He widened his stance, fighting to regain his balance. "What've you done?"

"I sold her—for the night."

A tremor ran through him, making the rifle in his hands shake. "You're lying. There wasn't time."

"I found a buyer crossing Front Street, an extremely eager one."

Rage made him dizzy and threatened to make his finger slip on the trigger. "Where *is* she?"

"Right now?" The corners of Gertie's mouth twitched. "On her back, I imagine."

A bullet was too quick. He'd rip her apart with his bare hands. He lunged for her. Only Bat's hold on his arm—a tether that hadn't been removed—stopped him.

Gertie's smile widened until she looked positively gleeful. "My buyer always was hot for her. I should've sold her to him, and not Edward, when I first got her."

Disbelief then anger clawed up his spine. He'd heard another person talk about wanting Sadie and being denied by Edward. He'd nearly punched the whoremonger when the man had stopped Sadie's buggy on Front Street and insulted her with lewd comments.

A growl shot from his throat. "You sold her to Wardell?"

Pressing her lips tight, Gertie ducked her head.

"Where are they?" he shouted.

The madam's gaze lifted along with her chin until they once more reached a confident angle. "What's the matter? Can't figure that out on your own? You lawmen, and everyone else in this town, are a pack of dimwits."

"We ain't stupid forever," declared a voice cold as January. Behind them, hands fisted at her sides, Cora stood in the doorway. She stalked forward, pushing past Noah and Bat without a word or a glance. She only stopped when she stood toe to toe with Gertie. "I know what you did to Orin. He's gone because of you."

Gertie snorted. "He's gone because he made poor choices."

"You as good as ran him out of town with your schemes an' your greed."

"Don't get all righteous on me, Missy. Orin betrayed us first. He wanted to leave town with Edward. He had to go. Good riddance, I say." Gertie flung her arms in the air as if she could cast out the man all over again. "Your brother was worthless."

"He wasn't to me!" Cora launched herself at the madam.

Noah helped Bat haul Cora, kicking and screaming, off the madam. While he'd like nothing better than to let the two women throttle each other, doing so wouldn't help him find Sadie.

Gertie dabbed her mouth. She glared at the blood that came away on her fingers. "You may've outlasted all my other sorry brats, but I'm done mollycoddling you. I don't give a whore's fuck about any nonsense you feel inclined to spout concerning Orin or anyone else."

Cora's spine snapped straight as a hickory switch. "You'll care when I say this." She finally faced Noah. "Your favorite whore is at the Great Western. You'll find her sharing her wares with Wardell in his room at the end of the hall. The same room where this murderous bitch—" she jerked her thumb over her shoulder at the madam, "—shot Edward Fiske."

Gertie sputtered with outrage.

Without a backward glance, Noah raced for the door. Sadie wasn't far away. He'd find her. He'd save her. He only needed a bit more time.

"You're too late," Gertie yelled after him. Bitterness made her voice brittle. "A year too late, by my reckoning. You can't turn back time. If you think otherwise, you're lying to yourself."

MID-FLIGHT FROM WARDELL'S ROOM, Sadie gaped up at Handsome John. Why was he here? Gertie's right-hand man stood equally frozen in the doorway. Then he blinked, and the spell was broken. His brow compressed into a scowl as if tightened by an invisible vise.

The expression was so familiar that Sadie's heart leaped with hope. Had Gertie changed her mind and sent John to bring her back to the Star?

Two men stood behind him. They pressed forward to ogle her with bold eyes. Even worse, they added another layer to the wall blocking her exit—while behind her, uneven footsteps shuffled closer. Wardell wheezed as if he'd been afflicted with the black lung. The men behind John craned their necks for a better look.

The skin between her shoulder blades prickled, begging her to turn and gauge Wardell's proximity. She concentrated on the doorway. If even the tiniest escape hole appeared, she must be ready.

"What happened to you, boss?" one of the men behind John asked. "You look like the dog that got the wrong end of the stick."

His words snatched the air from her lungs. *Boss?* That didn't sound right. If the men worked for Wardell, then why was John with them?

"What're you doing here?" Wardell croaked out.

"You told us to meet you here." The reply came without hesitation.

"I told you to wait for me *downstairs*."

"And you didn't show. Luckily, Cora came through the kitchen and told us you was back."

Cora? Sadie's head spun. The woman was supposed to be helping, not hindering Sadie's escape. Attempting to manipulate the woman hadn't been a wise idea after all. If it weren't for Cora, the doorway wouldn't be blocked. Sadie would be halfway down the Great Western's staircase.

John's expression retained its scowl. "Cora told us there'd been a change of plans. Said you wanted to talk to us in your room."

He worked for Wardell now? She'd never been able to outmaneuver John in the past. Her chances of escaping Wardell's room plummeted along with her stomach.

"Do I look like I want to talk to anyone right now?" Wardell's voice edged higher with each word.

John shrugged. "All I know is the last time we met, you was heading for the bank. What happened?"

"Nothing happened."

"But—" one of the men with John whined, "—we're still waiting for your orders."

"So go back downstairs and wait with the others!" Wardell's voice was now shrill.

The two men headed toward the stairs, grumbling. All Sadie caught were the words, "You'd better have our money."

A bolt of inspiration lifted her up on her toes as she strove to see the departing men over John's broad shoulders. "Do you mean the three hundred he gave Madam Garrett?"

The men crowded in behind John again. "You used our pay to buy a piece of tail, Wardell?"

"What if I did?" he replied. "It's my money."

John spat out a low, rasping sound, somewhere between a laugh and a growl. "I'm not much of a thinker, boys, but that don't seem right. So Mr. Wardell oughta make it up to us. He oughta pay us right now, or we ain't waiting no more."

Wardell swore. "Were you this goddamn particular when you worked for Garrett?"

"No. But then I only recently concluded I can't do the madam's bidding anymore. That's why I'm here, standing in this doorway wondering if I'm repeating the same mistakes."

"You'll get paid. *Later*." Wardell spat out the word. The puff of air that came with it brushed her hair.

Panic whipped her around. Wardell stood close enough for her to glimpse the sweat beading on his pasty brow. He wasn't looking at her, however, but over her head at John.

"Will I?" The question shot from John's mouth like a

storm brewing. "I learned my wages disappeared in the five minutes it took you to walk from the bank to this hotel. Might be a chance I'll never get paid."

Sadie couldn't stop herself from glancing at the door as she calculated her chances of squeezing by John. Same as the last time he'd stood between her and escape, he filled the doorway like an unmovable boulder.

Her chances were nil.

"Am I working for free now?" John asked. "If that's the case, I might as well throw in with whoever I damned well please. For instance, I could start working for you, Sadie."

Her gaze darted up to meet his. Fear that she might've misheard him rendered her speechless.

"This is ridiculous," Wardell hissed. "You cannot—"

"Tell me." John leaned down to her. "If you were my boss, what would you have me do?"

She found her voice. "Get me out of this room."

"Done." Spinning around, John pushed the two men behind him to the side, then grabbed her waist, lifted her through the doorway, and set her down in the hall.

Wardell and his two hired men now stood behind John's broad bulk. No one stood between her and the staircase. She backed toward it.

Wardell, trousers up but still without his jacket and waistcoat, pushed forward. John planted his palm on the doorjamb and stopped him from going any farther.

"Stand aside." Wardell's glare shifted from John to her. "She's mine."

She backed even faster down the hall.

"Sadie belongs to no one, and I've regretted every time I followed orders and kept her where she shouldn't have been. I won't be making those mistakes again."

"I paid good money for her."

John scoffed. "You used your men's pay. That's money poorly spent."

Red-faced with fury, Wardell fought to shove past John. When he failed, he thrust his hand as far as he could toward her.

Even though she was out of his reach, she jumped back. "Thank you for helping me, John. I'll find a way to repay you."

John shook his head. "The only payment I need is if you get the hell out of here."

She sprinted for the stairs.

"Remove him from my path—" Wardell's shout echoed along with her racing footsteps, "—and I'll pay you double what I promised."

Behind her, grunts and thumps told of Wardell's men's eagerness to now do his bidding. Ahead and somewhere below in the lobby, a door banged open, followed by many voices yelling.

She skidded to a halt and flattened her spine against the nearest wall. One stride from the top of the stairs. Out of sight of whoever created the ruckus below. Could one of them be Noah? Or were they the other hired men that Wardell said were waiting for him?

All she had to do to find out was take one more step and peek down the staircase. Uncertainty kept her pinned to the wall. The men below hadn't seen her. That gave her an edge.

"You can't go up. I won't allow any trouble in the hotel," a man she assumed was the clerk proclaimed in a lofty tone.

"Send them up!" Wardell's roar ripped down the hall.

John grappled with the two hired men, giving their boss sufficient time to slip by. John lurched after him and lost his footing. He hit the floor with the force of a toppled oak. As he did, he grabbed Wardell's legs. Wardell fell even harder. The floor shuddered under her feet.

Booted feet pounded up the stairs, adding to the floor's quaking.

She grabbed the handle of the nearest door. It didn't budge. The one directly opposite did. She sprang through, swung it shut, and wedged a nearby chair under the handle. With painstakingly slow steps, she retreated, intent on preserving the hush around her. She clamped her palm over her mouth for good measure.

On the other side of the door, running footsteps and angry shouts filled the hallway. Then the floor, and even the walls, shook as the fighting rose to a terrible din.

Expecting the door to open at any moment, she continued her retreat while her gaze clung to the thin wood separating her from the brawl. The backs of her legs hit something solid. Her hand left her mouth to shield herself from attack.

A brass tub sat at her feet. What little air remained in her lungs abandoned her in a whoosh. Her spine sagged, then snapped straight.

The game's not up. If you cannot escape, at least find a weapon to defend yourself.

She scanned the room's contents: a pair of brass tubs, a table with a pristine china washbasin and a wealth of perfectly aligned bottles, bowls, brushes and razors. She grabbed one and flipped it open.

The straight blade flashed. Pretty as a ribbon of silver. Sharp as death.

Did she have the gumption to sink it into someone's flesh and end their life to continue hers?

Gertie hadn't wavered when she'd pressed her knife to Sadie's throat. Davenport hadn't hesitated more than a handful of seconds before he'd set his derringer against her temple.

Behind her, something—or someone—crashed full against the door. She retreated as far as she could from a slab of wood that now creaked and rattled like a portal to hell. Against all odds, the door remained closed. On the other side, John must be putting up a mighty fight. But, no different from his days protecting the girls at the Star, he was only one man against many.

How many opponents did he now battle? Would his struggle be in vain?

Not if she had a say in the matter.

Whoever came through that door would get the surprise of their lives. She held the open razor hidden in the folds of her skirt. She'd learned from Gertie as well as Edward. Gaze locked on the door, she summoned every last drop of her courage. Memories of Noah colored everything. His need to protect her and shoulder her burdens. His glorious gift for making her smile—for real.

No more counterfeit smiles for her.

She recalled the first time she'd glimpsed his smile. That day, she'd finally thanked him for his help, and he'd given her even more. He'd rewarded her with his smile, a gift greater than any number of dollars, more precious than even her farm.

What would it be like to share his happiness every day? To be a part of his life with no more games between them? Or maybe better ones?

His childhood tale about his brother rose in her mind. They'd played hide 'n seek, and his brother had fooled him by hiding under an overturned washtub.

Her gaze dropped to the tubs between her and the door. Could such an obvious deception succeed again? If she overturned both, they might look as if they'd been flipped to let them drain as the girls had done in the Star's fancy room. They might be ignored as Noah had done all those years ago while searching for his brother.

An eerie quiet had descended in the hall. When had that happened? The silence spurred her into action. Careful not to break the hush, she closed and pocketed the razor, then turned the first tub. Kneeling on the floor, she tilted the second onto its side and began lowering it over her.

Footsteps paced the hall before halting outside her door. A mighty crack, like wood exploding, split the air.

Surprise made her lose her grip on the tub. It crashed to the floor. The resulting clang echoed loud as a church bell in the bowl now covering her. She seized the rim in a futile attempt to stop the ringing.

Next to her hand, through the narrow gap between the floor and the tub, only the bottom of the door was visible. It hadn't opened. Had they kicked in the door opposite?

Her relief didn't last long. Her door handle rattled. She released the tub and yanked the razor from her pocket.

The door burst open with a bang. A pair of booted feet stepped over the threshold and halted. The man's sudden stillness sent a shiver up her spine. A cold sweat slicked her palms. She clutched the razor tighter.

Was he scanning the room? Or staring at the tubs?

His feet pivoted to point away from her. He'd decided nothing of importance was inside the room. Her gamble had worked. The tension drained from her body. Only to return with a vengeance.

He hadn't left.

With a mind-numbing slowness, he turned and walked toward the tubs.

A sudden longing for the sound of Noah's spurs overwhelmed her. She clung to the memory of the jingle they'd made as he'd strode toward her when they'd first met on her farm. The man approaching had either given up his spurs or never worn them. He belonged to Dodge.

He wasn't the cowboy she longed to see.

The toe of his boot hooked under the tub next to hers and raised it enough to look underneath. Then he lowered it and advanced on her tub. When he halted, he stood opposite her razor. She braced herself. As soon as he touched her hiding place, she must use the blade.

The man's stillness returned. He didn't move. But his voice rumbled around her like a river. Deeply familiar. Endlessly loved. "I'm here for Sadie Sullivan. For her, and her alone. I told her I'd help her. I'd keep her safe." His voice lowered even further, vibrating with concern. "So far I've done a damned poor job. I just hope I haven't failed her completely."

Dropping the razor, she heaved the tub up. Large, work-roughened hands reached out to assist her, revealing strong arms covered in faded blue, a steadfast jaw, and amber eyes that once again warmed her like a shot of whiskey.

His grip remained on the tub, as if he were afraid to let go and reach for her. His eyes, narrowed with worry, searched hers. "Have I let you down again?"

She flung her arms around his neck and hugged him tight. "Not once since you came back." He'd accomplished what he set out to do.

She never wanted to let go of him, but she must. If she loved him, she had to give him what he'd given her. She released him and said, "You're free to leave Dodge."

CHAPTER 23

*N*oah stood on the jailhouse porch, observing Dodge's residents and new arrivals rush by. The town was the same as when he'd rode in a few weeks ago searching for Sadie—wicked and brash, and like no place he'd ever seen before.

Its time would come, though. It'd flex its muscles, run wild like a yearling colt, believe itself unstoppable, and then one day it would hit an obstacle that would shake it to its core.

That was when something amazing might happen. A path previously shrouded might become clear. If the townsfolk allowed, the town could rebuild itself into something more resilient. It would survive.

All things changed eventually.

He grasped this with a certainty now, because—this time —he'd been the one to change.

He'd come to Dodge looking for redemption in the salvation of a woman whose first name he hadn't even known. He'd found all of that and more. His remorse over his brother's death hadn't disappeared, but it no longer gnawed at him relentlessly. More often than not, when he thought of Jacob, he recalled the good times they'd shared working the ranch together.

That was another change. Texas was on his mind a lot lately. Ideas about how to make the land flourish and improve his home tumbled around inside him like rough-housing children.

It was time to go home. Time to build a life.

But something stronger bound him to Dodge.

Sadie.

How could he leave without her? He tried to picture his future without her in it...and failed. So that meant staying in Dodge. Or not. Was there a place for him in her heart? More than ever he wanted to ask her to marry him. New worries stopped him.

She was now a respectable woman with her entire future ahead of her. No one and nothing held her prisoner—not her promise to her friend or her fears that Gertie or John would catch and punish her if she ran. After Gertie had been arrested, John had left town without a word. So had a strangely silent Cora.

For the first time, Sadie had control over her life. Would she give up any of her newfound freedom to make a place for him beside her? After all she'd been through, did he even have the right to ask her?

He should take a step back, court her, and treat her like a lady. Approach her like he would've on the first day he'd searched for her in Dodge...before he discovered her working in a saloon. But he couldn't move forward until he took care of one piece of unfinished business.

He had to return her farm, show her the house he'd spent the last days improving with a few finishing touches. Or more than a few, as he procrastinated.

What if his offering stirred the old resentments?

Slipping his hand inside his pocket, he touched Edward's letter, although it was as much Sadie's letter now. He'd read her words so many times they were burned into his subconscious.

I won't let the best truth I've ever known die with me. I will always love you.

Why hadn't she said the words? Not once had she even mentioned the letter—not when he'd found her under the tub at the Great Western, and not in the days that followed. That worried him. She'd written the words hastily, under adverse circumstances. She'd been scared and feared she might die.

Did she remain silent because she regretted what she'd written?

He'd find out if he went to talk to her. But his feet remained rooted in place. If he didn't speak to her, he could hold on to the lie that her love might be true.

The door to the jail creaked open and closed behind him. He straightened his back, shrugging off his hunch but not the weight of his uncertainty.

Bat handed him a cup of coffee and set his shoulder against the porch post beside him. Two sentinels standing guard over Dodge.

"How's Gertie settling into her new home?" Noah asked.

Bat grinned. "She looks good sitting in Miss Sullivan's cell. Jus' sorry we didn't find a way to put her in there sooner."

Noah's fingers tightened around his cup. "Would look a helluva lot better if Wardell was locked up with her."

"True, very true. But knowing a person should be in jail 'n getting them there are two different things. Edward's letter might not hold up in court, but that don't matter after we caught the madam with his missing possessions. The judge will convict her for theft, but with Wardell, there wasn't a charge we could make stick."

Noah huffed in annoyance.

Bat released a low chuckle. "You should be happy Wardell obliged us 'n left town. Dodge's an interesting place, appalling 'n fascinating in equal measure. I reckon I'm ready to move on too. Either that or take my business here to a new level." He eyed Noah from under the brim of his hat. "How 'bout you, Deputy? You finally rustle up that plan we talked about?"

Noah stared at the cup in his hands. "I'd like to go home to Texas."

"But?"

He ran through all the possible excuses, then gave up and settled for the truth. "I'm not sure I can leave without Sadie."

Bat drew in a long breath and whistled it out.

Noah's skin prickled in anticipation, but Bat was silent.

"What? You got nothing to say?" Strangely, perversely, he wanted the lawman to needle him, give him unwanted advice, fill the void of uncertainty that surrounded him. "You've always got something to say."

The faintest of smiles curved Bat's mouth. "Sorry, not this time." He stepped down into the street. Without breaking stride, he tipped his hat to a pair of passing ladies before calling over his shoulder, "This time, my friend, yer on yer own."

INSIDE HER ROOM at the Dodge House Hotel, Sadie sat with her hands folded in her lap. Golden beams of afternoon sunlight spilled through the second-story window, caressing her skin like a loved one's tender touch. Not asking for, or taking, anything. Not clammy and overpowering, like the fever and chills that had overrun her body during the last few months. Not harsh and demanding, like Gertie's and Wardell's schemes for her future.

Everything was different.

She rose to her feet and wasn't overcome with dizziness or the slightest fatigue. Her vision didn't blur. Darkness didn't crowd in from the corners. She could see, with no impediments, her surroundings: a modest but homey room with not only a bed and a bureau but also a writing desk with an ornate clock and a chair with plump cushions.

A smile tugged her lips as she smoothed the folds of her skirt. Her dress was new, but what pleased her most was its neckline and hem. The highest button rested on her collarbone while the skirt swished the floor when she walked.

Bat had asked his ladylove, Lizzie, to help Sadie acquire new clothing. Lizzie had pulled the soft yellow dress from a trunk and proclaimed, with a wink, that it suited Sadie much better than her.

The color suddenly reminded her of the buttercup curtains in her bedroom at the Star. She willed her shoulders to relax. She'd never see those curtains, or that room, again.

She'd succeeded. Edward's treasures were no longer in the hands of his murderer.

Gertie had tried her damnedest to keep them to the very end, though. They hadn't been in her piano, and she'd denied any knowledge of their whereabouts. She'd also locked her safe and refused to open it.

When Noah and Bat had discussed ways to break into the cast-iron box—use dynamite or send for an expert from

Chicago—she'd offered another option. She'd given them the combination. The one she'd learned while hiding under Gertie's bed.

Noah finally learned how she'd gotten so dusty the night he'd first kissed her properly. He'd again expressed his concern for her risky behavior, but she deemed it well worth the danger.

In the end, that gamble had paid off.

After so much time and effort, finding the watch and jewelry box in a rough canvas sack in the safe made them appear smaller. But their true value couldn't be denied. It wasn't their size or even the amount of money they'd fetch at auction. They equaled her freedom, her debt to Edward repaid, her promise to avenge his murder fulfilled.

Your last moments were not in vain, my friend.

She'd accomplished what she'd set out to do. She hadn't regained her farm, but it no longer seemed important. Not when she had her health and her freedom, and something as precious.

New friends.

In addition to giving her respectable clothing, Bat and Lizzie had, along with Doctor Rhodes, called in several favors to secure her new living accommodations. She now resided in a respectable establishment, dressed like a lady with her future wide open.

No one could order her to stay in this room, or go anywhere else. She could do whatever she pleased. And still...something was missing.

Certain wishes were as far out of reach as ever: a home she could nurture and cherish, this time alongside a partner who'd make her stronger while she did the same for him. Her dreams had coalesced into a single point of longing.

Noah. She wanted to spend every day of her new future with him.

And him? What did he want? Each minute that passed, she became more certain he was waiting till he deemed her truly safe and he could leave. She hadn't seen him since they'd found Edward's possessions. Then today she'd received a message from the boy who'd delivered so many.

Noah had asked to visit her at four o'clock.

She reclaimed her seat in the chair she'd placed between the window and the desk. It provided the best view of the jail and the clock.

Almost time. Time to face the truth.

Noah hadn't mentioned the declaration she'd written on Edward's letter. He knew she loved him. Yet he'd said nothing in return. Maybe when he arrived, he'd speak to her in a different way. He'd take her in his arms, and his kiss would tell her everything she longed to hear.

The clock read one minute to four. The door of the jail opened. Her gaze never left Noah as he crossed the street. If today was the last time she saw him, she wanted to memorize every minute.

Too soon, and not soon enough, he entered the hotel below her window. Turning in her chair, she faced the door to her room. The clock ticked loudly in the silence. Her heart outpaced its rhythm, accelerating until she could no longer sit waiting. She leaped to her feet and wrenched open the door.

Noah stood outside. One bruised and scraped hand was raised to knock on the door. The other held his hat. More wounds from his battle with Gertie and Wardell's men marred his face. Nothing had stopped him. He was reliable and steadfast and everything her heart desired.

He lowered his hand. His gaze drifted down as well,

skimming her dress before returning to her face with a look of hunger. Her response came quick. A welcome rush of heat made her lean toward him.

He stared at his hat, now clutched in both hands. "I'm glad to find you looking so well, Miss Sullivan."

A chill snuffed out her hope. Only once before had he called her Miss Sullivan. Back when they were strangers visiting graveyards. Had the time for falsehoods returned? Before she could halt it, her false smile tightened her lips. "Thank you, Mr. Ballantyne."

A frown pinched his brow, but he didn't look up from his hat. An extended silence stretched between them. She racked her brain for a way to bring them closer, only to have him retreat a stride.

"Will you accompany me on an outing?" He gestured along the hall.

There wasn't anything in Dodge she wanted to see. She caught herself before she said no. He wouldn't leave her side while they walked wherever he wanted to go. She could hold on to him a bit longer. She collected her new bonnet.

Imagining him watching her, she fumbled to tie the ribbons beneath her chin.

"May I assist you?" he asked softly.

Not trusting her voice to remain steady, she nodded. As he tied the bow, his fingers brushed her chin and her neck. Did he feel her love pounding in her veins? Would he read it in her eyes? She kept her gaze averted.

"How's that?" A gentle tug tested the bow he'd made. "Not too tight?"

She shook her head. When his hands retreated, she summoned the strength to look at him.

The frown remained on his brow. "You're very quiet today. Aren't you curious where we're going?"

As long as I'm with you, the destination doesn't matter. She buried that wish and said, "Anywhere will be fine."

He led her out onto Front Street. At the far end of the hotel's hitching rail, a dainty chestnut mare stood next to his faithful gray. "I arranged for the livery to provide you with a horse.

They were traveling somewhere that required riding? When she was ill, she'd longed to ride on her own. Now she wanted to demand he fetch a buggy or wagon. Then she could be closer to him, like they'd been on their trip to the picnic.

Why was he acting so formal, like they'd just met? Why call her—?

"Miss Sullivan, may I help you onto your horse?"

She stifled her grimace. "That might be a good idea. It's been a while since I've ridden."

His hands were warm and solid around her waist as he helped her onto the mare. Unfortunately, he released her with the timeliness of a polite suitor, or a man full of disinterest. He untied her reins and gave them to her without touching her hand.

Then he swung into his own saddle and winced. The beating he'd taken behind the jail continued to bother him. Yet he'd suggested this outing. Her spirits deflated further. He must be very eager to speak with her, so he could leave Dodge.

Side by side, they rode south out of town. She didn't ask where they were going. She cared even less now. It was enough that he was with her. He hadn't said goodbye. Not yet.

They traveled along a swath of earth packed hard by the hooves of thousands of longhorns. As they continued, an increasing familiarity tugged at her senses. She ignored it, preferring to cocoon herself in the daydream that Noah might be taking her all the way to Texas.

The abrupt halt of their horses jarred her back to reality.

Noah had brought her home. But this was nothing like her home of a year ago.

In front of her stood one of the most idyllic houses she could imagine. A waist-high fence surrounded a small but solid looking house with windows flanking a door on a south-facing porch. She pictured herself sitting on that porch every evening, staring south toward Texas.

Alone.

The ember of hope in her heart sputtered and snuffed out.

Noah dismounted.

She scrambled down before he could help her. "You built this?"

"I wanted to replace the house my herd destroyed. This one will stand the test of time. It'll last." Despite his words, he eyed the house as if it troubled him. "Neither beast nor nature can easily tear this down."

She stared at the structure. She didn't see a home. She faced another prison. A solid one built—like he said—to last.

"Shall I show you the inside?" he asked.

The prospect of entering the house, and staying there alone, unleashed her panic. She stumbled away from it and Noah. "None of this is mine. I never earned those last acres."

"I shouldn't have asked that of you. I'm giving them back. All of them."

Her throat constricted. One word burst free. "Don't."

His eyebrows shot up. "Don't?"

She wanted to say, *Don't leave me*. She settled for, "Don't be so kind."

"I only want to help."

"Stop telling me that!"

The lines etching his face deepened.

"I'm sorry," she said. "I'm being ungrateful. It's a lovely house. Thank you."

"Now who's being kind? You're trying to spare my feelings." He scrubbed his hand across the back of his neck. "Tell me how to make things better, Sadie."

The sound of her name on his lips made her heart ache. She shook her head.

"I know not everything can be mended or replaced, but I hoped with time I could earn your forgiveness."

Tears blurred her eyes. She refused to let them fall. "I forgive you. I did a long time ago."

"Oh, hell," he muttered. "Not even at first was it so bad that you cried. Bringing you here was selfish. You need… something else. Maybe more time." He glanced at his horse. "I should go."

Of all places, he'd leave her here? Once again, she stood on her farm watching him destroy what she cherished most.

Anger ripped through her like fire along a tinder dry prairie. "If you leave me here, I'll burn down that house." She jabbed her finger at his beautiful offering. "Then I'll sell this land and turn my back on all of it, because it means nothing to me—the same way my letter meant nothing to you." Her voice rose higher and higher with each word. "Go on. Climb on your horse and leave."

He stared at her with an expression so full of worry that it left room for nothing else.

The ache in her heart swelled until it made her entire body hurt. Damn his concern. She neither wanted it nor needed it. "What're you waiting for?" She shoved his chest with both hands. "Leave me here. Like you did before."

When he didn't budge, she launched herself at him with all her strength. He caught her before losing his footing. He landed on his back with her on top of him. A groan vibrated deep in his chest. Too late, she remembered his injuries.

She cringed. This wasn't like before. She couldn't hit him like she had last year. She couldn't pretend she hated him. Not when he was the most precious thing in her world. A hundred times he'd earned her forgiveness and her love, but he deserved his freedom. He deserved a peaceful goodbye.

You have to let him go. Her body disagreed. With a will of their own, her arms rose to bring him closer.

In spite of his injuries, he hugged her in return. "I wasn't leaving you." His voice was quiet but firm. "I was only going into town. No farther. I came to visit you today with the intention of courting you."

"Courting me?" She raised her head to gape at him. "You called me Miss Sullivan like we were strangers. You kept me at a distance. You wouldn't touch me."

"Isn't that how courting goes? I wanted to treat you with the respect you deserve, the respect I should've given you when I first arrived in Dodge. I wanted to take things slow, do things proper." His jaw went hard with determination. "To hell with being proper. Tell me the truth. Tell me about your letter. If the words are true, say them." Despite his gruff tone, hope glowed in the golden depths of his eyes.

She adored his eyes. "I love you."

His mouth met hers in a scorching kiss that stole her breath, but promised more than it could ever take. When their lips finally parted, they were both breathing heavily.

"I love you, too," he said. "Will you come home with me to Texas?"

"Can we leave today?"

"If you want." A smile tugged the corners of his mouth.

"But first, what do you want to do with your farm? Shall we burn down the house together?"

She gave her smile full rein. "Let's give it to Bat and Lizzie."

"I imagine they both prefer living in the thick of things. Better to pick someone who needs to get out of Dodge as much as we do."

In unison, they both said, "Doctor Rhodes."

That they'd agreed so easily about anything concerning the doctor made her laugh.

Noah paused to pay great attention to exploring the curve of her lips before he continued speaking. "Living in the country when he isn't busy doctoring in town might bring him some peace."

"I hope he gives up that rum-hole across from the Star."

"Please don't tell me you've been there as well."

"I haven't. My bedroom window provided a limited view of life beyond the Star. For example, I could only watch while you talked to your friend Lewis as he packed his horse for Texas." Doubts crept in again and made her frown. "I feared you might go with him."

"Not without you." His words fell soft and soothing against her brow. "Lewis will be happy to see you come home with me. I'm certain I'll be even happier." His lips sought hers. He kissed her until she smiled again. "I'm looking forward to making you smile in Texas. Every day."

Pure joy coursed through her veins. She threw back her head and laughed. The sky arced high above them, endless with possibilities. But when she looked down again, the warmth in his eyes was all she truly needed.

EPILOGUE

Texas
May 1878

$\mathcal{A}$ single longhorn stood in Sadie's garden. The brute eyed her indifferently, chewing on a mouthful of greens.

She grabbed her broom and waved it at the beast. "Get out of my vegetable patch, you pointy-headed devil."

The steer sauntered through the broken fence, leaving her to survey the destruction.

"Some things never change," she grumbled.

"Having difficulties, Mrs. Ballantyne?" a deep, rumbling voice inquired from behind her.

A current of heat curled up her spine, leaving a tingle of anticipation in its wake. She laid her broom against the remnants of the fence but didn't turn around. "I seem to have the same trouble every spring."

Reaching around her, Noah gently drew her back until she leaned against his chest. "With cattle?" he whispered close to her ear.

"And cowboys," she replied on a sigh.

His soft laughter filled the shell of her ear, heating her straight through. "Didn't your husband tell you to stay inside the house?"

"Didn't I tell my husband to keep his cattle out of my garden?"

A rumble of appreciation vibrated in his chest as his hands moved to caress her swollen belly. Then he lifted her into his arms. "The baby's due any time, and you agreed to lie down and rest."

"I've spent enough time in that bed."

He nuzzled her neck. "Are you complaining about your husband's lovemaking?"

"My husband's made love to me in every room inside our house and many locations outside too, so my remark about the bed is irrelevant." She couldn't have stopped her satisfied smile even if she'd tried. She didn't try.

Noah carried her into the house and up the stairs. "You sound like a wicked woman. I learned you worked in one of the most notorious saloons up north. Do you deny it?"

"No." She held onto the word, letting it slip from her mouth with a slow deliberation that matched the pace of her hand exploring the muscles inside his shirt.

He swept through their bedroom door and rocked to a halt beside their bed.

Under her hand, his heartbeat raced in time with hers. So did the pulse in his neck. His strength, solid and warm as stone heated by the sun, continued in a nerve-tingling roughness as she traced the line of his jaw. The same determined line that had captivated her when he'd saved her from his herd while she'd cursed him for the Devil.

His arms tightened around her as if loath to let go. "And the lies that came between us?"

"I no longer need them." She added her lips to her exploration of the determined ridge that ended at his ear. "The truth is my husband was my first and only lover. And I wouldn't want it any other way. So you see," she said as she caressed the curve of his ear with her tongue, "my past isn't very scandalous after all."

The smile she craved lifted his lips. "I still think you're wicked." He set her on the bed, leaning over to nip her neck before drawing back. "Deliciously so."

She tugged him down beside her on the mattress and sighed when he wrapped his arms around her again. "So are you, Mr. Ballantyne," she whispered against his lips. "And thank heavens for that. It wouldn't be any fun being wicked without you."

Thanks for reading Sadie and Noah's story! If you enjoyed their adventure, I hope you'll write a review on Amazon, BookBub, or Goodreads. Or even all three. Every single review helps. No matter how long or short, they are a heartfelt gift that is sincerely appreciated. Hearing from readers makes my day and keeps me motivated to write my next book.

www.amazon.com/author/jacquinelson
www.bookbub.com/profile/jacqui-nelson
www.goodreads.com/jacquinelson

Are you ready to see what happens to Noah's friend, Lewis Adams? Keep reading to see an excerpt from *Between Home & Heartbreak* and more.

BETWEEN HOME & HEARTBREAK - EXCERPT
Gambling Hearts Series, Book 2

Who is Eldorado Jane?
Long-lost friend or scheming superstar?

Plain Jane Dority vanished while riding in a storm beside her childhood best friend. Eighteen years later, Wild West trick-riding superstar Eldorado Jane returns to claim her birthright: the Dority homestead, now owned by the steadfast Texan who never forgot Jane or forgave himself for her disappearance.

Lewis Adams would give anything to see his friend come home, but he's certain Eldorado Jane isn't his Jane. So why does this mesmerizing woman—with the talent and fame to have anything she desires—want the remote patch of land that he loves? There's only one way to find out: accept a wager with a deceiver who holds the power to bring back his friend or break his heart. The outcome rests in her hands. Or does it?

Friendship. Betrayal. Blackmail. Eldorado Jane holds every card...except the one that matters most.

PROLOGUE

Outside Juniper Flats, Texas
Spring, 1861

Lewis struggled to stay upright—and not hit the ground like some pretender grasping for a fool's gold. Kneeling on his galloping pony, he clutched the saddle horn and stuck his other arm straight out for balance. Tonight he'd succeed. He'd prove his worth.

He'd keep up with his best friend, the invincible Jane Dority.

Beside him, easily holding the same pose on her horse Scout, Jane called to him, "Forget your father. Focus on me. They say the best partners act in harmony."

"Who says?"

"The owner of *Gypson's Medicine Show*."

Gypson also claimed his elixir cured every illness and strengthened the sensational acts that alternated between his sales pitches. Lewis' father said practice and perseverance, not doctored-up whiskey, made good performances. But Jane had talked incessantly about Gypson and his horse-riding acrobat after watching them captivate Juniper Flats' cheering townsfolk an hour ago.

Trying to duplicate one of their maneuvers while racing through a twilight field with storm clouds thickening overhead made him suddenly wish he'd never come to town. "Everyone's obsessed with that show."

"You're the same with roundup. Have been for years."

He lowered his chin against the rain that began falling and Jane's perceptiveness.

"Bet your father takes you next year." Her words came quick, with conviction.

"You said that last year." And the year before. And still his father kept saying he was too young, especially with the ongoing range disputes. But this year, his father and Jane's had agreed to take their friend Noah, who was also eleven and had been the same height as Lewis—until this spring.

"One day you'll tower over me. Bet you're as tall as Noah next year."

"Get out of my head, Jane!" He huffed out a breath, trying to expel the expectations—his and everyone else's—that pestered him like a saddle cinched too tight.

"Partners should embrace connections."

"Enough quoting Gypson," he grumbled. "Just teach me to ride like you." Then his father might see him differently and let him help bring in the strays from the high country.

"Next year you'll work with the men every day. And I..." Jane's voice wavered. "I won't be riding."

Lewis shook his head in disbelief and swayed precariously on Sergeant. He pressed his knees against the pommel and stared straight ahead, searching for a balance that was difficult to find. "You'll always ride."

"My mom needs help cooking for the Ballantyne hands. No time for horses, she says. Next year you'll be a better rider than me."

Laughter burst from his lips. He'd never beat Jane on a horse. No one would. Not even the girl in the show they'd recently watched; the rider whose routine they now mimicked.

"I'll settle for being your equal at riding." That would impress his father. And that's all he wanted, tonight and tomorrow. *Hold on. Don't fall. Keep up with Jane.*

"Why should anyone settle?" Jane and Scout edged ahead.

He urged Sergeant to regain the lost ground. Jane kept pulling away. Sweat stung his eyes. Then the heavens opened up and washed away everything, including all sight of Jane.

"Come back!" Fear clawed up his spine until he

glimpsed the tip of her long brown braid flying behind her. She'd slowed down for him. "Let's go home."

"I'm not ready." Despite her curt reply, Jane continued slowing Scout until her entire silhouette was visible.

The tightness squeezing his chest eased. Only to return with a vengeance when she yelled, "I won't stop riding."

"It's raining too hard." The downpour pummeled his entire body, turning the saddle slick and slippery beneath him. "We have to stop!"

"The star of the show wouldn't let a little rain stop her."

Fear and frustration warred in his veins. "Stop pretending. You're no star. You're just plain Jane Dority!"

Her shoulders drooped and then snapped straight. He stiffened as well, with remorse. He'd finally said the name too many used. Despite being a dazzling rider, his friend was plain in every other way.

He'd let her down—with the worst words possible.

Thunder rumbled, chastising him, shaking him to the bone. He strained to stay on Sergeant and say something to dilute the sting of his foolishness.

Ahead, Jane's silhouette grew smaller, fainter. "Maybe I'll ride all night. All day tomorrow, too." She was leaving him again.

He couldn't let her ride into the night alone. A best friend deserved better.

He urged Sergeant to go faster. A chant built in his head along with the pounding of Sergeant's hooves. *Forget about falling. You can do this. You have to do this. Say you're sorry before you drive her away.*

"Jane—"

"No, I won't go home till I'm ready. Till I'm a star so bright, I'll blind you with my brilliance."

Lightning blazed, concealing Jane, Scout, and even

Sergeant, still galloping valiantly beneath him. A heartbeat later came the roar.

The blast of light and noise enveloped him. His body flew from the saddle, his hands lost the horn, the reins— leaving him with only the air.

CHAPTER 1

18 years later...
High country above Juniper Flats

Lying flat on his back, squinting at the sycamores swaying against a hazy blue sky, every bone in Lewis Adams' body ached, berating him for letting the half-broke Appaloosa Cayuse toss him out of the saddle and over the fence. The land he loved reverberated beneath him. He'd be tempted to stay here if he didn't have nine more prickly horses requiring his attention. Training them in time was all that mattered.

The silhouette of a woman, framed by a sunshine halo, leaned over him and cast a soothing shadow. "You almost had him." Her smooth-as-honey voice held a hint of amusement.

At last, an angel had descended from the heavens to ease his burdens. One bearing encouraging words as well as laughter. Exactly the kind he liked, and needed.

An easy smile lifted his lips. Now here was a reason for lying in the dirt. Damned if he'd move and spook her. *Stay with me. Don't disappear.*

She leaned closer, revealing deep brown eyes rich as polished heartwood.

"Your eyes are—" His breath lodged in his chest, then found freedom with the word, "stunning."

Her eyebrows shot up in surprise. Then her laughter floated down around him like a warm embrace. "I think your fall, not my eyes, stunned you. Next time keep *your* eyes on your mount's ears. They'll tell you which way he plans to jump."

His grin grew. Horse sense, a kind heart, and a sharp wit. His angel and her mesmerizing eyes were a dream come true.

The clatter of hooves swelled above the earth's fading tremors. Recognition shook the fog from his brain. His visitor was one of the three riders he'd glimpsed approaching before he'd been bucked off. Her mount had thundered ahead like a towering black cloud and now hovered next to the corral, looking at his rainbow assortment of horses.

The woman standing over him was real.

Who was she? Why was she at the Dority homestead? No one came up here for months on end. Craving a better look at her, he tried to push up on his elbows.

"Lie still." Crouching on her heels, she laid her gloved hand on his shoulder. Even wrapped in soft kidskin, her light touch jolted him like a lightning bolt, then held him hostage. He'd do whatever she said as long as she kept touching him...and staring at him with her angel eyes.

"We must talk before they join us." Her voice had dropped to a conspiratorial whisper. "I'm sorry. I'm going to hurt you again."

"Eldora, is he dead?" The not-too-distant bellow made them both flinch. The eagerness in that shout rang in his skull like the bells of hell anticipating a funeral.

To read more about *Between Home & Heartbreak*,
visit JacquiNelson.com

STORY INSPIRATION & NOTES

The spark for *Between Love & Lies* came from the letter
below and my collection of *Time-Life Old West* books
containing these lines: "The longhorns were carriers of a
microscopic tick. The Texas animals were immune to the
parasite, but the same tick produced deadly splenic fever in
local cattle."

I imagined a small farm, held together only by the grit and
hard work of its owner, might not survive such an event. I
wondered what might happen next, both on that unlucky
farm and in the nearest town: Dodge City, the Queen of
Cattle Towns—where life would be challenging for a
woman who luck had deserted.

~ Jacqui Nelson

January 1, 1878 - Letter in the Washington, D. C. *Evening Star*

"Dodge City is a wicked little town. Here those nomads in
regions remote from the restraints of moral, civil, social, and
law enforcing life, the Texas cattle drovers, from the very
tendencies of their situation the embodiment of wayward-
ness and wantonness, end the journey with their herds, and
here they loiter and dissipate, sometimes for months, and
share the boughten dalliances of fallen women."

Deadwood, Dakota Territory 1876...
In a gold rush storm, can an unlikely pair rescue each other?
Raven wants to save one person. Charlie wants to save the
world. Their warring nations thrust them together but duty
pulled them apart—until their paths crossed again in
Deadwood for a fight for love.

EXCERPT
RESCUING RAVEN - CHAPTER 1

Fighting a growing impatience fueled by rage, Charlie
Jennings drew his revolver and urged his horse through the
trees flanking the Deadwood Trail. Below him, an
Appaloosa with the strikingly similar color of his own horse
—white covered from head to hock in chestnut spots—was
rein-tied to the back of a buckboard. If the horse hadn't
caught his attention, he might not have given the transport a
second look.

He might not have seen her.

The wagon rattled forward carrying one silent and seven
grumbling passengers. When a bend in the trail cast the sun
in the eyes of the guards, one riding behind and the other in
front, he charged his spotted mare down onto the road.

Everyone in the wagon, except for the cowering raven-
haired woman, screamed. The driver jerked on the lines.

The horses skidded to a halt. The guards scrambled for their weapons.

The click of his revolver being cocked made them all freeze.

The silence that followed was as heated as the summer sun on his back. The guards glared at him through squinted eyes. He kept his focus on them as well—lined up in a neat row down the barrel of his Colt Peacemaker.

"Jennings," growled the closest man, who went by the name Big Bill. "You shouldn't be here."

"Yeah," hollered Bill's partner, a stranger who resembled a beanpole.

Frontier trails and towns had a way of attracting similarly named men, including the Charlies like him. They also had a fondness for embellishment. The deck was stacked in favor of the rear guard being called Skinny Sam or Loud-mouth Pete.

"We heard you were guidin' a miner 'n his four kids, the ones who lost their ma, away from Deadwood." At least Skinny hadn't heard, and used, the double-barreled moniker Charlie had been saddled with since arriving in the Black Hills.

"But you," he shot back, "didn't hear that my job finished ahead of schedule."

"Well," Bill said on a long breath, "ain't that a spot of bad luck."

"Not for one of your passengers." He didn't look her way. He'd already seen enough: a ragtag assortment of women, one hunched with her dark head over her wrists tied to the wagon.

To read the rest of *Rescuing Raven*, visit my website JacquiNelson.com and sign up for my newsletter.

ALSO BY JACQUI NELSON

GAMBLING HEART SERIES

Between Love & Lies - Book 1, Dodge City, 1877

Between Home & Heartbreak - Book 2, Texas, 1879

∾

STEAM! ROMANCE AND RAILS

Adella's Enemy - Kansas, 1870

∾

To learn more about my books, visit my website

JacquiNelson.com

PRAISE FOR THE LONESOME HEARTS SERIES...

Between Heaven & Hell

"A perfect, steady-paced book with poetic descriptions of romance and easy-to-follow fluidity of Callahan and Hannah's journeys." ~ Chanticleer Book Reviews

"A fire-cracker of a love story with the perfect blend of fascinating characters, intense emotion, historical drama and fast-paced action." ~ Scarlett Penn

"Beautiful writing and flawed characters it was easy to care about. A thoroughly engaging story I enjoyed tremendously." ~ Lark

"An exciting journey filled with perilous adventure, this is an original interesting tale with a woven plot line that comes full circle." ~ InD'tale Magazine

Following Faith

"The first story I'd read by Jacqui Nelson which put her on my watch-out-for-and-read-her-stuff list. Despite the short length, this story packed a big punch." ~ Michelle R.

"So well written and so descriptive, you easily get transported to the old west and are traveling on the trail with Faith and Eagle. A beautiful, sweet, romantic, heartwarming story you won't want to miss." ~ Barb

Jacqui Nelson "has a unique way of drawing the reader back

to the old west with colorful descriptions and characters who leap from the page." ~ Jacquie B.

Choosing Bravery

"Grand adventure. Mystery and excitement." ~ Sandra S.

"Action packed, fabulous setting and two main characters you could really root for" ~ N. Love

"One of those stories that just takes you away to a world of the wild west, filled with adventure, suspense and sweet romance. I couldn't put it down." ~ B

Rescuing Raven - **free for my newsletter subscribers**

"Grabbed my interest from the first page and did not let go until the end." ~ Babs

"Beautifully written...Don't pass this short story by. You will not be disappointed." ~ Sandy S.

"I loved this short story and you will too." ~ Dorothy R.

ABOUT THE AUTHOR

Fall in love with a new Old West... where the men are steadfast and the women are adventurous. You'll find Wild West scouts, spies, cardsharps, wilderness guides, and trick-riding superstars in my stories. Those are my heroines. Wait till you meet my heroes!

My love for historical romance adventures with grit and passion came from watching Western movies while growing up on a cattle farm in northern Canada. I've been nominated for over 20 awards and won the RWA® Golden Heart® & the Laramie® — but my best reward is hearing from readers who have enjoyed my stories.

Email me at Jacqui@JacquiNelson.com

For updates on giveaways, special events, and more, join my newsletter at JacquiNelson.com

amazon.com/Jacqui-Nelson/e/B00EE6GE88

goodreads.com/JacquiNelson

bookbub.com/authors/jacqui-nelson

facebook.com/JacquiNelsonAuthor

instagram.com/jacquinelsonauthor

pinterest.com/JacquiAuthor

x.com/Jacqui_Nelson

youtube.com/@jacquinelsonauthor

tiktok.com/@jacquinelsonauthor